TRANSCEND

Book One

by Jewel E. Ann

Copyright © 2018 by Jewel E. Ann
ISBN: 978-0-9990482-9-0
Print Edition

Cover Designer: ©Sarah Hansen, Okay Creations
Photo: ©Wong Sim
Cover Model: Elias Chigros
Formatting: BB eBooks

TRANSCEND

Dedication

For Shauna, Queen of Names

CHAPTER ONE

NEVAEH. IT'S HEAVEN spelled backwards and the name of the girl to my right with her finger five stories up her nose. I grimace while readjusting in my chair. It has nothing to do with her disgusting habit. One of the wings to my pad is stuck to my pubic hair. Mom worries about tampons and toxic shock syndrome. It can't be more painful than this.

The receptionist keeps glancing at us through her owlish glasses, tapping the end of her pen on her chin. "Nevaeh, do you need a tissue?" she asks.

My parents are not the weirdest parents in the world after all. Lucky me.

Roy.

Doris.

Cherish.

Wayne.

With over ten thousand baby names in the average name book, how does one settle on such horrible names?

Backwards Heaven glances over at me as if I have the answer to the receptionist's question. I'm not the tip of her finger. How am I supposed to know what it feels like up there? After inspecting her size—smaller than me—and her yellow hair in a hundred different lengths that looks like something my mom calls a DIY, I give the receptionist a small nod.

Without moving her finger, because it might be stuck, Nevaeh mimics my nod. The receptionist holds out a box of tissues. They both stare at me. When did I get put on booger duty?

"Swayze, do you need to go potty before we leave?" Mom asks, coming out of the office where I took my tests.

Swayze. That's me. Worst name ever—until five minutes ago when Nevaeh introduced herself and offered me a gluten-free, peanut-free, dairy-free, sugar-free, taste-free snack from her BPA-free backpack. My uncle thinks the millennials are going to ruin the world because they have no common sense, and all of their knowledge comes from the internet. He may be right, only time will tell, but then what's my parents' excuse? Or Nevaeh's parents' excuse? Common sense says you give your child a good solid name. Kids don't want to be unique. It's true. We just want to fit in.

I grab the box of tissues and toss it on my empty chair, turning before Nevaeh's finger slides out. Some things I don't need to know, like why it smells like cherry vomit in the waiting room, why there is a water dispenser but no cups, and what's up Nevaeh's right nostril.

"Restroom," I mumble, tracing the toe of my shoe over the red and white geometric patterns of the carpet.

"We can't hear you when you talk to your feet, Swayze," Dad says like he's said it a million times. Maybe he has.

I lift my head up. "No, I don't need to use the *restroom!* Or *potty*. Do I still look four to you?"

His blue eyes, which match mine, ping-pong around the room before landing on me. "Shh … you don't need to be so loud." He smooths his hand over the top of his mostly bald head, like I ruffled his feathers, what few he has left.

"Let's just go, dear." My mom reaches for my hand.

I jerk away.

"Swayze."

As if giving me such a stupid name wasn't enough, she has to draw it out. "Swaaayzeee." Who wants a name that rhymes with lazy and crazy?

"Well, you said you can't hear me when I talk to my feet. Can you hear me now?!"

They hear me. The guy who tested me peeks his head out the door, squinting at me. He hears me too. I can't find my inside voice. Something has tripped my volume and it's stuck on playground voice.

"Potty is what toddlers do. I'm not a toddler! I'm eleven. And I know stuff that other eleven-year-olds don't know. So what? That doesn't mean something is wrong with me. You keep bringing me to places like this to take stupid tests and sit in stinky waiting rooms with weird kids who have crazy names and like to chant unsolvable riddles, pull their hair, and pick their noses!"

Balling my hands, I resist the rare urge to pull my own hair. My parents each take one of my arms and drag me out of the office. Just before we reach the door, I give Nevaeh a small grimace of apology. She slides her finger back into her nose.

"Am I a genius yet?" I ask in a much calmer voice as my parents rush me to the elevator and down fifteen stories like someone's trying to kill the president. Next to our blue hybrid car is a red convertible. Maybe it belongs to Nevaeh's parents. Then again, that car is a little too cool for people who would name their child Heaven backwards. Heaven in the opposite direction ... wouldn't that be Hell?

After checking my seatbelt, as if an eleven-year-old can't be trusted to listen for the click and give it a tug, my dad glares at me, jaw clenched. He's too mad to talk. That's fine. I'll know when he's ready to talk; his first demand will be an explanation. There really isn't anything more I can say. My words, although louder than necessary, were self-explanatory.

After long minutes of some self-imposed timeout on himself, my dad looks at my mom and nods.

"Swayze?" She glances over her shoulder at me, curling her dark hair behind her ear. I don't detect any anger in her voice. It's sweet and juicy like the Starburst candy I get at the movies.

I fear her words will feel like the cavities I get from eating too much sugar.

"How would you feel about trying a new school?"

Yep. She's drilling without numbing anything first. I've attended four different schools. Every educational psychologist and child development expert in a fifty-mile radius has evaluated me. They figured out I'm gifted, but not in a typical way. Smart. But not necessarily a genius.

My random recollections of historical events, that are not at all noteworthy, are most puzzling. I'm not playing Chopin or speaking fluent Spanish. I enjoy talking with adults, but I fit in just fine with my peers as well. I can't name that many famous war generals. Even naming the presidents in order is a challenge. But random things that happened in Madison, Wisconsin, a few years before I was born seems to be my specialty.

"Move? Again?" I sigh as we pass the UW-Madison Arboretum, one of the places I like to go in the summer.

"We just want to find a good fit for you."

"I fit fine where I'm at."

"But they're not challenging you enough."

I shrug. "What does it matter? If I already know what

they're telling me, then I don't have to do as much homework as my friends."

"It's wasted potential." Dad shoots me a quick look in the rearview mirror. He, too, has lost his fight over my outburst.

"Potential means—" Mom starts to explain.

"Possibilities, prospects, future success. I get it." I'm fairly certain other eleven-year-old kids in sixth grade have heard the word potential before. It's not exactly a word I'd see on my word of the day calendar.

"You know, Swayze, the Gibsons are sending Boomer to a private school only an hour from our house. If we send you there, you'd already have one friend."

Boomer. Another hideous name. Sounds like a Rottweiler. Nice boy though. I like him, but not the way he likes me. At least I don't think so. He carries my backpack to the bus for me after school, but he also snaps my bra in class. The bra I don't need. My mom pressured me into getting one after several of my friends got them. I don't have breasts. Nope. Nothing there yet. Still, I wear it to feel like all of the other girls, and apparently Boomer's need to snap it during math every day means he likes me. At least that's the story my mom tries to sell.

Not buying it.

"I like my school." I twist my blond hair around my finger then slide it through my lips curled between my teeth.

Mom frowns. She has a thing about hair near the mouth. A hair in her food triggers her gag reflex to the point of vomiting, and then she can't eat that type of food for months. Dad always threatens to plant a hair in the ice cream she likes to sneak—his ice cream.

"You'll be in middle school next year. It's a good time for a change. The transition will be easier." Dad nods as if he only needs to convince himself and my mom.

"I like my friends."

"You'll make new friends," Mom says, shaking her head and scowling at the hair in my mouth.

I pull it out and flip it over my shoulder. "Why can't I just be normal and you be happy with that?"

"Swayze, if you just give this a try, I promise we won't ask you to switch schools again, even if it doesn't work out." Mom flinches like something's caught in her throat, probably bile from seeing hair in my mouth.

One last move. One last school. I'll do it. But I won't believe it's truly the last.

CHAPTER TWO

10 Years Later

"SWAYZE, WHAT MAKES you think your parents gave up on you?" Dr. Greyson asks.

Carlton Greyson. That is a well-thought-out name. Strong. Manly. Intelligent.

My father died of a heart attack last year. I'm good, but my mother suggested *we* use some of his life insurance money to help deal with the loss. I suggested a trip to Costa Rica. She decided on shrinks.

Again, I'm good. However, it appeases her to know that I'm expressing my emotions to someone since it's not her. I've been through a handful of psychologists and psychiatrists, looking for someone who doesn't annoy me.

This is my first visit with Dr. Greyson. It's too early to make any conclusions, but his name doesn't piss me off so there's that.

"My mom likes antiques. She used to watch this roadshow on public television. There's such excitement—high hopes— for people who think they have a hidden gem. I felt like that hidden gem for most of my life. We waited, visiting one expert after another, going from one private school to another, waiting for someone to tell them my gift—my worth. I imagined that lottery-winning look on their faces."

"What happened?"

I stare at his interlaced hands on his lap—the skin of a man who has never had an ounce of grease stuck in the wrinkles and crevices. Who knew manicured nails and the occasional steepled index fingers could be so enthralling? I find his command of the room both intimidating and comforting. Deep-set eyes almost silver in color match his graying hair that's receded into a sharp widow's peak. He reminds me of Liam Neeson. It makes me wonder if he has a "particular set of skills."

Meeting his gaze, I smile. "At my final evaluation, five years ago, my parents were told I was a perfectly normal sixteen-year-old girl with above average test scores but nothing at that point that exceeded all of my other peers. I was smart, but not a genius. They recommended I take as many AP classes as I could, but there was no mention of skipping grades or even testing out of classes. However, I did have my first year's worth of college credits by the time I graduated high school."

Dr. Greyson glances at some papers in my traveling file. I've learned to travel with my file of test results and records of my academic achievements. "You scored a thirty-one on your ACT and graduated with a three-point-nine GPA. That's really good. And you just graduated from college."

I shrug. "I wasn't valedictorian of my class. I didn't receive a full-ride scholarship to any college. No write-up in any medical journals. No national television appearances. No lottery ticket. No hidden gem. But, yes, I did just graduate from college. That's good, right? Not everyone has a college degree. I'm hoping to get a teaching job for this school year. Otherwise, I'll substitute teach."

"And now?"

"I do graphic design: websites, banners, book covers. That

sort of stuff."

"Do you like to design?"

No one has ever asked me that. It's always been an assumption that I must like it because I do it. Since when did everyone love their job?

"Not particularly. But I'm good at it. It's a job for now."

We talk about random stuff—a getting-to-know-me session. By the time we finish, I agree to make another appointment. A first for me.

Turning from the receptionist's desk and grabbing several chocolates from a ceramic bowl that looks like something a young child made in school, I see Nate. He's aged quite a bit, but I'd recognize that wavy, ginger hair anywhere. I've always had a thing for guys with wavy hair, especially the ones who don't fight it and just say "Fuck it." Really, there's nothing more appealing than unruly, fuck-it hair.

He's filled out too. No longer a boy, but a man with broad shoulders and a strong jaw. And a thick layer of stubble. Testosterone looks good on him. I smile when he looks up with those unmistakable blue eyes.

"Hey, how are you?" I ask just as his gaze diverts to the ground, arms resting on his sturdy, jean-clad thighs, hands folded in front of him.

He glances back up with no recognition on his face. His eyes shift side to side before focusing on me again.

"Nate?"

"Yeah?" he says in an uncertain tone.

"Wow, you're all grown up."

His eyes narrow. "You'll have to excuse me, but how do we know each other?"

"You lived on Gable Street. Faded green house. You played

hockey. That's how you got that scar along your hairline. Remember? You and some other kids were playing on the pond, no helmets or protective gear."

Nate's hand moves to his head, tracing the scar hidden behind his wayward locks. "What is your name?" he asks, narrowing his eyes even more.

"Swayze Samuels." How can he not know me? I know he likes pineapple and jalapeños on his pizza, extra butter on his popcorn at the movies, which is just soggy and gross, and he tells all of his friends that he likes video games, but secretly his passion is chess. Or ... was. I still can't get over how much he's grown up.

He shakes his head. "Do you have older siblings?"

"No." This is crazy. I know he's an only child, so how does he not know the same thing about me? He's a huge Chicago Bears fan which pisses his parents off because everyone who lives in Wisconsin should be loyal to their Packers.

"Do I know your parents?"

"Nate Hunt, how can you not remember me, we ..." I tuck my shoulder-length hair behind my ears and sigh. "We ..."

He's my captive audience; even the older lady sitting two chairs to his right, pretending to read a magazine, gives me a curious glance. This is ridiculous. It's clearly been years; he has a few wrinkles by his eyes to prove it, but ... I know him.

"How old are you?" he asks, breaking my stuttering that's doing little to formulate words that explain how I know him.

"Twenty-one."

"Well, I got this scar when I was fourteen. That was twenty-two years ago. You must know someone who knew me when I was a child."

I return a single nod, not really agreeing with anything.

"Um … my parents … Travis and Krista Samuels? My dad passed away a year ago." I don't remember ever talking about Nate with them, but we must have.

"The names are familiar." Nate nods slowly, lips pursed to the side. "But I'm not completely placing them. Then again, I've been a bit off lately." He nods to the door to Dr. Greyson's office. "Obviously, if I'm here, something must be off, right?" He chuckles, but more pain than humor radiates from it.

I know him, as in really *know* him, not a simple we met or someone I know spoke of him. It's more. Skin crawling, chills causing the hair on my neck to stand erect type of more.

"Good to see you." I leave him with a stiff smile and skitter out before he has a chance to say, "Wish I could say the feeling is mutual," because he has no clue who I am.

WHAT IF IT'S a brain tumor? I think about this more than I should. However, it might explain a lot of the unique, brilliant, advanced, inconsistent, often times meaningless thoughts that go through my head.

"Nate Hunt," I chant his name, pulling out of the parking lot, heading back to my apartment.

It's déjà vu in overdrive. Vivid thoughts and memories reside in my head, clear and detailed. Dreams leave gaps and push past the realm of reality. These aren't recollections of dreams. I know Nate Hunt.

After a shower and a burnt grilled cheese, thanks to Nate consuming my mind, I text my mom to let her know I won't be able to have dinner with her tonight—our Thursday night tradition. On my way down to my car, my phone rings.

"Job interview, Mom. I'm not ditching you for anything better."

"Swayze, I'm not calling to guilt you. Just wanted to make sure you're feeling okay. Clearly you are, so tell me about the interview. Is this a job-job or just a temporary job until fall?"

"Not sure yet." I put her on Bluetooth as I pull my black Elantra away from the curb. "It's a nanny job, evenings and some weekends. I'll let you know."

"Is it here in Madison?"

"Yes, just a few minutes from my place."

"How was your session?" Conversation whiplash.

"Fine."

"Fine is good?" She knows me too well.

I sigh. "Fine is a second session booked."

"I'm so glad to hear that."

Why? I'm not the one who still cries at the mention of my father's name. If I weren't recognizing seemingly complete strangers and recollecting things about them that happened before I was born, then I'd say I'm perfectly normal.

"Has Dr. Bunz suggested you sell the house yet?" Howard Bunz. It hurts my brain to even think about his name. I never even made it to a first session with him for reasons that are obvious.

"No. You're not a doctor, Swayze. I don't know why you're so adamant about me selling the house. Dr. B hasn't mentioned it, and I don't think he will."

"Dr. B, huh?"

She clicks her tongue. "That's what all of his patients call him."

"I can't imagine why." I grin as I pull onto the street, my navigation talking over my mom.

"Stop it. You and your obsession with names. Even if you don't think you have issues over losing your father, your name thing alone is enough of a reason to see a psychiatrist."

Eyes flitting between my rearview and side mirrors, I parallel park between two much more expensive vehicles on the street. This is a really nice neighborhood. I'm shocked to see any cars on the street at all.

"And by 'name thing' you mean my astute observations into the quirks of humanity? The need for people to be unique at all costs? The obsession with trend-setting?"

"Goodbye, Swayze. And good luck with the interview." That's her way of ending a conversation she knows she can't win.

"Bye, Mom. Love you."

I'm early, so I wait a few minutes before making my way up the long, tree-lined drive to the brick house with a high-pitched roof and white pillars at the door.

I press the doorbell and wait, sliding my hands into the pockets of my black dress slacks then dropping them to my sides. I cross them over my chest and end with tucking them back into my pockets just as the door opens. Nerves are crazy little creatures.

My eyebrows shoot up as my head jerks back. "Nate."

CHAPTER THREE

NATE BLINKS A few times before craning his neck out the door, surveying the area. "What are you doing here?"

My eyes follow his line of vision around the lush, manicured yard and tall evergreens dividing his property from the neighbor's. Are clowns going to jump out? Are there hidden cameras? What am I missing?

"Well, I'm..." I pull out my phone and show him the email "...here for an interview. See?"

His back stiffens as I shove my phone in his face, not meaning to come an inch from smacking him in the nose. My nerves were a little shaky on the way here. Nothing crazy. Typical interview jitters. But Nate answering the door has me trembling like an earthquake.

"S. Samuels?" He squints at the screen.

The whole world doesn't need to know my name. S. Samuels makes me sound more mysterious like an author who doesn't want to reveal her gender—or one with a shitty name. "It's Swayze. In case you forgot."

Nate rubs his forehead like he needs to erase the day from his memory. Something must be going wrong in his mind if he needs Dr. Greyson. It might be a little *pot calling the kettle black* of me to think that. I feel sorry for him. It's not my intention to be one more thing he doesn't want to deal with today.

"I didn't forget. My sister-in-law scheduled these inter-

views. Sorry, I didn't make the last name connection from..."
his lips twist "...earlier."

Earlier. Not years ago. What is going on? I'm losing it.
Cancer. It has to be cancer in my brain—or aliens. Every year I
get a physical. Cancer seems unlikely, but they miss shit.
Happens all the time. Aliens are a better possibility. They must
be real. Why else would NASA spend so much money to search
for life beyond Earth?

His lip trapped between his teeth and the nervous pull to
his brow says he's not comfortable letting a stalker into his
house, let alone interviewing said stalker for a nanny position.

I don't *need* this job. Even if money gets tight, I can take
on a few extra design jobs to get me by until fall. But this is no
longer a job interview; it's a mystery I have to solve. *Nate? Why
are you in my head?*

"I have to apologize for earlier. I figured out how I know
you or 'of' you. My older cousin used to date your friend, Toby
Friedman. She told me about the hockey story and where you
grew up—four houses down from Toby's house. I've been
down that street a million times. The house is still green.
Anyway, she had a photo of you and Toby. I think your blue
eyes made you unmistakable and ... *familiar.* Hope I didn't
freak you out."

Toby grew up four houses down from Nate, and they were
both on the pond the day of the accident. But I don't have any
cousin who dated Toby. I'm just praying to God that Nate
finds my explanation believable.

After a few seconds, he returns a sharp nod. "I haven't seen
Toby in years. Not since we graduated from high school."

"Neither has my cousin." A non-creepy smile attempts to
settle on my face. Damn! I hope he buys it.

"Please, come in."

I step inside, slipping off my shoes because the dark wood floor before me doesn't have a single scuff mark on it. Trapping my tongue between my teeth, I don't tell him what a beautiful house he has and what a huge step up it is from the green two-bedroom house on Gable Street.

I'm dying to know what he does and how he can afford to live in such an expensive house. Nate swore he'd never be one of those rich, snobby people he always despised—like the bastard who had an affair with his mom, until she broke it off and begged for his father's forgiveness; he forgave her and took her back. Like Nate, he's awesome.

How the hell do I know all this shit about him?

"Follow me." He leads me to a set of double doors to our right. The woody, slightly sweet bergamot and vetiver of his aftershave rattles my senses. It's sharp and sophisticated like the man before me.

"Wow." I inspect the story-and-a-half library or office. I'm not sure which it is. There's an imposing antique desk surrounded by three walls of bookshelves and a ladder—the cool kind that glides on rollers along the shelves. The other wall is all windows, and the far ends have panels of medieval stained glass like something salvaged from a church. Slivers of late afternoon light cutting through the trees filter in as a splattering of Technicolor around the room. "This is an amazing space."

"Thank you. Have a seat." Nate sinks into the leather desk chair while I take a seat on the cream tufted accent chair in front of his desk.

"Nice skeleton." I chuckle at the life-sized anatomical human skeleton on castors next to his desk.

He gives it a quick glance before opening his laptop. "I'm an anatomy professor."

"Really? That's awesome and to think—" I bite my tongue again. This is so hard.

"To think what?" His arched brow calls me out.

Nate wasn't going to college. Hockey. That was his life.

"Uh ... to think that for the longest time I thought these life-sized skeletons were real skeletons. You know, when I was younger. Crazy, huh?"

More blinks from him make me feel like my chance at getting this job is nil.

"You didn't castle. What's up with that?" I shoot a nod to the chessboard on his desk.

He eyes it and then frowns, apparently realizing I'm right and he's two moves from losing his king. "You like chess?"

"No."

"No?" His eyes shoot up at me.

I don't. Never played the game in my life. But looking at the board, it's all very familiar. Just like Nate. "It's long, tedious, and boring. No offense."

A smirk plays across his lips as he leans back in his chair and folds his hands over his stomach. Since I saw him at the shrink's office, he exchanged his jeans and tee for gray pants and an eggplant button-down shirt with the sleeves rolled up just below his elbows. God! He looks sexy as hell, which is insane because he's aged so much since ... I don't know. But I can't stop admiring his sophisticated sexiness. When did I start having a thing for older men?

"You have a degree in education, but no teaching position?"

I clear my throat. "I'm hoping to get one for this fall. I've put in several applications."

"No current employment?"

"Freelance graphic design."

"Married? Children?"

"No."

"Experience with children other than working as an associate teacher?"

"In high school, I babysat for neighbors and worked as a nanny full time for two summers during college. It's on my résumé."

He nods, without looking at my application and résumé, which I assume is what's on his computer screen.

"CPR? First aid?"

"It's …" *On the résumé.* "Yes. Both."

"Ever been arrested?"

"No."

"Speeding tickets?"

I chuckle. "No."

"Parking tickets?"

The lunacy.

"No."

"Smoker? Ever used any drugs? Consumption of alcohol? Medical issues like depression, diabetes, epilepsy?"

Who is this guy? Nate Hunt was laid back. The world could have ended and he would have said, *"It's not as bad as you think."* He worried about nothing. Trusted everyone. Totally chill all of the time.

"Not a smoker or drug user. I like candy, but it's never put me into a diabetic coma. No epilepsy. As you know, I see a psychiatrist, but I'm not depressed. I'm doing it for my mom. She thinks I need to talk to someone about my feelings since my dad died. But really, I'm good."

"Do you have questions for me?"

It's my turn. That wasn't so bad. This guy is older than I am, yet I feel a tremendous sense of pride. That seems condescending. He's asking all the right questions. I want to give him a ribbon or merit badge for a job well done. "How many children? Your ad didn't say."

"One." Sadness washes across his face as he glances back over at the chessboard and the matte-silver picture frame. I can't see the actual picture from my chair.

"How old?"

"One month."

"Oh, wow. Short maternity leave."

Nate flinches. "My wife died giving birth."

Grabbing the arms of the chair, I start to stand then sit back down. Shit! My instinct is to hug him. What the hell? He lost his wife. But … we don't know each other—supposedly. Nate got married. It's been too long. There's so much I don't know in spite of all that I do know.

"Nate … I'm so sorry."

He bites his lips together for a moment before meeting my gaze again. "I go by Nathaniel. I haven't been Nate since I was a kid."

"Sorry, my cousin said Nate. Probably because you were a kid when she was dating Toby."

"I leave for work by noon Monday through Friday. My sister-in-law, Rachael, will be here until 4:30, so I'll need help from 4:30 until 8:00, except for Friday. I'm home by 6:00 on Fridays." He drums his fingers on his desk.

"Weekends?"

"Every other Saturday from 7:30 until noon. And I have

several conferences I'll be attending in July and August, and I will require some additional help during those weeks. Now ..." He stands. "I have two more interviews tonight. I'll make a decision by the end of the week. Thank you for coming."

His hand hangs in the air waiting for me to shake it—the huge hand of a gorilla, with callouses and knobby knuckles from jamming fingers. A sizable mitt made to wrap around a hockey stick, not hold a red pen to grade papers. I stand and hook my purse over my arm and slip my hand into his. Part of me expects his touch to be familiar, but it's not. I don't think. No light bulb. No electrical tingling. I don't think so anyway. My hand's too shaky to really feel anything.

"Thank you, Nate—thaniel." I bite my lip in a grimace.

"I'll show you out." He follows me to the front door.

I slip on my shoes as he opens it. "Do you have a son or a daughter?"

When he smiles, it's the ghost of the boy that I recognized at Dr. Greyson's office. For a few seconds, he beams with happiness and pride. "Daughter. Her name is Morgan."

Once I step out into the warm June air, I turn. "Morgan. That's a great name."

"I named her after ..." His eyes and mouth turn downward as he stares at his hands, his left ring finger still wearing a platinum reminder of what he lost.

After what? Now I need to know that too. But I can't cause him any more pain by asking, and I can't hug him even if he desperately needs a hug. And believe me, no human has ever needed a hug more than Nathaniel Hunt does at this very moment. He has the defeated appearance of an NFL kicker who just lost the winning field goal for the Super Bowl.

"I named her after ..." He clears his throat and glances up

at me again with a pleading vulnerability—nothing like the stranger shooting questions at me just minutes ago.

"Someone special or something meaningful?" I smile because it's all I have to give to a man who doesn't know me. My words are sincere, even if wholly inadequate to comfort him.

"Yes," he whispers.

I take another step backwards. "I'd love the opportunity to meet Morgan. But if you find a better fit, then it was nice meeting you and good luck." My teeth scrape along my bottom lip several times as I nod. "You're going to be just fine, Nathaniel. I'm certain of it."

CHAPTER FOUR

T HE ALL-BLACK HARLEY Davidson Breakout parked on my
street brings a grin to my face as I pull in behind it. Two
months ago I met Griffin Calloway, a Harley Davidson
technician and mechanic with tattoos and muscles of a gym rat
which my mom assumes come from steroids.

Griffin is clean. The guy owns some high-end blender, a
juicer, and he's always shaking a protein drink in one of those
flip-top bottles with the stainless steel blender ball. I've gone
grocery shopping with him twice, not counting our first
encounter. Yep, we met at the grocery store. Over half of
everything he buys is produce, and the other half is lean meat,
nuts, and protein powder in bulk.

I forgot my wallet the day we met. He handed the cashier a
fifty to pay for my bottle of wine, the bag of chipotle lime corn
chips, two 55% dark chocolate bars, and a twelve count box of
super absorbent tampons.

When I insisted he give me his address so I could send him
a check, he wrote his number on the back of my receipt and
told me to call him when I was ready to buy him dinner as
payback. I was on day three of my five-day cycle. I called him
two days later.

"I tried texting you." Griffin keeps his gaze on the TV.
NASCAR.

Eventually, I'll stop pinching myself at the sight of this

man in a sleeveless shirt and jeans as ripped as the body that wears them when I walk into my dinky one-bedroom apartment. He usually has a bandana covering his smooth shaven head, but not today. Griffin Calloway is two-hundred and thirty pounds of raw sex, and he's mine.

Pinch.

"Sorry. I had my phone silenced, and I forgot to check it before I headed home." That and an all-too-familiar stranger crashed into my world today, and I haven't been the same since.

"Another lover?" The corner of his mouth quirks, but his eyes don't move from the TV.

"Griff, I have many lovers. How do you think I pay for my groceries?" I slip off my shoes and hang my purse on the hook by the door.

He rubs his hand over his mouth, hiding his grin. "Get over here so I can fuck some sense into you."

"I have to finish a website design by morning."

"Then you'd better do less talking and more stripping." Griffin shrugs off his shirt revealing a sea of taut, inked skin. Another pinch-me moment.

I'm an average girl. Average height. Average weight. Average boobs. My hair is just past my shoulders, an average shade of blond. My eyes are blue, not too dark, not too light—average.

Griffin is the opposite of average. I'm still trying to figure out his attraction to me. Maybe I'll have to discuss my average self-esteem with Dr. Greyson at our next appointment.

"Tell me about your day." He stands and removes his jeans and boxers in one fluid motion—still watching the race.

I'm not having sex with him while he watches NASCAR.

Even this average girl has standards. Crossing my arms over my chest, I wait for him to make eye contact with me. He hasn't shown me his sable eyes since I walked through the door.

Griffin sits on my black leather sofa. "Swayz, your day. Hop on and tell me about it." He strokes himself.

Still no eye contact.

It's not easy to act unaffected by his large hand fisting his thick cock, but who says "hop on?"

"You're not one of your bikes you work on." I grab the remote from the arm of the sofa and shut off the TV. "I'm not *hopping on.*"

Playful brown eyes finally focus on me, accompanied by a cocky grin.

"It looked like you were masturbating to NASCAR." My teeth trap my grin. I want to be mad at him for this anti-romantic gesture, but he keeps stroking himself, and all I can do is squeeze my legs together.

"I love NASCAR." White teeth peek out from his full lips. "How was your appointment with the new shrink?"

Stroke. Stroke. Stroke.

I may need to figure out why he's attracted to me, but I don't have to figure out why I'm crazy about him. He's sexy, comfortable in his skin, and so damn goofy it's ridiculous.

"Stop!" I grab the yellow blanket from the back of the sofa and toss it over him before tackling him.

"Oof!" He chuckles.

I wrap my arms around his neck, burying my nose into his skin while taking a deep inhale. He's all cedar wood and spice. Warm and delectable. I feel small pressed to the hard planes of his body. And safe. Griffin makes me feel safe.

"I missed you, hot stuff." He palms my ass and gives it a

firm squeeze, adjusting me over his erection covered by the blanket.

"I missed you too." His scent is crack to my senses. My nose refuses to move from its lodged position in the crook of his neck.

"Tell me about your day?"

Begrudgingly, I lift my head. "For real? Or just because you like background noise when you're having sex?"

Griffin sits up, setting me aside like a throw pillow. He has a dragon tattooed on his back, and the tail of it runs down his right butt cheek and ends partway down the back of his leg. When he stands, my eyes go straight to it.

"I love that tattoo."

"I know you do."

"So cocky."

"Nope. I've just heard you say it a million times. I love your tattoo too."

"It's a birthmark."

He gets dressed. Such a shame. It should be illegal for Griffin to put on clothes. But I know why he's doing it, and I kinda love him for it.

"Every detail. You have my undivided attention." He sits down and pulls me onto his lap so I'm straddling him.

"I don't deserve you, Grocery Store Guy." I kiss him.

The day he wrote his number on the back of the receipt, he signed it *Grocery Store Guy*.

Fisting my hair, he deepens the kiss. It's sensual, familiar, possessive, and utterly intoxicating. I think I'm falling in love with this man, but I'm still too deep in lust to know for sure.

He pulls back, rubbing his lips together like he's savoring my taste. "Go."

I grin. "Coffee with sugar."

He rolls his eyes. "Sugar with coffee, but go on."

"Barre class. Shower. A bit of design work. Then Dr. Greyson."

"Good name."

My eyes double in size. "I know. Right? And his appearance fits his name too."

"Bonus." Griffin gets me. That's huge. That's everything.

"I made another appointment."

"So a good day?" He gathers my hair and moves it away from my neck before ducking down to kiss me. "Didn't you have an interview too?"

Yep. Totally falling for this man. Griffin may be a grease monkey some days, but he's smart and attentive when he wants to be, and he remembers stuff that most twenty-three-year-old guys would not remember. Hell, most guys of any age wouldn't remember the little things that Griffin does.

"Yes." I stretch my neck to the side to give him better access. "Funny thing … I met this guy in the waiting room at the doctor's office. I totally recognized him, but he didn't recognize me. Then I get to the interview, and it's the same guy. What are the chances?"

His hands rest on my legs, sliding upward until his thumbs brush over the spot I want them most. "One in a million," he mumbles into my neck. "So how do you know him?"

"I don't know."

"You don't know?" He unfastens my pants. The guy is a multi-tasking god. His dick hasn't lost focus; I can feel it bulged against his jeans. He devours the skin along my neck, but he's still one hundred percent engaged in this conversation.

We've had full conversations during sex. I suck at it; my

mind goes blank like too much blood is needed parts, leaving an inadequate amount in my brain to fu properly. But Griffin can fuck me into next week, coming hard—almost violently—without missing a single detail or comment, even if his words are strained, breathy, and grunted out with each thrust.

"I know him and things about …"

His hand slips down the front of my panties. "Keep going." His finger brushes my clit.

"Um … Griff." My eyes blink heavily.

"Things about?" He sucks my earlobe, teasing it with his tongue the way his finger teases my clit.

"His past. But I don't know how because it doesn't coincide with my past, or at least I can't make the connection. It's so … Jesus …"

Griffin slips his middle finger inside of me. "Biblical?" He chuckles.

And the shift has happened. There's no longer enough blood left in my brain. "Just fuck me, Griff." I grab his face and pull it away from my neck, smashing my lips to his.

"YOU HAVE TO leave." I block the doorway to my bedroom when naked, insatiable Griffin follows me down the short hall connecting my bedroom and bathroom.

His gaze slides along my naked body, and that's why he has to leave. "You've stopped by the shop, and I've kept working. Why can't you work when I'm here?"

"Because it's late and my bed is inviting enough without you in it. *With* you in it … I don't stand a chance. I need to ın pay rent and stop whoring myself

ıirt over my head. "Then stop looking at
.nore."

ıng only his bare feet step into his boxers and
jea.   snags the shirt from my head, a killer grin on his
freshly-ʃ.   en face. He slips it on as I turn and grab a nightshirt from my dresser. This room could not be any more
cramped. I have a full bed, desk, and dresser crammed in here
with barely enough space to turn around.

"Congratulations on the job, baby." He hugs me from behind and nuzzles into my neck.

I close my eyes and ghost my fingers over his arms. "I don't
have the job yet."

"You'll get it. Anybody would be a fool not to hire you."

"You might be biased." I laugh.

"Slumber party at my place this weekend."

I turn in his arms. "Slumber party?" This guy puts the best
smile on my face. My cheeks hurt when we're together.

"Ask your mom. Maybe you can ride home with me on the
bus after school on Friday." He winks.

"You have too many sisters." He does. Three. And they're
all younger and still in school.

He lifts me off my feet and kisses me, one hand sliding to
grip my ass. Website? What website?

"Goodnight," he whispers over my mouth before easing me
back onto my feet.

I rub my lips together as I follow him to the door, admiring
his backside when he shoves his feet into his black leather boots
by the door. "Will there be pillow fights?"

Griffin chuckles while still bent over tying his laces. "Yes."

He stands and turns toward me. "Wear something pink and lacy and put your hair in pigtails." Biting his lower lip, he nods slowly. "Dear God yes ... pink lace and pigtails, baby."

I laugh and head back toward my room. "Goodnight, Grocery Store Guy." As soon as I hear the roar of his Harley out front, I sit at my desk and start designing. Two seconds later, I'm on the internet searching up Nathaniel Hunt. "Why are you in my head," I whisper.

CHAPTER FIVE

"WHERE ARE YOU off to so early?"

Halfway down the stairs I pause, glancing up at my neighbor bent over the railing. A loose ponytail corrals her black curls as she scrutinizes me. Her lips hug the red handle of a toothbrush.

"Erica, are you spying on me?"

"Nope," she mumbles around foam. "Just keeping an eye on *things*." Her gaze flits between me and the door across the hall from her apartment.

"Dougly at it again?"

Erica holds up a finger before dashing back into her apartment. Doug Mann, her new sixty-something playboy neighbor with orangish hair plugs—that elicit a cringe every time I see him—possesses a hidden sex appeal that we can't figure out. And his nose ... let's just say it should have its own zip code. Since he moved in a month ago, he's had a steady trail of women pass through his revolving door. Young women. Pretty women. Hookers? We're not sure. It seems like the only plausible explanation for the old and ugly (Dougly) man (Mann) entertaining that many women.

"Two. There were two of them willingly following him into his place when I got home last night around eleven." Erica hoists her backpack on her shoulder as she scuttles down the stairs toward me.

"Ew …" I wrinkle my nose and swallow the bile crawling up my throat. "Maybe he's rich."

"I don't think rich people live in this building."

Our footsteps echo in sync as we approach the main floor. "You're a cardiologist and you live here."

"Second year resident. Dirt poor. Buried in school loans. I'm not rich. Nor do I have a ridiculously hot boyfriend who rides a Harley."

Musings of Griffin and his overabundance of hotness elicit something between a chuckle and a dreamy sigh.

"In fact…" her blue Saab parked behind my car beeps when she unlocks it "…I'm quite certain I'm the only one in the building not getting any."

"But you're saving lives." I hop off the curb, riding my Griffin high.

She tosses her backpack in her car and leans on the top of the open door. "When your inked god is in your bed, do you wish you were saving lives instead of …" Her eyebrows waggle.

I open my door. "Are you asking me if I'd rather have sex with Griffin or save the world?"

"Yes."

"No brainer. Griff all the way."

Erica shoots me the bird and slips into her car. "You never said what has you out and about so early." Her head pokes back out before she shuts the door.

"I got a callback for a nanny job. So I'm off to meet the baby today."

"Oh, good luck!"

MY TEETH CHATTER, fed by a bad case of nerves. Nate's sister-in-law, Rachael, called me Friday to set up a time to meet Morgan. Her father, this familiar stranger, resides in my head, entangled in my thoughts and dreams. Hours of online research led me to repeated dead ends. He's listed under the university website. I found his wife's obituary. The county assessor's website gave me the value of his home—with a dizzying seven-digit value.

My gut tells me to proceed with caution. Especially when I know I'm of sound mind. Nate has to be the crazy one. After all, he, too, is a patient of Dr. Greyson's. The poor guy's wife died. Maybe he's had a breakdown. Memory loss or something like that.

My knuckles rap three times on the rich wooden door, hard enough to be heard but hopefully soft enough to not wake a sleeping baby.

"Swayze?"

My gaze lands on the swaddled baby hidden in the white blanket dotted with pink bunnies. A tiny patch of dark hair peeks out from the top. The woman holding the baby looks like a statue. Why do people get so stiff the moment they pick up a baby? Her earthy-toned eyes blink. Okay, she's alive. A constipated smile creeps up her face, marring her natural beauty accented by strands of chestnut silk sweeping along her chin in a reverse bob.

"Yes," I say with muted enthusiasm. If I scare her, she could crack and send the baby tumbling to the floor.

"Come in." She grimaces at the baby without moving the ridged cradle of her arms.

If the baby wakes, the world will end. That much I can deduce from this situation.

"I'm Rachael," she mouths. Good thing I can read lips. Not really, but her exaggerated jaw flapping makes it easy. "It's a pleasure to meet you."

I fight off a giggle. Babies also turn perfectly-put-together humans into buffoons.

Slipping off my shoes, I browse around for any signs of Nate. "Thank you. It's nice to meet you too. And thank you for the callback. This must be Morgan?" I refrain from saying the obvious "*she's so tiny*." But she really is tiny, even for a one-month-old.

Rachael's back stiffens on a silent gasp. I spoke beyond a whisper and the world may end.

An exhale tiptoes past her parted lips once she realizes babies don't require complete silence to sleep. "Yes…" Rachael watches Morgan "…she's being lazy this morning." She tests a few more words. Morgan doesn't flinch. "Only took half her bottle before drifting back to sleep."

When her wonder-filled gaze meets mine, I lift my brows a fraction. *Wow!* Did she just now realize it's okay to talk in front of a sleeping baby? Poor girl. And by girl I mean young lady because I'm certain she's older than I am, at least by five or so years, but younger than Nate.

I follow her to the living room filled with oversized leather furniture and a wall of curtain-framed windows overlooking dense woods. There's a newborn living here. Where is the baby swing sitting in a corner? Or the dark wicker basket of diapers and other baby essentials that should be on the wooden coffee table? Toys. Why are there no toys that Morgan is too young to play with but they can't resist trying to entertain her with them anyway?

No blankets.

No tiny baby hats.

No knitted booties from a grandma or great aunt.

"Would you like to hold her?"

I lift up my hands. "Mind if I wash my hands real quick?"

Rachael's smile grows a fraction like I passed the first test, but I honestly don't think it's a test. That would require more knowledge of babies and a confidence she doesn't possess.

"Do you have kids?" I ask, washing my hands at the kitchen sink, but I think I know the answer.

"No. Never been married. I don't even have a boyfriend. But I'm getting a crash course in motherhood." Her smile dissipates as her brow tightens.

"I'm very sorry for your loss."

Rachael smiles as if she feels the need to make a quick recovery. Her sister died a month ago. I don't think forced smiles are necessary yet.

"We're doing well." She hands Morgan to me.

I bring her up on my shoulder. She burps, let's out a squeaky cry, and falls right back to sleep.

"Wow. She never burps for me."

I sit in the rocking chair, and Rachael sits on the love seat, tucking her legs underneath her.

"Burped babies are happy babies." I nestle my nose into the blanket and take a hit of that new baby smell.

"You have siblings?" she asks.

"No. I did a lot of babysitting in high school and took on summer jobs as a nanny during college. What about you? Any other siblings?"

"An older brother in Washington. But he's not married either. Our mom died a few years ago, but our dad lives here in Madison. When Jenna died, I was the only one who stepped up to help Nathaniel, aside from his mom. But she's had some health issues, so we don't like to ask her for too much help. And Nathaniel doesn't have any siblings, so ..."

"So you're all figuring this out as you go because no one has any real baby experience."

She chuckles a bit. "Pretty much. I was supposed to start grad school this fall, but I'm going to take a year off to help with Morgan. Nathaniel works long hours, so that's why he needs you. He insists I find a life beyond Morgan. But ..." Rachael traps her bottom lip between her teeth and focuses on Morgan in my arms. "I feel guilty handing her off to anyone else. Jenna wouldn't have wanted that. No offense." Her nose wrinkles when she glances up at me.

"None taken. But I'm a little confused. You asked me here to meet Morgan. I assumed you're still making a final decision, but you just said Nate-Nathaniel needs *me* ..."

"He does. He just doesn't know it. You're the best fit. The youngest, but most experienced. And watching you with her confirms it, but Nathaniel's a little uneasy about ..."

I know where this is going. She doesn't have to say it. "I recognized him from pictures. I get it. Our first meeting was weird. Totally my fault. I shouldn't have said anything until I figured out the connection." I shrug. "It was no big deal. But I understand how it might have freaked him out at first. This is his child. He should be skeptical to a fault."

"Well, after a slightly heated argument last week, he agreed to let me hire you if I still felt all 'gung-ho' after meeting you. Honestly, I don't think he knows what he wants other than ..."

We share a painful look. His wife. Nate wants his wife back.

"I want the job, so don't take this the wrong way. Were the other applicants so bad that I looked *that* good just from my résumé?"

"Not bad, just old. I'm not trying to discriminate, I just wanted someone younger but experienced. Taking care of a baby can be an exhausting job. So the job is yours if you want it. I can send the contract home with you today to look over."

I pull in a deep breath, suffocated by the sterile air.

No lavender candles.

No sugar cookies baking in the oven.

No baby powder lingering in the air.

Morgan starts to fuss, so I stand and walk around with a gentle bounce to my step. Below the TV mounted to the wall is a fireplace mantle holding framed pictures. I recognize Nate's parents; they're on the beach holding on to their big floppy hats so they don't blow away. There's one of *Nathaniel* and Jenna on their wedding day at the doors to a cathedral, rose petals floating around the happy couple as they make their escape. I haven't seen that smile from Nate in a long time. Maybe it died with his wife.

With each step around the room, my heart cracks a little deeper. There are no pictures of Morgan. There should be the classic hospital mugshot that only the parents can love and one with Nate. Why hasn't anyone taken a picture of him asleep on the sofa with Morgan nestled into his chest, the official daddy and baby first date picture?

It's a cricket kind of silence in the house, only without any crickets. At least a few chirps would be some sign of life.

No TV murmuring in the background.

No music or soft static from a white noise machine.

No little wind-up toys playing "Mary Had a Little Lamb."

It's almost too painful to be here, but I can't walk away. This house—this family—needs two paddles and a jolt of life put back into it.

"When do I start?" She should question my taking the job before reviewing the contract or negotiating my wage. But she doesn't.

"Tomorrow too soon?"

"Tomorrow is perfect as long as everything looks agreeable in the contract. I'll read it over when I get home and message you. I don't anticipate any issues."

We small talk for another hour while I give Morgan a bottle and change her diaper.

"You're good at that. It takes Nathaniel and me forever to do that." Rachael's eyes illuminate with wonder like I just demonstrated levitation.

It's a diaper change and three snaps on a onesie. This poor child may be doomed if a twenty-one-year-old stranger is the foremost expert on her.

"TELL ME ABOUT your day, Swayz."

Griffin nods to the upside-down five-gallon bucket a few feet to his right. It's where I like to perch when he's doing his thing in his anal-retentively organized garage. Shiny red tool chests and pegboards of more tools and cords line the wall on either side of his workbench. Behind me, his Harley hides under a custom cover, flaunting its reserved parking spot while his black truck weathers the seasons parked in the drive beneath a canopy of mature oak trees on both sides.

"I want a baby."

He raises an eyebrow at me as he works on his neighbor's motorcycle. I love his two-bedroom house and one-car garage that he uses for side jobs like this. It's in the middle of an older neighborhood with lots of trees and houses that have character, not the cookie-cutter homes in the newer neighborhoods. The fact that it's two blocks from his parents' house is also a lovable trait.

He's close to his family. Sometimes I envy his life. It's not glamorous, but it's rich in the really good stuff that I feel like I missed out on during my parents' quest to discover something brilliant in me.

"Before I put my foot in my mouth or you put yours in my balls, can you clarify if this is an announcement or a request?"

I scrape the worn bottoms of my flip-flops along the gray-speckled sealant on his garage floor and wiggle my toes. My blue nail polish has seen better days.

"I got the nanny job. I start tomorrow."

"Yeah, that's right. You went to meet the baby this morning … Morgan, right?" His socket clicks in quick succession.

I find that sound mixed with the hum of the fan hanging in the corner quite soothing. Watching Griff work on bikes has become my favorite pastime. He's magical with his hands. Heat spreads along my skin, settling between my legs, just thinking of his strong, capable hands.

"I love you, Grocery Store Guy."

He stops his motions and looks at me with those sable eyes that won me over at our first grocery store encounter. I've stopped pinching myself and settled into the fact that he sees something in me that I don't see in myself. We've "loved" many things about each other: his tattoos, my birthmark, his body, my hair, his fingers, my mouth. But neither one of us has used "you" without the "r" after the word love.

"You're pregnant."

I grin, not offended one bit by his assumption. "If I were?"

His gaze flits over my face. If I were pregnant, I might fear the thoughts rolling around in his beautiful head. But I'm not, so my thoughts revel in the anticipation of his next words.

"I'd have to design a sidecar to accommodate a car seat."

"And that's why I love you."

He drops the socket and walks on his knees to me, keeping his sweaty body and greasy hands a few inches from touching me. I happen to love him in any state. Every inch of my body would welcome his touch, even if it left a few smudges.

"Did I get one past the gate?" He rubs his nose against mine then nips at my lower lip. He smells like grease, sweat, and spearmint from his favorite xylitol gum. It's not a marketable combination, but it's my addiction.

"No." I giggle. "It's a thing. When women hold babies and get a whiff of that newborn smell, our ovaries go into overdrive."

"So, you're not pregnant, but you want to be?" His eyes shift from my face to my neck then slowly ease down my body, doing all the things I know his hands and mouth want to do.

"No," I say a little breathy. I know that look of his and so does my body.

"But you said…" his gaze makes a quick return to mine "…you love me."

"I do. But I love you because you ask me about my day—every day. And you *remember* everything I tell you. And you're observant. You know my favorite flower because you know the scent of my favorite lotion. You know the size of my clothes because you've peeled them from my body so many times. You hand me a tissue five seconds before I cry during a sad scene in a movie, but you never actually look at me. You just ... know."

He shrugs, staring at me so intently a shiver snakes along my spine. "It's because ..." His teeth dig into his lower lip.

"That's my point." I grin and lean toward him, teasing his lips with mine until he rewards me with a smile.

"It's because I love you," he whispers over my mouth.

"Thank you..." I kiss him once "...for remembering Morgan's name." I kiss him again—longer, deeper—as my fingers flick open the button to his jeans.

"Baby," he mumbles, "my hands are greasy."

I ease down his zipper. "Then put them in your back pockets. I don't need your help with this."

He moans into my mouth as my hand slides inside his boxers, and like the good boy he is, he stuffs his hands into his back pockets. I love his body too, and the way his deep hums of pleasure vibrate my lips each time I stroke him.

"Swayz ..." He tears his mouth from mine and tips his chin down, watching me stroke him. "Fuck, baby ..." His abs tighten on each labored breath.

"Mom said you'd buy raffle tickets for my show choir fundraiser."

Griffin and I both snap our heads toward his sister, Chloe, standing at the front of the garage. His back is to her, hiding my hand wrapped around his cock. We have a terrible habit of tuning out the rest of the world when we're together. It might have been a good idea to shut the garage door before expressing my recent declaration of love.

"What are you guys up to?" She fans herself with a big white envelope.

Griffin turns back to me. "Let go of my dick and go buy

some raffle tickets," he whispers.

I'm not sure why I'm still holding it. Frozen in shock, I guess. "K." I give him a toothy grin as I release him and stand. "Of course we'll buy raffle tickets." I step past Griffin leaving him to tuck the goods back into his jeans.

Chloe's fifteen, a sophomore, and I think she's still a virgin, but I'm not sure. Regardless, there are some things she never needs to see, and my hand stroking her brother's cock is at the top of that list.

"Great! How many?" She opens the envelope.

"Uh ... ten?"

"They're ten dollars apiece."

"Maybe three?" I give her a wrinkled-nose grin.

"Thanks, Swayze. How many for you, Griff?" Chloe rubs her lips together, mischief alight in her brown eyes as she bats her dark hair away from her face but loses her battle with the evening breeze.

The clicking of the socket wrench starts again. "Swayze said three."

"*She* did. But how many are you buying. You two aren't married, so you can't make joint purchases yet."

She's good. I like his sisters. Hell, I like his whole family. They paint happily ever after using all the colors of the rainbow.

"I'll take one."

"Five it is, Griff. Thanks! You're my most favorite brother ever." She tears off eight raffle tickets.

Griffin tips his chin up from behind the bike and raises a single eyebrow until it brushes the edge of his orange and black bandana. I take the tickets and slip them into the back pocket of my denim shorts.

"Wallet?" I smirk at him.

He sighs and stands holding up his greasy hands. "Front right pocket."

With my back to Chloe, I slide my hand into his pocket grazing his lingering erection. His lips twitch as he eyes me with promises of things that will happen when we are alone again. Heat spreads through my body, converging deep in my belly.

I pull out his money clip and count out eighty dollars. "Mind loaning me thirty dollars to buy raffle tickets from my boyfriend's sister?" Batting my eyelashes, I glance up at him, trapping my lower lip between my teeth.

"I'll let you work it off." His gaze leaves no question as to how I will be working this off.

"I'm not five. Your innuendos are weirding me out. Just hand over the money before I mini-vomit."

I giggle because she's only six years younger than I am, but there's this invisible wall between adolescence and adulthood that makes six years feel like thirty. In a few more years, that gap will be indistinguishable. However, for now, we're the gross adults and she's the innocent child who we're *weirding out*. How innocent? I don't know. Cheerleaders and football players get the bad rap for parties and sex. In my experience, more sex happens in the band room than any other place in school.

"Here. What's the prize?" I hand Chloe the money.

"Caribbean cruise."

"Really?" My head jerks back.

"No. Not really. A subscription to the Madison Symphony Orchestra."

"Fucking great," Griffin mumbles from behind the bike.

"Language, Griff." I roll my eyes.

Chloe laughs. "I'm familiar with the word. He's said it more than once around me. Anyway..." she stuffs the money into the envelope "...thanks again. I'll see ya around."

"Bye." I give her a wave when she makes one last glance over her shoulder while walking down the driveway. "I love your sisters." With a content sigh, I plop back down on the bucket.

"Kinda takes away from the specialness of you declaring your love to me. Don't you think?"

"I assumed you and your family are a package deal. If I love one of you, I have to love all of you."

"Well, I sure as hell love all of you. Now, tell me more. Are you going to like watching after this Morgan?"

Perfect. He's so damn perfect.

"I think so. The hours are good. She's tiny and precious beyond words. It's a pretty cool house. The sister-in-law, Rachael, is really nice, but she has no experience with babies. It's a little weird that the twenty-one-year-old nanny has the most experience of anyone, but I think it may be true."

"And the dad?"

"Nate, er ... Nathaniel is troubled. But he lost his wife, and now he's trying to work, grieve, and raise a baby—his first baby. I think that earns him a pass for any psychological issues he might have. There's a reason they say it takes a village to raise a child. His village is quite small. So ... yeah, they need me."

"Sophie has a dance recital this weekend."

"It's on my calendar."

"And the motorcycle rally in August?"

"I'll ask for that time off. I'm not sure how my ass will feel after that long on the back of your bike, but I'm in. Even though your biker buddies look at me kinda ..." *Like lunch-meat dripping with mayo.*

"Like you're beautiful?" he says it so matter-of-factly.

"Sure. We'll go with that." I twist my lips to hide my grin.

CHAPTER SIX

A BONUS TO this job is its proximity to my apartment. Summer in Madison delivers temperatures in the mid-eighties with the occasional stray thunderstorm. I wear tennis shoes with my shorts and tee and toss an umbrella in my backpack to make the twenty-minute trek to Nate's house.

"She's napping in her crib." Rachael turns on the TV in the living room and a live feed of Morgan appears.

"Not your average baby monitor." I grin.

"Only the best. Jenna and Nathaniel didn't skimp on much."

I'm not sure who this Nathaniel guy is because the Nate I knew was frugal. It took at least four holes in his socks to warrant tossing them.

Threadbare clothes.

Secondhand sporting equipment.

Even the occasional trip to the food pantry when money got really tight for his family.

"He can monitor her as well from his computer or phone. Cameras throughout the house, so don't try and steal anything." Rachael winks and laughs.

"Bummer. I brought my tape measure to see if that sofa would fit in my apartment. And the Viking stove too."

"Do you have any questions? Everything you'll need is in the nursery. My number and Nathaniel's number is on the kitchen counter. Help yourself to food, but other than beer and baby formula, I don't think there's much in the house. I bring my own stuff. You might want to do the same."

I nod.

Rachael sucks in a deep breath and holds it before releasing it on one big huff. "I'm nervous."

"No need to be. We'll be fine."

"I know." She curls her hair behind her ears and smiles. "Leave her in her crib until she wakes up. Nathaniel's trying to train her to be self-soothing. Holding her yesterday was an exception so you could meet her. It's hard to let her be, but it's really for the best."

"Got it." I give a sharp nod.

"Okay then …" Her eyes make a quick sweep of the room. "I'm off. If you need anything our numbers are—"

"On the counter. I got it. No worries."

"And if it's a real emergency—"

"9-1-1. Got it." I fight back a chuckle because while it's funny, I can feel how much it pains her to leave. The need or guilt to fill her sister's shoes is palpable.

"Duh." She shakes her head. "I'm out of here, then. See you tomorrow."

"Bye."

After the door clicks shut behind her, I turn in circles several times. Here I am. And he could be watching my every move. There's nothing unnerving about that. I wonder if there's audio enabled with these surveillance cameras.

"Hey, Professor Hunt." My gaze roams the room until I spy a camera in the corner. I grin and wave. "Thanks for the job. Morgan is in good hands." I shoot two thumbs-up at the camera and grab my backpack to retrieve a book. "*The Power* by Naomi Alderman." I hold up the red covered book so he can see it. "Have you read it? Probably not. You should. It's quite thought-provoking. I don't want to ruin it for you, so I'll just say it's some stimulating insight into what the world would be like if women were deemed the stronger sex. I finished *We Were Liars* by E. Lockhart last week. Mind-blowing." I find my page and start to read.

An hour later Morgan stirs, more like a muscle twitch, but I'm in charge, so I make the executive decision that she needs out of jail. "Hey, Lazy Daisy." I kiss her head and lay her on the changing table. Her fisted hands and springy legs jerk as I unwrap the burrito. "Why is your diaper dry? That's not good."

Morgan makes a weak attempt at scolding me as I dress her and carry her to the kitchen to heat up a bottle. My phone on the counter chimes with a text from a number I don't recognize.

It's not time for her to eat.

Snapping my head up toward the nearest camera, I shoot it a stink look.

Swayze: *Her diaper is dry.*

I add the number to my contact list with his name.

Professor: *Are you sure? They're very absorbent.*

Swayze: *It's a nice day. After I give her a bottle I may take her for a walk. Is that okay?*

He doesn't respond until I take the bottle from the warmer.

Professor: *She can't walk yet.*

I giggle and look at the camera. *This* is the Nate Hunt I remember. Total smart-ass.

> **Swayze:** *Good point. Maybe I'll put her in the baby carrier.*
>
> **Professor:** *Don't give her the whole bottle.*
>
> **Swayze:** *I won't. Just the milk inside it.*
>
> **Professor:** *You know what I mean.*

I carry Morgan to the rocking chair. "I do, Professor Hunt," I mumble, hoping he can hear my voice but not make out my words, "but I'm still going to let her feed until she pops off like a stuffed tick."

She sucks down the whole bottle while my phone vibrates and chimes on the counter. After I burp her, change her diaper, and get her secured in the baby carrier, I check my phone. There is a string of texts spaced about five minutes apart.

> **Professor:** *That's enough milk.*
>
> **Professor:** *That's enough.*
>
> **Professor:** *Stop.*
>
> **Professor:** *Why are you ignoring me?*
>
> **Professor:** *I can't believe you let her drink the whole bottle.*

I slip the phone in my back pocket and wave at the camera in the living room, the one in the hall, and the one by the front door. "Say 'Bye, Daddy.'"

NATE ARRIVES HOME an hour early—if seven at night can be considered early. He sets his messenger bag on the counter, stares at the screen of his phone, and fetches a drink of water before making eye contact with me.

I don't have to acknowledge the downward curl of his lips to know he's disappointed. His weary eyes say it all. They say, *My wife died. I'm miserable. And after a long day, the last thing I need is to come home to the nanny breaking rule number one— don't hold the baby.*

Reclined in the chair with a book in one hand and my other hand drawing circles on Morgan's back as she slumbers in the comfort of human touch, I regret nothing. On a sigh, he marches toward me and lifts her from my chest.

No kiss.

No nuzzling to inhale her baby scent.

No words.

He takes her to her nursery with the sentiment of carrying a paper grocery sack in from the car.

I pack my bag and attach it to my back just as he returns.

"Thank you for today. Tomorrow I'll have Rachael explain a little better the self-soothing process we're using with Morgan. Too much off-schedule feeding and holding today."

His ginger locks look like his hands tugged the hell out of them today, probably while watching me overfeed and over hold his daughter. Those eyes, they feel like an intimate embrace, so damn familiar. How can he look at me with such detachment? What happened to him that he doesn't remember me?

"I'm sure you saw me peek into the room beyond the nursery."

"It's stuff from baby showers," he says in a thick voice.

I nod, rubbing my lips together. There's wall-to-wall baby things in that spare bedroom. Nice things. Brand new. Waiting to be used. "I figured. You have six different baby seats and two swings. Have you thought about bringing a few things out here or setting one in your office? It would be *hands-off.*" I don't grin. It's not funny. It's utterly heartbreaking.

"She's good in her crib, and I can monitor her, so what's the point?" His body shifts as he clears his throat.

"Well, you could at least talk to her. Stare at her. I don't know. It was just a thought."

"She's good." He regards me like I'm his student and his words are final.

I feel all fifteen years between us.

"She's good," I echo. Morgan's not good. She's been out of the womb for four weeks. Her mommy died, and the people who are supposed to love her think casting her into some oblivion of bullshit self-soothing is what she needs. I have nothing to base this on, but I feel in the depths of my soul that babies grieve too. Nate has his family, Rachael, his co-workers, and Dr. Greyson. Who does Morgan have? A blanket and a half a bottle of formula?

Her cry echoes into the room. Nate's shoulders tense as his jaw clenches. It's not a fussy cry, it's a desperate save-me cry. On instinct, I turn to go to her.

"Leave her. She'll calm down."

My hands fist. It's all I can do to keep them from wrapping around his thick neck and shaking some sense into him. I should leave. My job for the day is over. But I can't. And as upset as I think he is with me, he's not telling me to go because he's not sure she will settle down, which means he will have to deal with her.

Pick her up.

Hold her.

Soothe her.

Love her.

Of course he loves her. How can he not? But why is he fighting it?

We stand in the same spots for ten minutes. I know this because the clock on the microwave is in my line of view. The cries have not subsided, not even a little. They've grown like the anguish on Nate's face.

"I'm going to pick her up. You can physically stop me, but I will fight you, or you can fire me, but I'm. Picking. Her. Up." With a quick pivot, I make long strides to the nursery, my aching heart ready to bust through my chest.

As a nanny, there's this point of no return. It's the moment when the child matters more than the idiot parents. The point where the only way to get the nanny out of the house is to fire her because she's not there for the paycheck. It's a heroic need to save an innocent human, to fight for them when they cannot fight for themselves. It's long days of contemplating the unfairness of undeserving humans having everything but not giving a damn about anything.

"Oh, Little Daisy," I hold her close to me as her cries subside.

"Why did you call her *that*?"

I turn toward Nate's imposing form in the doorway.

"I don't know. Why? Are pet names not allowed?" I'm asking to get fired. But damn him for being such an ass when I know that's not who he is … or was.

"Daisy. Why did you call her *that*."

Cupping the back of her tiny head, I whisper, "Shh shh shh" while dancing in small circles. "I don't know. She sleeps a lot, so I called her Lazy Daisy earlier and the daisy must have stuck because little daisy just…" I shrug "…came out. Why?"

He shakes his head. "Nothing ... no reason."

Within minutes, Morgan drifts off to sleep, and I ease her back into the crib. Nate backs away from the door as I shut off the light.

"Do you have nightmares about losing your wife?" I whisper as we stand toe-to-toe in the hallway.

Nate's brow knits together. I wait for him to answer.

"Sometimes."

"Maybe she does too." I press my palm over his heart.

He stiffens under my hand.

"I'm not hitting on you. I'm just reminding you that touch is a basic human need, and it's an expression of love. If you were self-soothing you wouldn't be seeing Dr. Greyson." I remove my hand. "Touch is the only kind of love Morgan can feel right now. So remember that the next time you count the hours I spend holding her while you're at work."

Gathering every ounce of emotion desperate to explode from my chest, I grab my backpack and run out the door. After several blocks, I slow to a stop, bend over, and rest my hands on my knees as tears well in my eyes. "Jesus, Nate. What's happened to you?" Standing, I stare at my hand. The second I pressed it to his chest, it remembered the feel of *his* heartbeat. My fucking hand remembers a heartbeat. How is that possible? And why can't he remember me?

CHAPTER SEVEN

THE TRICKLE OF the fountain in the corner of Dr. Greyson's office drowns out the muffled voices in the waiting room. Someone needs to water the sad, wilting fern on the window ledge. The aroma of coffee fills the air, but I know by the time I leave, it will be replaced with peppermint.

Five.

Dr. Greyson averages five mints during a session—the strong kind that come in a little tin with a white paper liner.

"Can we discuss something new today?" I ask while hugging a navy throw pillow with a white compass embroidered on the front. Maybe he likes to sail or maybe it's symbolic of helping patients find direction.

"We can discuss whatever you'd like to discuss." Dr. Greyson has three postures: hands folded in his lap, hands folded on his desk, and hands folded at his chest with his chin resting on steepled fingers.

Right now he's giving me hands folded on his lap, which is where we usually start each session. In another twenty minutes they will be on his desk, and by the end they will be steepled—his most contemplative position.

I notice random stuff.

"Lately I've had some déjà vu moments, but not the kind that feel weird for a few seconds and then go away. They're not just fleeting feelings of 'I've experienced this before.' They're vivid memories, as vivid as the memories of my sweet sixteen birthday party or the look on my mom's face when the doctor told us my father died."

Dr. Greyson skips hands-folded-on-the-desk position and goes straight to steepled fingers. "Tell me about these memories."

My fingernail traces the cross of the compass on the pillow hugged to my chest. "I recently saw this guy, and I know him, but not like 'why do you look familiar, I know I've seen you before.' I mean I *know* him, but not the *now* him; I know the *then* him."

"The 'then' him?"

"Yes."

"So you knew him when you were kids?"

The million-dollar question.

"No."

His lips purse as his brow draws tight.

"I know things about him from when he was a kid. Not *us* as kids." I laugh. Saying those words aloud sounds even crazier than they do in my head.

"Does he know you?"

"No."

"You switched schools a lot. Are you sure you weren't classmates at some point?"

I shake my head slowly. It's funny and confusing and insane and ... heartbreaking because I remember his *touch*—the rhythm of his heartbeat.

"Do you have old yearbooks you could look through?"

My head continues to turn side to side. "He wouldn't be in any of them."

"How can you be sure?"

"Because he's fifteen years older than I am."

The lid to his mint tin snaps open and the white paper crinkles as he plucks out a mint and pops it into his mouth. I think he uses this time to think of another question or maybe an appropriate and professional response that doesn't involve the word crazy. "Can you be more specific about the memories?"

"What do you want to know? His favorite color? The layout of the house he grew up in? His quirks and mannerisms? How much his father hated the way he scuffed his feet along the floor like he was too lazy to pick them up and walk like 'a normal person?' I know everything about him, or that's what it feels like."

"But you don't know how you know?"

"Yeah." I cringe.

"Have you confirmed that what you think you know about him is factual?"

"Yes. Well, not everything. I don't want to freak him out completely. He's my new boss."

"You got a new job?"

"Yes. I'm a nanny for a one-month-old. Her mother died giving birth. The dad is a professor and works odd hours."

I wait for recognition on his face. He has to know I'm talking about Nate—Nathaniel Hunt.

The pace of his blinks increases for a few moments. He's making the connection.

"He's your patient. Nathaniel Hunt."

Dr. Greyson wets his lips methodically.

"I know you can't tell me. That's fine. I saw him in your waiting room after our first visit. That's how I know. You don't have to speak, just listen." I chuckle. "Nothing new, right?"

He relinquishes the tiniest grin accompanied by the lift of one eyebrow.

"I think Nate ... that's how I remember him ... has some type of emotional trauma from his wife dying. Not the average grieving, but something deeper that's affected his ability to remember things like ... how we know each other."

"I can't discuss—"

"I know. Really, I don't expect you to share anything with me. I'm just throwing it out there. Food for thought. Whatever. I guess..." I blow out a slow, long breath "...what concerns me the most is that *I* can't make sense of how I know him. Like ..."

Little balls of anxiety bounce around in my gut, bringing on a familiar nausea. It's the same feeling I used to get every time my parents took me to be tested or evaluated. I can't remember a single time in my life where I felt normal. Experts have been trying to "figure me out" forever.

"It's hard to explain, but it's the *us* factor. I remember my past and his past, but not *us*. And it feels ridiculous, even impossible, to know so much about him if there wasn't an us."

Not a single blink from Dr. Greyson. I expect a team of people in white scrubs to burst through the door at any moment, plunge a needle into my arm, and haul me to a place with padded walls and no windows.

Seconds, maybe minutes, drag on until he taps the keyboard at his desk, slips on a pair of black-framed reading glasses, and tips his chin up reading over his nose.

"Are you reading my health history again?"

Questioning eyes shift, shooting me a scrutinizing gaze. His honey-brown eyes are kind but tainted by something that feels like concern. It's the first time I've seen that look from him.

Stuffing the compass pillow behind my back, I fix my sunken posture. Crazy people don't look confident, so I'm going to be the mascot for confidence even if insecurity eats me alive on the inside. "No head trauma. No history of abuse—drug, physical, or otherwise. My last drink was half a glass of wine several days ago. No prescription meds. No pot. Nothing."

He slips off his glasses and returns to the steepled-finger pose. "Are you sleeping well?"

"Define well."

"Eight hours of sleep. Ideally six *good* hours straight."

"Depends on the night and how much coffee I've had for the day. But you can't honestly believe that my knowledge of Nate is from a lack of sleep. Like … his past has wormed its way into my dreams. No. Not buying it."

"I think you're struggling to remember how you know him, and it could be caused by a myriad of things. A lot of physical and emotional things affect memory."

"Do you think Nate losing his wife is what has caused him to not remember me?"

"Swayze, I can't discuss that with you."

"What if he weren't your patient? What if I told you about this guy, and his wife dying, and you didn't know him. Would you say it's 'hypothetically' possible that he's suffering from memory loss due to the emotional trauma in his life?"

Dr. Greyson sighs. He's not been a sigher with me. The man is a pillar of control, but as he squirms in his chair, fighting all three of his favorite positions, I see his demeanor has shifted to a little off-kilter.

"*Hypothetically* it's possible."

That's all I need to know right now. The only way I can

keep a shred of my own sanity is by believing Nate's mental health might be impaired.

RACHAEL ANSWERS THE door with Morgan in a carrier strapped to her chest. A smile settles on my face as I fight the urge to lift an eyebrow in question. Since last night's confrontation with Nate, I half expected to get a phone call that my over-holding baby services were no longer needed. Yet, here she is, *holding* Morgan.

"No need to knock. You're welcome to come inside when you get here each day."

"Thanks." I slip off my shoes inside the door and follow her to the main room. My eyes go straight to the camera in the corner.

"Ignore them." Rachael grins, sliding Morgan out of the carrier.

I turn my back to the camera. "It's weird," I whisper. "Yesterday we were talking about your family, Nathaniel, and losing your sister …" I sneak a quick glance back at the camera. "And he was watching and *listening* to us the whole time."

She chuckles, kissing Morgan on her peach-fuzz covered head. "We weren't saying anything about him that we wouldn't say in front of him." Rachael winks at the camera and lowers her voice. "But I'll show you the safe spots in the house to talk behind his back."

My muscles relax a fraction. "Oh, good to know."

Rachael hands Morgan to me and drapes the carrier over the back of the sofa. "I'll leave it here in case you want to use it."

"To hold her?" I can't resist questioning the sudden baby-holding policy change.

"Yes. Apparently Nathaniel has decided the self-soothing method might not be the right fit for Morgan. I'm not sure what brought about this epiphany, but I love holding her, so ..." She smirks in the direction of the camera.

"Lucky Morgan." I rest my cheek against the top of her head, warm and soft. Gloating is one of Nate's pet peeves, so I won't gloat over being right. Closing my eyes, I try to shake off that thought because I shouldn't know that about him. These memories feel like a cancer gnawing at my sanity.

"Bye, baby girl." She rubs Morgan's back. "You know where to reach me if you have any questions or issues."

I nod.

Rachael retrieves a few items from the fridge and sets them in a black canvas bag. "She had a bottle about an hour ago, and I just changed her diaper before you showed up. See you tomorrow."

"Bye." Tiny grunts accompany jerky hands as I reposition Morgan and sit in the rocking chair. "Hey, Professor Hunt." I offer the camera a smile after I hear the door click shut behind Rachael. "This is so weird," I murmur to myself without moving my lips.

The next four hours pass without incident. And by incident I mean no nose-picking or butt-scratching on my part.

"Good evening, Swayze." My ginger-haired ghost from the past fills the doorway to the nursery, looking handsome in his blue button-down shirt with the sleeves rolled up to his elbows.

"Professor." I finish dressing Morgan.

"Nathaniel." He chuckles. It's familiar. Too fucking familiar.

Nate.

His last name isn't Hawthorne. I cannot call him Nathaniel. "She had a blowout clear up her back. But I'm sure you saw that on the spy cam. So I bathed her and now she's in her jams." I lift her off the table. "All nice and clean, Little Daisy." I give her a gentle hug before passing her off to Nate.

His brows knit together as he takes her in his burly hands while looking at me with confusion lining his forehead. I've avoided staring at him too long until now. For the first time I sense a flicker of recognition behind his questioning gaze.

This is it. He's piecing everything together. The anticipated ah-ha moment dangles on the horizon. Finally, we're going to connect the dots together.

Thank God!

"It's odd that you call her that."

"What?" I reel in my anticipation before it bubbles over into a joyous "*Finally! You recognize me.*"

"Daisy. That's not a common pet name for a baby. Are daisies your favorite flower or something?" He cradles Morgan to his broad chest and bounces her gently.

My shoulders lift into an exaggerated shrug. "No, but daisies are nice. I find them to be one of the happier flowers. Lilies and carnations have a real funeral feel to them, and roses are just risky. There are too many meanings behind the colors. But honeysuckle is my favorite scent."

Flowers. Really? He baits me with that look and then asks me about my favorite flower. Yes, daisies are nice. I think I just convinced both of us that they are the perfect flower, a topic I hadn't given much thought to until now. But if he wants to talk about flowers, then maybe we should discuss the lilac bush he stole from a neighbor and transplanted behind his parents' green house on Gable Street as a Mother's Day gift—all between the hours of midnight and two in the morning.

"Are you feeling okay?"

I blink a few times. "Uh, yeah. Why?"

"The color has drained from your face, and you look like you're a million miles away."

I flip off the light switch, forcing him to retreat down the hall in front of me as I pinch my cheeks to regain some color. "Deep in thought. I had a session with Dr. Greyson today."

"Oh."

I wait.

That's it? *Oh?* It would seem I lack the baiting skills of a good fisherman. *Yes, Nate. I saw* our *psychiatrist today. We discussed my memories of you. What do you discuss with him? Your missing memories of me? Your PTSD?*

"Did you eat dinner?" He adjusts Morgan so she's nestled in one arm like a football while he uses his other hand to flip open the pizza box on the kitchen counter.

Pineapple and jalapeños. I knew it before he opened the box.

"Not yet."

"Have some." He folds a flimsy slice in half and engulfs it. "I haven't eaten all day." His words mumble past his mouthful of pizza.

I take a piece and tear off a corner of the crust and pop it in my mouth. "Interesting choice of toppings."

Morgan's fists jerk in front of her face as her eyes cross trying to focus on them. Nate's gaze affixes to her while he finishes chewing. "I used to love jalapeño and sausage pizza." His forehead wrinkles a bit. "My best friend liked pineapple and mushroom pizza. She didn't like sausage. I didn't like mushrooms. We decided to try pineapple and jalapeño. It was stupid really. We could have just ordered half and half, but we both ended up loving the pineapple and jalapeño."

I pick off both of the oddly-paired toppings and drop them back in the box.

Nate's chewing slows while his lips turn up into a slight grin. "Not your thing?"

"Plain cheese. I'm sure that makes me boring, but I'm good with boring. Too many years of high expectations and unwanted attention can do that to you." I shrug and take a bite.

"I can relate to high expectations."

I chuckle. "You have a doctorate degree. Surely you've met or exceeded all expectations."

"Except my own." He tosses the end of the crust into the box next to my discarded toppings and grabs another piece.

He still doesn't eat the crust. It's the best part.

"You've always been an over-achiever."

Jesus! Knock that shit off, Swayze.

Before his questioning look settles into an irreversible frown, I make a quick save. "I don't mean you. I mean people like you are always over-achievers." I nibble at my pizza like a rabbit grazing in a yard of clover. Some people chew their fingernails or twirl their hair to release nervous energy. I'm a nibbler. As if my awesome name isn't enough, I have unique habits like nibbling food and knowing personal things about complete strangers.

"People like me?" Nate inhales another piece of pizza and bounces Morgan as she begins to fuss a bit.

"Success breeds greed."

Nate's stony posture softens a bit because I'm wrong. Where most people would be offended by my statement, he's not. It's not just me battling a case of the crazies. He's fighting it too. I see it every time his gaze lingers on me like it did in the nursery. Something about me is familiar to him too.

"I'm not greedy." He tosses a second pizza bone into the box and grabs a glass from the cupboard.

Nate isn't greedy. I know that. Kids who grow up with very little don't turn into greedy adults, but that doesn't mean they're not driven. He doesn't need the house, the car, and the expensive security cameras; knowing he *could* have them is enough.

"Don't be fooled by the house. I'm not rich and snobby." He fills the glass with water as my heart rate doubles.

I need him to say that he knows me too, because this strange familiarity is like an out-of-body experience. Of course he's not rich and snobby; he simply swore he'd never have to add water to milk or ketchup to make it last longer or duct tape on the sole of his shoe to mend a worn hole until he could get a new pair.

He turns back to me, gulping down the water like a dog on a hot day.

"Sorry. I shouldn't judge you."

"Success breeds success." The glass clinks against the granite counter as he sets it down.

Morgan's grunts begin to escalate into a full-on cry.

"I'd better get going so you can get her fed and down for the night." I grab my bag. "Thanks for the pizza." Shooting him a quick smile, I head for the door.

"Swayze?"

I stop and turn just before grabbing the door handle.

"I just want you to know that I didn't have a lot growing up, so I've always worked hard to ensure my life wouldn't revolve around unpaid bills and a lack of food on the table. My wife had a good job. The house ... the *stuff* is a reflection of her more than me." He grimaces and shakes his head while repositioning a crying Morgan against his shoulder, rubbing circles on her back. "And I don't mean that like it probably sounds. She didn't *need* the stuff either, but she grew up with it so ..."

"It's fine. Really, I wasn't trying to sound judgmental. Just ... poor word choice on my part. Goodnight."

For the second night in a row, I run until my lungs burn so my thoughts can only focus on oxygen instead of the ghost from ... my past? I just ... don't ... know.

CHAPTER EIGHT

S COTT AND SHERRI Calloway have the all-American two-story house clad in white paint and black shutters.

Four kids.

Four bedrooms.

Four animals.

Black chain-link fence borders the property line in their backyard complete with a fire pit and an old, rusting swing set, but it all feels white-picket to me.

The imperfections are character.

The chaos is my favorite music.

The inked guy at the grill is every girl's fantasy. And he's mine.

"Tell me about your day, Swayz," Griffin in his "Hands off my meat" apron flashes me a lopsided grin over the lid of the grill as he flips the burgers.

My parents never flirted in front of me. No sexy grins. No PDA. No whispers that elicited pink cheeks. The Calloways are the complete opposite. His parents can't keep their hands off each other as they go in and out of the sliding deck door, setting the rest of the food on the table beneath the big red umbrella. Scott not-so-discreetly pinches Sherri's butt, and she shoos him away while biting back her flirty grin like a teenage girl with a crush.

I love this family.

It's been two weeks since I last ran out of Nate's house, filled with adrenaline, fear, and nausea. My new routine involves handing him Morgan and sprinting for the nearest exit as soon as he walks in the door. Since Dr. Greyson and I seem to be at a stalemate, unable to figure out why I know things I shouldn't, I've decided to use distractions to keep my brain from wandering into crazy land. Griffin is my favorite distraction.

"Typical Friday. My grocery store guy forgot to wake me up before he left for work." I glare at him, but within seconds my lips curl into a grin. Ten seconds is my record for staying mad at him. The adoration in his eyes every time he looks at me is too disarming. "Coffee. Exercise. I finished a business card design and trade show banner. Then I got my Morgan fix."

"You mean baby fix?" His right eyebrow lifts a fraction.

I fill the blue plastic cups with lemonade as his mom yells into the house, calling his sisters to come eat. "No. Morgan fix. Baby fix implies my uterus is speaking to me, and I'm pacifying it in other ways. I told you Morgan started smiling this week, real ones, not the newborn reflex. She's such a happy baby. Not colicky. She fusses when she wants to eat, but that's it."

"Enjoy it now." Sherri winks at me as she takes the nearly-empty pitcher from my hands. "If you end up married to my rebel child and have children with him, there is a good chance you will have chronically fussy babies. *All* of our kids were colicky. The grumpy gene is strong in the Calloway bloodline. All from Scott's side."

Scott hands Griffin a plate for the burgers. "I know nothing of this grumpy gene. My wife has a vivid imagination."

It's all smiles and laughter. Griffin doesn't recoil in fear at the mention of marriage and babies with a girl he's known for only a few months. I like to believe in fate. Really, I like to believe in anything that involves a lifetime of Griffin and his family.

"Swayze, how's your mom? We haven't seen her in a while. You should have invited her to dinner," Sherri says.

"She's good." I take a seat at the table. "She misses our traditional Thursday night dinners now that I'm working late on Thursdays, but I met her for frozen yogurt last night. And Griff told me to invite her tonight, but she's taking a wine class or something like that. Her psychiatrist suggested she find ways to socialize more."

"I want a tattoo." Hayley takes a seat next to me. "And I'm no longer eating meat." She covers her plate with her hand as Griffin tries to hand her a hamburger."

"I want a tattoo too." Chloe tips her chin up and grins.

"Shut up. You're only fifteen." Hayley scowls at her.

"I want my nose pierced like Angie's mom." Sophie taps the side of her nose.

"I want my oldest spawn to apologize for being a terrible role model." Sherri gives Griffin the hairy eyeball as he takes a seat on the other side of me.

"Dear Lord…" Scott bows his head "…please grant me the patience to raise three girls. Please help scientists find a cure for cancer and the Calloway grumpy gene." Everyone chuckles. "And thank you for Swayze, a refreshing breath of normality in our crazy family. Amen. Let's eat."

Griffin rests his hand on my bare leg and gives it a gentle squeeze. Yep. Knowing intimate details about the life of a complete stranger is one hundred percent normal.

"I'm serious. I want an infinity symbol on the back of my

neck." Hayley adds a slice of cheese, pickles, ketchup, lettuce, and tomato to her bare hamburger bun.

"You're seventeen. You can't legally get a tattoo." Sherri gives Hayley a dismissive headshake.

I'm not only the mistaken "normal" one at this table. I'm also the only blonde with blue eyes. All of Griffin's family have dark hair and rich brown eyes. His mom is forty-eight—two years older than my mom—and she looks like the oldest sister in the group, not the mom. Four women with long, thick brown manes and two men with athletic bodies, flirty smiles, and a constant twinkle of mischief in their eyes. And now there's me—Goldilocks.

I love this family.

Sometimes I wonder if my life would have been different had I not been too smart too early—then ultimately nothing but average. Would my parents have had more kids? Would we have been the family grilling out every night and disputing typical parent-teenager problems like tattoos and piercings?

"I might be able to get it with parental consent. You can in some states."

All eyes shift to Griffin. He shakes his head. "Don't look at me. I wasn't a minor when I got mine. I don't know the laws in Wisconsin."

"It's a moot point because you don't have parental consent." Sherri gives Hayley a smug smile.

"No one will see it unless I pull my hair up in a bun or high ponytail."

"No one will see it because you're not getting one," Scott says.

"It's one tiny freakin' tattoo! Griffin has them everywhere, probably in places we don't know about. I bet his ass has a tattoo on it."

Griffin keeps his chin down, mouth full, so everyone looks to me for confirmation. My skin feels like it matches the color of the umbrella above us.

"Does he, Swayze?" Chloe asks.

"I … well …" This is great. Two curious parents, and three girls—seventeen, fifteen, and eleven—wait for my reply.

My love for this family is waning at the moment.

"Would it just be easier if I showed everyone?" Griffin pushes back in his chair and stands while unfastening his worn, faded jeans.

I twist my body away from him and slap my hands over my face.

"Leave your pants on, Griff." A deep chuckle rattles from Scott's chest.

"I wanna see it!" Sophie bounces in her chair and giggles, not realizing that seeing her older brother's ass is inappropriate, especially during dinner. She's eleven. She'll figure it out in a few years.

Hayley grumbles and shoves a bite of coleslaw into her mouth, and everyone gets back to eating.

Griffin leans over and whispers in my ear, "Really, babe? Out of everyone at this table, *you* hid your face at the prospect of seeing my ass?"

I press a napkin to my lips and finish chewing. "Reflex." I laugh.

After dinner we have a badminton tournament in the back-yard. Of course, Griff and I win. Then he takes me for a long sunset ride on his Harley. This is the life I love. My parents were loving in the only way they knew how to love me, and I see it now with greater clarity and gratitude than I did at the time. But I never felt one hundred percent good enough for their standards. Behind the love, I could always see that tiny dark smudge of disappointment.

"Don't move." I hug Griffin's back tighter as he kills the engine to his bike.

He interlaces his fingers with mine, gripping his chest. "You okay?"

After a few more seconds of relishing the feeling of our bodies pressed together, I release him and pull off my helmet. "I'm great."

He removes his helmet and his bandana while I slide off the Harley. I could watch him all day. The meticulous way he puts our helmets on the shelf and wipes the bugs off his bike mesmerizes me. Griffin takes care of everything he owns—the new shiny things as well as the old, weathered things like his house and garage.

"I think you're an old soul, Griffin Calloway."

He hangs the rag on the hook and shoots me his sexiest grocery-store-guy smile. "Why is that?"

"My parents used to tell people I was wise beyond my years because I knew stuff most kids my age didn't know. That was just knowledge, random facts, not wisdom. But you ... you have an appreciation for things and you take care of them like someone twice your age might do."

"My parents always took care of things. They still do. It's just how I was raised." He shrugs.

"No. Hayley and Sophie are complete disasters. I've seen their rooms. Chloe is a little tidier but still not you. I don't think you were conditioned to be this way, I think it's nature more than nurture."

"An old soul, huh? From another time?" He pulls me into

his chest and nuzzles my neck while lifting me off my feet.

I hug him with my arms, legs, and entire being. It took twenty-one years, but I finally found where I fit in life, and it's every inch of my body pressed to his.

"You make me feel safe," I murmur but it sounds more like a moan warring between physical pleasure and emotional pain. It's an unsettling feeling that I have such a strong need to feel safe. I don't understand it.

"You are safe," he says between kisses beneath my ear.

"You make me feel like I belong." My breaths race to catch up to my pulse.

"You belong with me." He walks us to the garage door, shuts off the light, and closes the door behind us.

He's my mind's favorite place to go. When I think of him—of us—I don't feel crazy. And maybe I should feel crazy because we're both young and inexperienced in life and love. But I don't want to think about the numbers that make up our ages or the months we've been together.

We crash through the front door like the first big gust of wind at the front of a storm.

"You make me feel needed," I whisper just before his mouth claims mine.

His house is bigger than my apartment, but only by one bedroom. We don't make it to either bedroom. He deposits me on the sofa and shrugs off his shirt.

"I need you." He unties his boots and kicks them off while unfastening his pants as I shimmy out of my clothes. "In fact, I am pretty fucking sure you're *all* I truly need."

Twenty-three-year-old guys don't say that. His soul is not simply old, it's ancient like that of a great poet ... who may have said fuck a few times.

I tug at his partially unfastened jeans.

He grabs my hand. "Close your eyes."

"Why?" My head cocks to the side.

"Because I know you don't want to see the tattoo on my ass."

"Shut. Up." I bat his hand away and tug down his jeans with both hands. A few moments of silence settle between us as I stare at his form before me. "I still blush when I look at you." My gaze trails up to meet his eyes.

Griffin steps out of his jeans and briefs and kneels on the sofa between my legs as I lie back. "I know what else makes you blush." He slowly dips his head between my legs, and my fingers curl into the sofa cushion.

"RISE AND SHINE."

The covers are ripped from my naked body.

"It's Saturday." I blindly search for a sheet, blanket, even a discarded T-shirt. Nothing. They're gone, so I rub the sleep from my eyes and peel them open.

"There she is."

I lift up onto my elbows. "Here I am. Naked. In your bed. Yet…" my lips twist "…you're dressed. How are we supposed to have Saturday morning sex with you so overdressed?"

"The real question is how are we supposed to have Saturday morning sex when you're supposed to be at Professor Hunt's house in less than thirty minutes?"

"It's not my Saturday to work—SHIT!" I fly off the bed. "It is! I said I'd watch Morgan for an hour this morning." My legs wobble a bit as they fight to keep up with my adrenaline rush.

"You did." Griffin chuckles.

"Don't laugh at my forgetfulness," I holler from his bathroom. "Instead, be helpful and get me some coffee."

"It's already on the kitchen table next to your purse and car keys."

After throwing on clothes and brushing my teeth in record time, I race past him toward the kitchen.

"Wait." He snags my arm and pulls me into his chest. "Drive safely." And there it is, that adoration, that complete feeling of safety and security that comes with Griffin's affection.

"I love you, Grocery Store Guy."

He tips my chin up with his finger and kisses me. "I love you too. Now go, before you get fired."

I smile. I'm late, but I take a few seconds to bask in the moment of being so incredibly in love with this man. If my father's death taught me anything, it's that last goodbyes don't RSVP. Take lots of mental pictures of favorite moments. And being present with the ones that matter most is the wisest investment of time.

"Your place or mine later?" I grab my stuff neatly lined up on the kitchen table.

"Yours. It's a mess. We should clean it up tomorrow."

"Great. Your place it is. Bye, Griff."

He slowly shakes his head as I close the door behind me.

I arrive at Nate's three minutes late thanks to traffic and my oversleeping. A shower and clean clothes would have been nice. I really need to keep more than a toothbrush and a stick of deodorant at Griffin's, but he hasn't asked me to move in, so actual clothes might feel a little too intrusive and presumptuous.

"Hello?" I step inside the front door and slip off my shoes.

"In here," Nate calls from his office.

"Sorry I'm a few minutes late. Traffic was—"

"It's no problem." He keeps his eyes on the computer screen, fingers playing hunt and peck with the keyboard. Typing would have been a useful skill, but I'm not surprised he never learned it.

I'm only surprised that I know that. Here we go again …

"Where's Morgan?"

"Sleeping. She was up early, so after her bottle she fell back to sleep." He shuts the top to his laptop. "I won't be gone long."

"Meeting?"

"Cemetery."

"Oh, you have an actual plot?" Last week Rachael told me Jenna was cremated. I suppose some people still want a physical place to feel close to the departed.

"No. It's …" He shakes his head. "Hard to explain."

"O-kay. No explanation necessary. I'm here, no major plans today so take your time."

Nate studies me with that scrutinizing look that feels pained and confused at the same time. I glance around the room, out the window, at the shelves of books. Anywhere but directly at him.

"My best friend died."

This statement demands eye contact. "I'm sorry."

He shakes his head a half dozen times. "Thank you, it was many years ago, but I still go visit her grave every year. I named Morgan after her."

My eyes widen a fraction. "Your best friend was a girl?"

"Yes."

"That's ... wow. And you named your daughter after her ..."

He nods again.

Thinking back, he did say "she" when he discussed his best friend's favorite pizza. It didn't sink in until now.

"That's really ... special. Did Jenna know your friend too?"

Nate hesitates, distracting me with nervous gestures like clearing his throat and checking his watch. "No," he says so softly I can barely hear him. But I know that's what he said.

"Well, I'm still very sorry for your loss. Clearly you must have been close if you named Morgan after her, and you still visit her grave every year."

Nate stares at his feet while scratching his head, ruffling his already wayward curls. "We met when we were seven." He sighs slowly and makes his way toward the windows.

I guess he's not leaving quite yet.

"I never talk about her. I never told Jenna about her. She never knew about my yearly visit to Morgan's grave."

"You should share this with Dr. Greyson."

With his back to me, Nate shakes his head. "My sessions with him revolve around Jenna and my 'feelings' about being a single parent—a widower. But ..." He sighs again.

"But what?" I rest my hands on the edge of his desk and lean back against it.

"I need to tell someone. I need to let it go ... I need to let *her* go."

I'm a twenty-one-year-old girl he's known less than a month. He can't seriously be suggesting *I'm* the one who he's going to tell—"

"The first time I saw Morgan she was picking a fight with a

boy twice her size because he wouldn't move his leg out of the aisle when she got on the school bus. She had room to pass, but nope, not Morgan ..."

CHAPTER NINE

Nathaniel Hunt – Age 10

"NATE AND MORGAN sitting in a tree ... K I S S I N G. First comes love, then comes—"

"Shut up before I knock your teeth out with my fist and you go crying to your mommy like a baby in a baby carriage." Morgan spit on the kids below us as they marched toward the lake, fishing poles in one hand, tackle boxes in the other, dodging saliva bombs.

I ignored their snickers and smooching sounds. Morgan didn't ignore anything. Her parents called her Little Firecracker, but not me—I called her Daisy because her middle name was Daisy and she hated it when I called her that.

"Have you ever hit anyone?" I asked as we continued our game of Go Fish, perched high in the old oak tree on the abandoned property a mile from our neighborhood. At least we thought it was abandoned. No one knew for sure. An old couple owned it, but there hadn't been any sign of them in over three years. All that mattered to us kids was that we could hide from our parents in what had to be the best treehouse ever built and fish off their dock along the lake.

"Yes. I've hit someone. Do you have any kings?"

"Go fish. Who have you hit?"

She drew a card and grinned as she got her final match. Game over. "My cousin, Austin. He's an idiot."

ANN

"So you hit him because he's an idiot?"

Morgan poked her head out of the glassless window. Her cheeks puffed out and rolled in waves as she collected more saliva for ammunition.

"Don't." I grabbed the back of her shirt and tugged her away from the window.

The cards on the floor scattered when she fell on them. Her giggles gurgled as she tried to swallow the excess spit without choking on it.

"Every time you act all tough, I end up in a fight, protecting you from them. I *wish* you'd hit them so I wouldn't always be the one getting in trouble for fighting. I'm tired of my parents saying, 'Why can't you be more like Morgan?'"

"I don't like them teasing us." She sat up facing me, crisscrossing her legs. "You're not my boyfriend. We've never kissed."

"We did kiss."

"That doesn't count." Her eyes narrowed at me.

"It counts." I smirked because I could never forget the day I met Morgan Daisy Gallagher. We were seven. She'd just moved to Madison mid-school year.

"I whispered over your mouth. Remember? I asked you to scoot over and let me sit by you after I kicked Benji for not moving his stupid leg."

"Our lips touched."

Morgan's brown eyes looked like marbles rolling around in their sockets. "The bus driver went over a speed bump and we…" she sighed "…bumped lips."

"A kiss. You kissed me so I would protect you from Ben. You always try to fight with people bigger than you."

More eye-rolling. "So what? You think you should be my

boyfriend?"

"Yeah." I grinned because Morgan was my best friend and pretty. Man was she pretty, like a real life princess with hair so long and blond it looked like a gold waterfall flowing down her back.

Boys chased her because they liked her, even if she kicked them in the balls, and girls wanted to be her—popular, pretty, smart.

"Fine. I'll be your girlfriend, but only until I find a real boyfriend."

"A real boyfriend?"

She pulled her hair over her shoulder and started braiding it. I could spend all day watching her braid her hair.

"Yes. A *real* boyfriend. One who brings me flowers and chocolate and opens doors for me like my dad opens doors for my mom. And one who kisses me right here." She pointed to a spot on her neck just below her ear. "My dad kisses my mom there and it always makes her giggle."

I shrugged. "I can get you flowers and chocolate and hold open doors for you." My hand dug into the front pocket of my shorts and pulled out a half-melted candy bar. "Here, chocolate. And I call you Daisy which is better than giving you flowers."

As if I were asking her to eat my vomit, she frowned in disgust. "Fine. But the next time your dad gets popsicles for you, you have to give me all of the good flavors."

"The red ones?"

"And the orange."

"That only leaves the purple. Nobody likes the purple."

"Do you want me to be your girlfriend?" She finished her braid and tossed it back over her shoulder.

"Yeah."

The grin that slid up her face was equal parts evil and sweet. "Then you'd better learn to like purple popsicles." She thought she'd won. Morgan's personality bled of competitiveness and confidence.

"Now the kiss." I licked my lips and rubbed them together.

Everything that wasn't her idea came with a heavy sigh. "One kiss. For two seconds."

I leaned forward.

"Wait!" Her head jerked back. "Let me get ready."

"Huh? What's there to get ready for?"

She straightened her back, drew in a deep breath, and closed her eyes. "Now." Her lips drew into a tight pucker.

As my lips neared hers they decided to take a last-minute detour landing on her neck just below her ear. In that moment, the best thing ever happened. Daisy giggled.

Nathaniel Hunt – Now

THE SMILE FROM my face fades. The memories? They haven't faded one bit.

"I should go."

Swayze blinks but *her* smile doesn't fade. "You're a romantic, Professor Hunt."

"I don't know about that."

She pushes off the edge of my desk as I head toward the door. "Look…" she holds out her arm "…I have goose bumps from your story."

I continue toward the garage. "You have goose bumps because I keep my office five degrees cooler than any other room in the house—except my bedroom."

"Well, at least now I know why you were so weird about me calling your daughter Daisy."

As if she hears us, Morgan starts to fuss.

"I won't be long." I open the door.

"Has she met her?"

"What?" I turn.

Swayze rubs her lips together as her eyes narrow into a slight squint like she's afraid to say anymore. "Has Morgan met Morgan?"

"One is dead and the other is a newborn."

"Yet … you visit dead Morgan's grave."

"So?"

"Do you talk to her?"

"What does it matter? She's crying. You'd better go pick her up."

"She's barely fussing, and I will get her in a second. Your best friend … you named your daughter after her. Hello? Of course you should introduce them. I introduced my boyfriend to my dead father." Swayze cocks her head to the side. "It went much better than I expected. My father didn't say much, and I felt certain he'd have something to say about my boyfriend's tattoos."

"You're morbid." I don't want to laugh. It's not the right time, and the context of this conversation has taken a wrong turn. She's crazy. I've hired a crazy young woman to watch my child.

"Says the guy who has a skeleton standing next to his desk."

My jaw clenches to keep myself in check. I refuse to laugh. "I'm an anatomy professor. Now, go do your job. She's crying."

"I'll grab her, a bottle, and the diaper bag. You get her car seat."

"No. I'll see you both in about an hour."

Swayze turns and jogs away, her voice fading as she retreats farther down the hall toward the nursery. "We can stop for iced coffee on the way. I need a pick-me-up. My treat."

I'm the boss, yet no means yes in the nanny world. If I weren't convinced Swayze is a true baby whisperer, firing her for insubordination would be the next logical step. But she's magical with Morgan. I'd say it's the breasts. Women have nurturing pillows that babies seem to love. But Rachael has them too, and Morgan fusses with Rachael as much as she does with me. That can only mean one thing: Swayze has magical breasts.

"What's that smirk for?" she asks as we pull out of the garage.

I clear my throat and remove the grin from my face. Magical breasts. What is wrong with me? The thought entered my mind in the most maternal, anatomical way possible, yet ... now that she's unknowingly calling me out on it, I feel like a dirty old man.

"I didn't realize I was smirking." I slip on my sunglasses to hide as much of my face as possible from my scrutinizing nanny who doesn't miss a thing.

"Were you thinking about Morgan, your friend? I can't stop thinking about her. She sounds like everything I wasn't. I'm a little envious of her."

"She died." I give her a quick sideways glance, my glasses hiding the slight raise of my brow.

"Yeah ... okay, I'm not envious of that, but she had a boy-friend at ten. I had a boyfriend at like ... I don't even want to say. It's embarrassing. Anyway, I was smart but not confident and I was *never* popular. She got a kiss on the neck and it made her giggle. I got my bra snapped and it nearly brought me to tears."

"You seem to have turned out okay."

"Sure." She grunts a laugh. "Barely. It was close. Could have gone either way. Wanna know the crazy part? My father's death was a pivotal moment in my life, but in a good way. And I know how morbid that sounds, but it's true. I've discussed this with our shrink."

Our shrink. That's cringe-worthy. She makes us both sound like fuckups.

"When my father died, I was no longer the focus. The expectations died with him. I guess if something good can come from something bad, then my freedom came from his death. Like … someday if you find another woman to love, it will be bittersweet. Something good from something bad."

I shake my head a half dozen times. "That won't happen. I'm done."

"Done?"

"Unless Morgan gives me a granddaughter someday, she is the last woman I will love."

"Ouch. That's a little pessimistic. You're still in your thirties. A lot could happen." She points to the coffee shop on the right side of the road.

I turn in. "I loved Morgan—Daisy—and she died. I loved Jenna and she died. See any pattern?"

"Oh … wow. I can't believe Dr. Greyson has let you get away with that train of thought."

"I haven't told him. We're still in the why-does-God-hate-me phase. I'm pretty sure we're stuck there. What do you want?" I stop at the drive-thru to order.

"Grande caramel iced coffee with cream."

"Two grande caramel iced coffees with cream," I yell into the speaker.

Her jaw unhinges. "You're getting the same thing?"

I shrug. "Sure. Why not?"

"Griff never as in *ever* gets naughty coffee drinks with me. He's an icon of health. I'm not exactly complaining, but sometimes it's fun to have a partner in crime. You know what I mean?"

"The boyfriend?"

"Yes. Griffin. He's a mechanic and technician at the Harley dealership."

"A guy with tattoos *and* a motorcycle? Now I too am surprised your dad didn't have *something* to say about that." And it's happened. She's brought me to a new low. I'm taking my newborn baby to meet my dead childhood girlfriend while indulging in copious amounts of caffeine, fat, and sugar—*and* making inappropriate jokes about dead people.

The laughter that fills the vehicle feels like Daisy is here with me, like Jenna never died, like God doesn't have it in for me. I want to bottle it and save it for the nights that leave me wondering what the hell has happened to my life. This … this feeling is the remedy for my fucking pity parties that seem to creep up at the worst time, like when Morgan refuses to take a bottle from me or when she won't stop crying and I swear she's grieving her mom and … it. Fucking. Kills. Me.

"Jesus, Nate …" She sighs with a soft, satisfying hum. "I've missed your humor."

I stop so fast at the drive-thru window my seat belt locks up. We stare at each other in silence. The same ghostly paleness washes down her face like it did that day in the nursery. It's a strange familiar. She's known me only as a single dad and grieving widower. That is the indisputable truth. But ... she *looks* at me like she's been looking at me my whole life.

"Swayze ..."

She shakes her head, eyes wide and unblinking. "That came out wrong. Don't—"

Tap. Tap. Tap.

The barista at the window smiles, holding up the two iced coffees. I roll the window back down and hand her a twenty, not waiting for change before handing one to Swayze and pulling out of the parking lot.

"Nate—"

"Nathaniel." It's not my intention to snap at her, but I'm on edge for some reason I can't explain.

We don't speak the rest of the way to the cemetery. As soon as my white Escalade is in *Park,* I open the door. "Just wait here."

Swayze pauses. I can't look at her because I don't know whom I'm looking at, and I can't handle the way she looks at me. It's so fucking haunting. She shuts the door. Out of my peripheral vision, I see her nod once.

It's a long walk to Daisy's grave. She's at the far corner next to her mom's parents. They watch over her. Over two decades, a marriage, a baby, and the loss of my wife later ... I still can't visit her without a lump in my throat and an ache in my chest.

The only true love I have left fusses as I reposition her so she's flush to my chest, head tucked under my chin. "Shh ... you're okay, sweet girl. I want you to meet my friend, Morgan." I stop at the glassy black headstone.

Morgan Daisy Gallagher
Beloved daughter, dreamer, beautiful angel.

"Hey, Daisy." I swallow back the lump as the wind howls through the tall trees. There's so much to say. I've never allowed myself more than one visit a year. But a lot happens in a year.

Morgan continues to fuss, so I bounce her a bit. "I'm a dad. Can you believe that?" Damn tears. I cried in front of Daisy once in the eight years we were together. It was the day she died, so she couldn't really see my tears. Since then, I've cried every year, just once—until Jenna died—on the anniversary of her death, here, where she rests for eternity. "So ... you probably know by now ... Jenna died giving birth to our daughter. We named her Morgan. Crazy right?"

Swallowing again and again, I try to keep my emotions contained. "Have you seen Jenna? I bet you've both been sharing stories and laughing about all my faults and the stupid stuff I've done."

My lips press to Morgan's head as she gets worked up even more. "I suck at this dad thing. But ..." I laugh through the pain. "It's only for eighteen years, right? That's... fuck..." I sniffle and hold Morgan secure with one hand while I wipe my face with my other hand "...three years longer than you got." The words fight their way into existence. I'm not sure I'll ever understand the reasons why. What kind of god takes away a daughter, a friend, an angel?

Morgan lets out a shrill scream.

"Let me."

I turn toward Swayze's voice. She rubs Morgan's back without meeting my gaze—my pathetic tear-filled gaze. I hand my daughter to Swayze and within seconds, she calms down.

Magical breasts.

Yes, it's a perverted sounding thought but it helps me regain some composure, so I let it chase away the grief.

Turning back to the headstone, I squat until her name is inches from my face.

"I met my soulmate when I was seven. She didn't care that I was poor and living in a dysfunctional home. She always gave me half of her allowance. When I refused to accept it, she'd leave a bag of groceries on our front doorstep with a note that said, 'For now ... I love you.' She agreed to be my girlfriend until she found a real boyfriend. That went on for nearly five years."

I pick at the grass. "I was her now. She was my always. And I thought that would add up to forever." My jaw grinds side to side as I blink away more emotion.

"She didn't care that I loved hockey more than anything ... except her. She didn't care that we would probably live in an old shack because the chances of making it to the NHL were slim. And she dreamed of being a famous poet, but I told her the only famous poets were dead poets, like all famous artists."

"So she's famous now," Swayze murmurs.

I grin at the ground. "In my eyes, yes." Standing, I take a few steps back and rob a single flower from a freshly-laid bouquet next to another grave.

"What are you doing?" Swayze asks in a hushed voice like we're going to get caught committing a crime.

I set the single flower on Daisy's headstone and take a foil-covered chocolate out of my pocket and rest it next to the flower. "She made me promise flowers and chocolates, but I rarely had the money to buy them. In fact ... I never bought them. So ..." I shrug.

"You stole them."

I nod.

"Did you steal that chocolate?"

I laugh. "One of my colleagues has a bowl of them on her desk. I pocketed several when she ran to the restroom."

"Wow."

I glance back at Swayze. "It's stupid. I know. I can afford them. It's just—"

She shakes her head. "That's not what I meant. It's the way you loved her. It's ..."

"Pathetic?"

"Beautiful." Tears fill her eyes as she smiles, but she quickly blinks them away and averts her gaze to Morgan.

"I've spent my entire adult life trying to convince myself I was too young to really love her. It has to be the trauma of losing her so suddenly at such a vulnerable age. Some people think kids are resilient. They heal faster because their cells divide faster. It's true on a physical level. But ... emotionally, I think what happens to us when we're young changes us forever. A broken bone is nothing compared to a broken heart. One is a scratch. The other leaves a scar on your soul."

Morgan fusses.

"I'm going to take her back to the car and give her a bottle. Take your time." Swayze turns and takes several steps.

"Have you ever had your heart broken?"

She glances over her shoulder, blond hair whipping across her face. "No."

"I hope you never do."

Her lips turn down ever so slightly as she nods. "Me too."

CHAPTER TEN

NATE FELL IN love with a girl who died. To this day, he still feels like they were soulmates. I don't know how to deal with that because of all the things I *do* know.

I know the tree house he talked about. He fell from it and broke his arm, but he told his parents it happened on his bike so he didn't get in trouble for trespassing.

I know his cast was covered in signatures and pictures from his friends, including a hockey stick drawn along the entire length of it.

I know he wanted to shave his head when his uncle lost his hair from chemotherapy.

Every day I seem to know more about him than the day before. But ... I don't know a thing about Morgan Daisy Gallagher except what he tells me.

"Look, Professor, she has a new roll. I'm certain it wasn't there last week." I glance at the camera in the nursery while running my finger along the tiny new roll on Morgan's back as I pull her onesie over her head. I don't know if he's watching right now, but acknowledging the cameras in the house makes me feel more comfortable than trying to ignore them.

Morgan is two and a half months now. In just six weeks she has stolen my heart, and I wonder if I'll be able to love my own children as much as I love her. It's like she's a little duckling who imprinted on me. I don't know why she seems to choose me over Rachael or Nate. But I feel like she needs me.

"And…" I continue talking as I snap her pajamas "…I have a job interview tomorrow. It's not a permanent position. It's for a maternity leave. But with school just around the corner, I think all of the permanent positions have been filled. This is a good place to start. Something to add to my résumé."

"I think you're right."

"Oh, jeepers creepers!" I jump at the sound of his voice.

He grins, standing at the door. "Sorry."

I pick up Morgan and hug her to me like she's the one who just had the crap scared out of her. But she's fine. It's my heart that's still in my throat. "You're home early."

"Yeah." He grips the back of his neck. "Fighting a headache. Has she been fed?"

I nod.

"Good." Nate takes her from me with his strong hands. I swear I could draw every line of them from memory.

"Maybe my little girl will go down easily for me so I can get some sleep and get rid of this headache." He sits in the rocking chair by her crib.

She fusses.

"You're off an hour early. Go do something fun. Make me envy your youth." Exhaustion wraps around his words as he attempts to smile, but it, too, is weak.

Morgan squirms and her lungs start to stretch releasing a shrill cry.

"Not tonight, pumpkin. Please." He kisses her head as she continues to thrash and wail.

My lips twist to the side. "Take off your shirt."

"Huh?"

"Let her feel your skin, hear your heart, smell your scent.

Here …" I take her from him.

He regards me with hesitation for a few seconds before unbuttoning his shirt.

One button.

Two buttons.

Three buttons.

Without warning, my eyes fill with tears. "Nate …" I whisper.

Unbuttoning the last button, he glances up, concern pulling his eyebrows together. "What's wrong?"

I close my eyes, but I still see his hands working the buttons to his shirt, a white shirt, not green like the one he has on now. And he's not in a nursery, he's in his bedroom on Gable Street. Something like water drips onto his hand. He pauses and then continues with shaky hands.

"Nothing," I say while blinking open my eyes.

"Doesn't seem like nothing."

I sway back and forth, soothing Morgan, but my eyes don't leave his shirt. "Promise not to fire me?"

"Swayze—"

"Just say it."

A slow breath leaves his chest. "I won't fire you."

"Two …" My voice cracks as I start to speak, so I swallow past the thickness in my throat and start again. "Two inches above and to the left of your belly button there is a mark. It's like a birthmark, but there is no pigment. It's most visible during the summer when the rest of your skin has more color."

The only thing more painful than memories that have no place in my life is seeing the confusion on his face. He has to be trying to recall a time that I've seen him without a shirt on or photos on the mantel—of which none are of him without a shirt.

"It's a heart shape."

"Give her to me," he says with cold words.

My gaze moves up his unbuttoned shirt that he's not removing any further. Our eyes meet with a clash of emotions— my sympathy and confusion, his anger and pain. I hand Morgan to him.

"Go home," he says, no longer looking at me.

A million feelings race between my head and my heart, but I can't bring a single one to life with words. Words are definable and they can be arranged to make sense. Nothing about the images and memories I have of Nate are definable or make sense. So ... I leave.

I'VE CANCELLED MY last three sessions with Dr. Greyson. Avoidance may be the coward's way out, but it feels like I'm asking him to solve the unsolvable. I'm so tired of being a mystery.

Griffin has a bike he needs to finish working on for a friend. I told him earlier that I have a design I need to finish so we should hang out tomorrow. Yet, I can't think about my project, and I can't wait until tomorrow to see him. My car navigates to his house without any other reason than I need to see him.

The second I step out of my car, I inhale the earthy scent of Griffin's neighborhood. It's black dirt and fresh-cut grass. The lawns are dotted with dandelions and patches of clover instead of carpets of perfect grass and pungent chemicals that keep them so perfect. Clothes hang from clotheslines instead of perfume-laced air flowing from dryer vents.

It reminds me of the neighborhood where Nate grew up.

"Hey." I smile at the unexpected gathering in Griffin's garage.

His parents, Sophie, and Chloe greet me with the usual Calloway enthusiasm that I love.

Griff looks up from his stool where he's working on his friend's motorcycle, black bandana soaked in sweat, grease smudges covering his face, hands, and arms. His gaze makes a head-to-toe assessment of me—it's endearing, possessive, and erotic. The muggy ninety-degree temperature doesn't begin to compare to how he's looking at me.

"Swayz." A naughty grin, that I hope his family can't see, pulls at his mouth. "Didn't expect to see you here tonight."

I gather my hair off my neck and hold it into a ponytail for a few seconds. It's so hot. No breeze. Just sticky heat. "Am I crashing the party?"

Sherri laughs. "No party. We made the mistake of thinking it was a good night for a bike ride. It was a short one." She fans herself. "Chloe wanted to stop and see Griffin on our way home."

Typical Griffin. His family stops by, but he continues to work. I admire and hate his focus, but it's fun to be his distraction when he lets me.

Sophie stands in the path of the fan. "It's so hot." She holds out her arms.

I grab a water from the small refrigerator below one of his workbenches and twist off the cap. "No Hayley?"

"She has a date." Scott rolls his eyes. "I don't approve."

"Stop." Sherri shakes her head. "Simon is a nice young man."

"He's nineteen." Chloe's eyes widen like it's a crime.

"He's in a fraternity," Scott grumbles.

Griffin flips over the five-gallon bucket near him and slaps the top. "Sit." He glances up at me and winks.

I take my usual spot.

"So, what's up?" He returns his focus to the bike, but I know he's engaged in me. My grocery store guy is the king of multi-tasking.

I shrug, looking around at his family as they wipe sweat from their brows, suckle from their water bottles, and inspect Griffin's perfectly-organized garage like they haven't seen it a million times before. "Just … I don't know."

His hands pause while he brings his focus back to me. I'm dying to say something, and he knows it. Griff reads me like he wrote the book on Swayze Samuels.

"Thanks for stopping by," he says, giving a particular look to his parents.

I cringe. He's clearly dismissing them for me.

"You're kicking us out?" Sherri says, but the glimmer in her eyes negates her attempt to sound offended.

"Unless you're going to get your hands dirty helping me, then yes, you're dismissed."

"You *don't* have to leave." I love his family. The last thing I ever want is for them to think I don't want to be with them.

"Sophie's going to overheat. We do need to leave." Sherri kisses the top of Grif's bandana-covered head, and then she kisses the top of mine like I'm one of her own. "I love you two."

"Love you too." I smile.

They mount their bikes and give a final wave as they ride off.

"Spill." His hands resume their work.

"Why do you think I have something to spill?"

"Then shut the garage door and take off your clothes."

D*a—amn!*

I'm dating the sexiest man alive. It's a fact.

A part of me wants to shut the door, shut off my mind, take off my clothes, and let Griff do what he does best—make me feel like we are the only two people who exist in the world. We make love like one soul—his pleasure is mine and mine is his.

But ... tonight I can't come undone from his touch. I need him to put me back together because Nate's existence in my world has shattered me.

"Something is wrong with me."

"Who told you that? They're an idiot. You're perfect."

Gah! If only it were that easy. I'm fine—perfect—because my grocery store guy says so. I've never been anyone's perfect.

"No. That's not it."

He pauses, giving me a concerned quirk of his brow. "Are you sick?"

"I don't think so. It's ... something really hard to explain."

"Try."

"I think I can read minds."

He chuckles as he should because it's crazy. "Really? What am I thinking right now?"

"That's easy. You're thinking I'm cuckoo."

Another chuckle. "No. Well, maybe. Go on. I'm listening."

"It's not really mind reading. It's more like I can access memories, but not with everyone. Actually, just one person and it's not all of his memories, just some ... from when he was younger."

Griff nods once. "And by 'his' you mean mine?"

"Nate's."

"The professor's?" He gives me a quick sidelong glance before returning his attention to the motorcycle.

"Yes. Remember I tried telling you this the day I saw him at Dr. Greyson's office. I said I knew him, but he didn't know me?"

"Then we had sex."

I chuckle. "Yes. I think all of our conversations end in sex."

"As they should," he mumbles while spraying something onto one of the bike parts. "But I don't really understand the mind reading."

"You don't have to understand. *I* don't understand it either. I just need to talk to someone about this because I know it freaks Nate out, and I don't want to lose my job. But keeping this to myself makes me feel like I'm losing my mind. And I don't really want to lose that either."

"What does Dr. Greyson say?"

I rest my elbows on my knees and wring my hands together. "I tried to tell him, but then it got uncomfortable and I was worried he'd think I'm crazy, so I haven't been back in several weeks."

"He's a shrink, Swayz. I think crazy is his specialty."

"So you think I'm crazy?" I jump up and the bucket crashes on its side. Preserving my sanity has taken priority in my life, and I can't stop my need to defend it.

"No, that's not what I mean." He grabs a towel and wipes his face and hands as he stands. "I just need you to explain it to me better so maybe I can wrap my head around it."

I cross my arms over my chest and pace the length of the garage. "How can I explain it to you better if I can't explain it to myself?"

"Babe …" He grabs my arm and I jerk away. "What do you want me to say?"

"I don't know!"

"Then why did you tell me?"

"Because I had to tell someone." I stop and move my hands to my hips. This isn't about him. I don't know why I'm taking it out on him. But I can't stop. And I hate that I can't.

Griffin pushes out a long breath and rubs his lips together, mirroring my pose. "Okay. You told me. Now what?"

"You think I'm crazy."

He drops his chin toward his chest, shaking his head as he chuckles. "If I say no, you're going to call me a liar. If I say yes, you're going to be pissed off." Glancing up, he shrugs. "I'm fucked either way."

"I have to finish a design. I'll just see you later."

"Swayz, don't leave."

I keep walking to my car.

"Fuck …" Griffin's parting sentiment fades behind me.

ON THE WAY home I stop for chocolate and wine. This time I have my wallet so there's no need for a grocery store guy to save me. Too bad. I already miss him even if I'm mad at him for no good reason. Maybe I should grab tampons just in case.

"What's in the bag?" Erica yells down as I unlock the door to my apartment.

"Wine and chocolate."

"You break up with Sex on a Stick?"

I grunt a laugh. "I hope not, but he may break up with

me." I glance up. "Are you on neighborhood watch or something?"

"Date. Blind date. Well … not like he's literally blind. You know what I mean."

"And you're waiting for him in the hallway?"

"Too desperate?" She rubs her glossed lips together.

"You're asking the wrong girl. I won the man lottery. I didn't have to work for it. I kinda went from nothing to everything with one trip to the grocery store."

"Yeah, yeah. I know. Stop bragging. The dress though, it's good. Right?" She does a quick three-sixty so fast she has to grab the railing to keep from stumbling in her high heels.

"Short, black, and cleavage. I'm sure it's every guy's dream. And the hair—" I whistle.

"It took me over an hour to straighten it."

"It's like one hundred percent humidity outside. You know that, right?"

"Don't remind me." She frowns while smoothing her hand along her silky black hair.

The door to our building slams shut below.

"Shit! That's him." Erica stumbles again and runs into her apartment.

Just as I open my door, the figure ascending the stairs snags my attention.

"Your friend's motorcycle," I say with a weak voice.

"Fuck the bike."

"I have a design to—"

"Fuck it too."

My grocery store guy climbs toward me wearing clean, ripped jeans, a white tee, and black boots. His woodsy just-showered smell makes it up to my floor before he does. The bouquet of flowers sticking out of a brown paper bag hides part of his face.

One step.

Two steps …

He climbs his way toward me with such confidence I want to cry.

Six steps.

Seven steps …

Griffin is so certain about life, and I'm not certain about anything because Nate Hunt has blurred my reality.

My sanity.

My existence.

He pulls out the flowers and presents them to me with that smile that cures cancer, ends wars, and melts hearts. "We'll figure it out. You're not crazy. And you're not alone."

"Griff …" My voice breaks as I wrap my free arm around his neck, our paper bags smashing together. "I love you, Grocery Store Guy. It's the only thing I know with complete certainty."

Griff wraps an arm around my waist and holds me. Protects me. Loves me.

"What's in your bag?" he asks.

I release him. He looks in my bag as I look in his. We both grin at the other's bottle of wine and chocolates.

"Tampon time?" He cocks his head to the side.

"Shouldn't be." I lead the way into my apartment. "But after my emotional breakdown at your place, I questioned it."

We don't fight. That's not us. No jealousy. No immature demanding of each other's time. No goals of where our relationship is going or where we should be. We just fit.

Griffin opens a bottle of wine and pours two glasses.

"You don't drink wine."

He hands me my glass and takes a seat on the sofa, guiding me onto his lap. "I do. Just not very often."

I sip my wine. His calloused hand slides under my T-shirt, resting on my belly. Parts of it feel like fine sandpaper. I love all of his rough edges and the way they smooth my frayed nerves and lull me into a safe, peaceful place.

"I'm sorry about earlier." I lean my back against him.

He rests his chin on my shoulder. "No apologies."

"Still … I was out of line."

"So, these memories … tell me about them."

I set my wine glass on the coffee table before wrapping my arms around Griffin. Then I tell him *everything*. He's my guy—my person. And I should have known it and shared these memories on the day I saw Nate at Dr. Greyson's office. Griff asks about my day—everyday—because my life is his life.

Without a diamond ring.

Without a legally-binding agreement.

Without ever saying the words …

Griffin. Is. My. Person.

An hour later, I've run out of words. I put it all out there so he can share this burden with me.

After the silence becomes loud in its own way, I slip off Griffin's lap and tuck my legs under me. "Weird. Paranormal. Right?"

His forehead tenses, eyes narrowed a bit. "You think you know what he looks like naked?"

"No. Well … I'm not sure." I close my eyes and rub them. "God! This is crazy. It's not just Nate either. I've seen other people that I feel like I know—really *know*. This couple at my bank about a year ago. I wanted to describe their house to them to see if reality matched what was in my head, but you just don't walk up to people who don't seem to know you and start saying crazy things like that."

"Yet, that's what you did to your boss at Dr. Greyson's office."

Arching my back and stretching my hands over my head, I yawn. "Yeah, but I honestly thought he knew me. It wasn't until three shitloads of diarrhea were out of my mouth that I realized I didn't know *how* I knew him."

Griffin stands, doing his own stretching from side to side. "We'll figure it out. Just get some rest and don't let it consume you."

"How can I do that when I see him every day?"

"Maybe you need a new job." He takes my hand and pulls me to the bedroom.

"I have that interview tomorrow. Hopefully they offer me the job. But it's temporary, and I can still watch Morgan after school and on Saturdays."

"What I'm saying is maybe you *shouldn't* watch her anymore." He pulls off his shirt and tosses it on the back of my desk chair.

"I can't just leave them."

His head jerks back. "Them?"

"Her. She needs me and he needs me to watch her." I grab his shirt and push it into his chest. "We can't." I shake my head and frown. "I'm going to be up late finishing my project and I know you have stuff to do too."

He studies me with an intense expression, chin tipped down, eyebrows knitted together. "Are you saying no?"

"Yes."

"That's my girl." He slides his hands up the back of my

shirt and unsnaps my bra before I can get a single word out.

I step back, hitting the edge of my desk. "I meant *yes* I'm saying no."

Griffin nods slowly, still scrutinizing me like I'm something he needs to solve. "Huh," he says like a half laugh filled with disbelief.

"Don't be mad."

"No." He shakes his head and slips on his shirt. "I'm not mad. I just wondered when we'd get here."

"Here?" I follow him to the front door where he puts on his boots.

"When one of us doesn't want sex. I'm not complaining. We've had a good run."

"We're over?" I say with a screech to my voice.

"No." Griff laughs, grabbing my face and pressing a firm kiss to my lips. "We've changed. That's all. We're comfortable with each other. I no longer feel the need to warn you before I come in your mouth, and you have no issue sharing paranormal experiences and your lack of desire to have sex with me."

I can't believe I called him an old soul. Right now he's the epitome of a young twenty-something.

Crude.

Selfish.

Cocky.

"You think I'm crazy. Just say it."

He opens the door, steps out into the hall, and turns toward me. "I think you're sexy as fuck."

"But crazy."

After one last kiss to my forehead, he descends the stairs. "Crazy for not wanting to get naked with me tonight, but I love you. Night, babe."

CHAPTER ELEVEN

FIRST OFFICIAL TEACHING job.

Okay, official might be a stretch. I'm covering for someone on maternity leave, but for eight weeks I get to mold the minds of twenty-five fourth graders.

After shooting off the same *I got the job* text to my mom and Griffin, I haul ass across town to make it to my other job—if I still have one. The way Nate dismissed me last night felt final. As close as I feel to him for whatever unexplainable reason, I can't forget he's my boss and *he* wasn't the one who wanted to hire me.

"Hello?" I call just above a whisper as I slip off my shoes and set down my backpack.

Rachael usually greets me with a fed Morgan, clean diaper, and a smile of gratitude. Not today.

"Hell-ooo?" I peek around the corner down the hallway.

"In the bedroom."

I cringe at the sound of Nate's voice. Why is he here? Let me guess ... I'm fired and he's home early until they find a replacement for Crazy Swayze.

"Hey." I drag my feet into his bedroom. I've never been in here before. This will be a first and last, all-in-one big "you're fired."

Morgan's swing ticks softly in the corner by the window as she kicks and coos, hands and feet jerking in every direction.

The master bedroom is … wow. Curiosity tugged at my conscience many times, but he always has the door shut and those pesky cameras spying on my every move.

A modern king-sized bed engulfs the middle of the room— not next to a wall, just … in the middle like the centerpiece. Everything is gray and white with accents of yellow, not what I expected. Then again, I'm not sure what I expected. Maybe dark blues or black—something more manly. Crazy. This was *their* bedroom, not just his. Light slants in through the white shutters. I think Morgan is trying to kick and punch the sun's rays.

I grin. "She's in a good mood."

"And without you. That's rare, huh?" Nate emerges from the closet with a box. He drops it on the bed.

Without me. I think that says a lot, as in they don't need me.

"Did I miss a message?" I go for the innocent approach. "Did you tell me you were going to be home and I forgot or missed a text or something?"

He disappears into the closet again. "Nope. I'm working from home today."

Am I fired?

"So … you don't need me?"

With another box hugged to his broad T-shirt clad chest, he glances at me while repositioning it next to the other box. "I'm about done here. I still need to work on my paper I'm writing for a journal."

"Okay." We're good. That's good. Well, I'm still not good, but that might be a lost cause by now. "What's in the boxes?"

"Clothes." Nate plants his hands on his hips and watches Morgan.

Her clothes. He's clearing out Jenna's clothes. That's good, I suppose. My mom still hasn't done a damn thing with my dad's stuff, but that's between her and Doctor B for Bunz.

"I had an interview for a teaching job, just temporary, but … I got it."

Nate's gaze shifts to me, a wrinkle of concern creasing his brow. "Well, that's bad timing."

"I think I can still be here by four."

His chin dips as his teeth drag over his bottom lip again and again.

It's not familiar. It's not familiar.

Gah!

It's so familiar. He has something to tell me, but he can't find the words. That bottom lip of his takes the brunt of his worry. It has for years. Fuck my stupid brain for knowing that or reading his mind. Whatever the hell this is.

Keeping his chin low, he glances up at me. I smile. Nothing to see here. I'm not thinking weird shit at all.

"Rachael wants to go to grad school, but she insisted on taking a year off to help with Morgan."

I nod. "Yes, she told me that."

"It's not fair to her. I told her to go."

I nod again, even though I'm not following where he's going with this, especially since his words are so pensive.

"I want you to watch Morgan for me. Full time."

My eyes widen as he chews more on his lip. This is the opposite of firing me. I don't know what to say.

"But … you've taken a job now and I knew this could happen, so … it's my loss." He slips his fingers in the pockets of his cargo shorts and they slide down exposing the gray waistband to his briefs. Nate's all boy right now with his casual attire, turned in shoulders, and nervous grin. Not a hint of Professor Hunt anywhere to be found.

"You're offering me a full-time job?"

"Yes, but I understand it might be too late."

"Yeah. I'd have to turn down the job I just accepted."

"You would." He says it like he's not trying to sway me in either direction, but I think that means he wants me to turn down the job I just accepted, otherwise he'd tell me to forget about it and insist I keep the teaching job. Right?

"I thought ..."

Morgan's coos escalate to grunts that we both know will lead into cries of frustration. When Nate makes no move to get her, I stop the swing and lift her to my chest, nuzzling my nose in her hair that's growing in thick with ginger highlights like her daddy's.

"You thought?" He grabs her sock that fell off when I lifted her out of the swing.

Why does Nate's hockey player hands slipping Morgan's sock onto her tiny foot make my ovaries hurt? I've said it a million times, she's a Morgan fix, not a baby fix. I'm twenty-one. My biological clock hasn't even started to tick. I may have a knack for taking care of babies, but it doesn't mean I'm ready for my own.

"I thought..." my mind shakes off the aching-ovaries internal monologue "...you were going to fire me today."

He blinks a few times, twisting his lips, but I don't get the impression my confession shocks him. That would have elicited a head jerk. No head jerk. Just a contemplative expression.

"Because ..."

Well played. He's going to make me introduce him to the gigantic elephant sitting in the corner of the room.

"I know things about you. That's why you asked me to leave last night."

As he busies his hands with folding in the flaps to the boxes of Jenna's clothes, he gives a tiny shrug. "It was late. You looked tired. I just said you could go home. That's all."

"You've never told me to 'go home,' until last night. There have been many, 'thanks, I'll see you tomorrow' or 'I appreciate all you do' or even 'have a good night,' but not the cold 'go home' you gave me after I said I know you have a birthmark in a place we both know I haven't seen."

Keeping his gaze on the boxes, he grunts. "It just surprised me a little that you thought you knew it with such certainty. I was worried about you, but clearly my concern came across as anger." He glances up. "It wasn't my intention. I'm sorry."

"So..." my eyes flit side to side before locking to his again "...you're saying you don't have that birthmark?"

Nate stacks one box on top of the other and lifts them. "Nope. Maybe one of your old boyfriends had that mark." He carries the boxes down the hall.

I sit on the edge of the bed and bounce Morgan a bit until he returns. "I think you should show me your stomach."

"What?" He scoffs, avoiding eye contact as he shuts the closet door.

"Your shirt. Take it off."

"It's inappropriate." Nate leaves the room again. "I have about two hours of work to do. We can order in dinner if you'd like."

"You're a man." I cradle Morgan and chase after him, not interested in dinner. "Taking off your shirt would not be inappropriate."

"Ask my boss if taking off my shirt in front of a student

would be considered inappropriate."

"I'm not your student." I stop at the entrance to his office as he plops down on his desk chair and opens his laptop.

"You're my nanny—my twenty-one-year-old nanny. I'm one hundred percent certain taking off my clothes in front of you would be inappropriate."

"Shirt. I didn't say 'clothes.'"

He chuckles and it's condescending. "Chinese?"

"I'm not hungry." I'm starving, but my curiosity has a bigger appetite.

"There's a takeout menu in the top drawer by the fridge. Order me something with chicken. Rice, no noodles."

I frown, bouncing Morgan as her eyes roll back in her head, eyelids too tired to stay open. "That menu in your drawer is a Thai menu not a Chinese menu."

He shifts his attention from the screen to me for a brief moment. "What's the difference?"

"Thai is spicier and made with less oil and curry. Fresher ingredients. Healthier."

Nate blinks a few times. "I like spicy."

"I know."

"Do you?" He leans back in his chair, lacing his hands behind his head.

What has happened? He's gone from spooked to actually challenging my knowledge of him.

"Yes. You eat pineapple with jalapeños on your pizza. You have to like spicy food to eat that shit."

"She can hear you." He shifts his attention to his sleeping baby in my arms.

"She's asleep."

"She can hear you." He grins, something between a smirk

and a grimace.

"Sorry, Professor Anatomy. I'll go order you a *Thai* dinner with chicken."

"Swayze?"

I stop before I get two feet past his office door. "Yes?"

"What have you decided?"

"About?" I take a step backwards so I can see him.

"My offer."

I have a degree in education. I want to teach. That's the goal. I need to jump at any chance to build my résumé.

"She's attached to you," he says.

He's not playing fair.

"How long?"

"What do you mean?"

"I mean, how long will this job last? Until she starts school? Until you find a good replacement?"

"Until you no longer want to watch her."

So. Damn. Unfair.

I adore Morgan, and I can't foresee a day in the future where I don't *want* to be with her. But … she's not my daughter, and being a nanny isn't my goal in life. A drop-dead sexy guy with a motorcycle could decide he wants to marry me. And … eventually my ovaries could ache for a child of my own—of *our* own. Then what? What if Morgan is not in school yet? If she's attached to me now, what will it be like in another year or two?

The job I worried about keeping has turned into the job I can't shake.

"I'll call them tomorrow and tell them I have to regretfully decline the job offer."

Nate's lips curl into a small grin. "Thank you. Rachael will be thrilled to know she can go to grad school without feeling guilty about Morgan."

I'm not doing this for Rachael. It's not that I don't like her, but it's a little unfair and ridiculous to choose her future over mine. I'm doing this for Morgan. I think I'm doing this for Nate too. But what scares me the most is that I'm doing it for myself because Nate has my every thought held hostage in this vortex of the unexplainable. It's dizzying. I can't make sense of it or even see straight when I'm with him.

I have to figure this out. *That's* why I'm agreeing to this.

After our dinner arrives and Morgan is fed and asleep in her crib, I edge the conversation toward my newest addiction—his past.

"Have you always liked 'Chinese-Thai' food?" I'm pretty sure I know the answer, but I want to see where it takes this conversation.

He grins over a mouthful then covers his mouth with the corner of a napkin. "No. Daisy loved crab rangoon and fried rice. *Asian* food made me—" He swallows.

"Thirsty." It's not a question. I'm just finishing his sentence before he does.

Lifting a questioning eyebrow, he takes a drink of water, studying me with an intensity that would have left me squirming in my seat a few weeks ago. Not now. Now I want to push him into acknowledging what's going on between us. This familiarity can no longer be ignored or I'll have a breakdown that will dwarf anything that's happened to my mom since my dad died.

I'm not going to push him. There's no need to start a fight, but I'm not going to censor every memory I have of him—or every thought I read from his mind. I'm still not sure which it is.

"Yeah." His eyes narrow.

I return a tightlipped grin, a small challenge of sorts.

"I'd be up half the night running to the kitchen for a drink and then to the bathroom because of all the dang water."

"And now?"

Nate chuckles, adjusting the barstool beneath him. His knee brushes mine, and we both share an awkward glance and look away.

Wow.

An innocent brush of skin. Knee skin. Not lips. Not caressing hands. Why did this happen again?

His touch.

It shouldn't be familiar, and it shouldn't spook me because it's already happened once. But it does because the first time *I* felt it—Crazy Swayze. This time we both felt it. There's no denying what just happened. And each contact feels stronger and more familiar.

"Um…" he clears his throat "…now it still keeps me up at night, gulping down gallons of water and running to the bathroom, but occasionally it's worth it. Jenna loved this restaurant."

We let a few moments of silence fill the room. It's a weird thing humans do after mentioning the name of someone who recently died—an unspoken moment of reflection and respect. I see many flashes of reflection cross Nate's face when he doesn't realize I'm watching him. There's such sadness in his eyes. Sometimes it's when the photo of him and Jenna on the mantle snags his drifting gaze, and sometimes it's when he watches Morgan sleep.

"I like when you tell me about Daisy."

A glint of something resembling life breaks through the grief that just stole his handsome facial features. "You're snoopy." He winks.

"If I'm Snoopy then you're Charlie Brown." I poke at my lo mein with my chopsticks.

"Jesus …" he whispers.

"What?"

Nate's lips part like he's silently gasping. So many of his expressions are eerily familiar, but not this one. Shock? Fear? I can't decipher the meaning behind the look he's giving me, but it sends an icy tingle along my spine.

"Tell me." I can barely get the words out.

His jaw muscles clench a few times then his Adam's apple bounces with a hard swallow. "I have some …"

Where'd he go? His gaze is locked to mine, but I don't think he's really seeing me. And his words are jumbled and broken.

"I need to … uh …"

"Just say it."

Nate squeezes his eyes shut and shakes his head while pinching the bridge of his nose. "Say what?"

"What we both know is true."

He grunts a laugh. "And what's that?"

"I can read your mind."

The pregnant moment lasts longer than I anticipated. If he doesn't open his eyes and say something, I might die because I'm holding my breath. I can't—I won't—breathe until he looks at me.

In the tiniest of increments, he opens them and they trail up just as slowly until we connect. "What am I thinking?"

"Not those thoughts."

"Then what thoughts?"

"Your past."

Blink.

Blink.

His moves are robotic. He tips his chin up and drops it into a slow nod with as much ease as he lays his sleeping daughter in her crib. "I ... see. Why do you think this?"

"It's the only logical explanation for how I know so much about your past."

"Elaborate." He leans in a fraction like I'm going to whisper it to him.

"I lied. That day at Dr. Greyson's office, I knew you. I knew about your scar. Later I told you it was because I heard the story from my older cousin who dated your friend Toby Friedman."

Another slow nod accompanied by a tightly-knitted brow.

"I don't have an older cousin who dated Toby. I wanted the job, so I tried to set your mind at ease by making up a story that you might consider believable."

Blink.

Blink.

"How do you know Toby?"

"I don't think I do know him. I think I can read your memories of him. He lived four houses down from you. You teased him about his buckteeth, then he lost the two front ones after taking a nosedive off his bike. His parents didn't have dental insurance, so their church took up a special offering to get him a retainer thingy that had two flipper teeth. It was cheaper than implants or a bridge. *He* called it a retainer. You called it a denture just to be mean."

Another pregnant pause.

"What else?"

"What do you mean?"

"Right now. What am I thinking?"

"I told you I can only read the past—"

"I'm thinking about my past. So tell me what I'm thinking."

I frown. "I don't know."

"But you just said—"

"I know what I just said." Stabbing my fingers through my hair, I glance down the hall toward the nursery to listen for Morgan, hoping my outburst didn't wake her. "I don't know. Maybe there's something like an active and passive memory. Like … maybe next week I'll be able to tell you what you're thinking right now. I don't know."

"Then tell me more. Tell me what you do know."

"It's …" I shake my head. "It's too much."

"Like what?" He digs, and I hate the irritation in his edgy tone, like it's my fault I know what I know. I thought I wanted to have this conversation, but now I'm not so sure.

"You kept nudie girl magazines under your mattress."

"Twenty, twenty-five years ago every boy kept nudie magazines under his mattress. Now you're just sounding like a fortune teller making broad and rather obvious assumptions."

I huff out a sigh. "You liked chess more than video games."

"You've seen the chess board in my office."

"You're a Chicago Bears fan and it pisses off your Packer-fan father."

"I have Bears beer mugs in the kitchen cabinet. Statistically my father would be a Packers fan."

I cross my arms over my chest. "Why are you doing this? What reason do I have to make this shit up? I'm not a fortune teller. I have nothing to gain. I …" I shake my head. "What do you want to know?"

He stands, gathering the takeout boxes and shoving them in the white plastic takeout bag. "Forget about it. If I have to tell you what I want to know, then that just proves you don't actually know it."

I follow him to the garage where he tosses the trash in the large bin. The door closes behind me leaving us trapped in the late summer heat and humidity. It's so thick in here I think I need to chew and swallow instead of inhale.

"You cheated to pass your final in Spanish. You had straight A's and one D going into finals."

He stops like an invisible wall appeared in front of him. "H-how do you know that?" he whispers, continuing toward me like I could bite him.

This hurts. *I* hurt for him because moments like this feel personal. But I can't give him an explanation. I can't make this better for either one of us. He climbs two of the three garage steps, putting us at eye level. Everything about him invades my space—his woodsy scent, his familiar gaze, the essence of his touch, the curve of his nose, even the way his ginger hair curls around his ears.

"How. Do. You. Know. That?"

I pinch my lips together to keep them from quivering. These memories scare me. They come with this vulnerability that reaches my bones.

"You wrote notes just above your knee because teachers paid attention to arms and hands. So you wrote answers on your leg and wore a pair of jeans with holes in the knees so you could slide the leg up just enough to see the notes."

The pain in his blue eyes sends a wave of nausea through

my stomach. I thought sharing this burden would help, but it's just compounding my own pain and bringing him down with me.

"I'm sorry." Unshed tears burn my eyes.

Nate has lost so much. He doesn't need this. What am I doing?

I flinch as his hand reaches for my face. He pauses a second before wiping his thumb along my cheek. It's wet. I don't remember blinking, but I must have because I'm now aware of the wet trails of tears on my cheeks.

"Something's wrong with me," I whisper while choking back a sob.

There's a lifetime of concern etched into his forehead as he slowly shakes his head. "No. Nothing's wrong with you."

It's too much to hold in. I cover my face with my hands as a cry rips from my throat. Nate pulls me into his chest.

It's warm.

It's comforting.

It's familiar.

But mostly ... it's terrifying.

CHAPTER TWELVE

I T TOOK YEARS to come up for air after Daisy died, but I did. That breath's name was Jenna. With a single smile she showed me love never dies. We just experience it in different forms, ever-changing like the tides and the stars in the night's sky.

Since she died, Morgan has been my life support—my new form of love. She's my purpose for holding my shit together instead of drinking myself into the grave. Being her everything leaves no time for self-pity. No time for mourning. No time for letting my mind be anything but sharp and focused on working, raising a child, and being a role model.

Dr. Greyson helps me navigate the hard parts. I let go of my insecurities and confess my fears in the safety of his office. Then I put on my responsible father mask and do what needs to be done.

However, this week I cancelled my session with him because I need answers that I'm not sure he will have for me. There's only one person I trust with these questions—a fellow professor at the university. She was my old professor of psychology. With a twinkle in her eye, she used to say pieces of many souls lived inside of her. The most unnerving part was her vast knowledge of everything. More knowledge than anyone could acquire in a single lifetime. Her students say it's because outside of the classroom, she lives the life of a recluse.

No close family.

No friends.

No pets.

Just books—writing them and reading them. I've read several of her books and that's why I'm here to see her.

"Nathaniel Hunt." Doctor Hazel Albright peeks out from behind a pile of books on her desk, shoves a bookmark into the one in her hand, and slips off her reading glasses.

At eighty-four, she's the oldest professor at the university and probably the shortest and skinniest. I think my bag of golf clubs weighs more than her—it might be taller than her too. Her short, gray hair and eyes too big for her head make me think of an aged Tinker Bell.

"What a lovely surprise."

"Thank you." I gesture to the door. "Mind if I shut this?"

"Must be serious." She takes a sip of her tea then removes the teabag, depositing it in the garbage can next to her desk. "It's a bit early for a nooner, so I guess you're not here for that." She winks, moving some of the books on her desk to the shelves behind her.

I chuckle, easing into the red leather chair. "I doubt I could keep up with you."

"Don't sweat it, young man. No one can." She takes another sip of her tea. "Well, Professor Hunt, to what do I owe the honor of a closed-room conversation with you? Things not going well with Dr. Greyson?"

Hazel referred me to Dr. Greyson.

"Things are good with Dr. Greyson. He's been helpful. It's just ..." I rub the back of my neck and grimace. "I've read several of your books."

"That's a lovely compliment. You might be the only one

who's read them." She uses a cotton handkerchief with a yellow embroidered edge to wipe the pink lipstick mark from her tea cup—not a mug, but a delicate white teacup.

"Most of your books have landed on best-seller lists. I don't think I'm your only reader."

Her lips press into a soft smile. "And I don't think you're here to discuss my book rankings. Maybe if you told me which books you've read, I could make a better guess as to why the door is shut."

"Your books on reincarnation."

Her eyebrows lift a fraction. "My dear, I do believe you have my attention."

"I hired a twenty-one-year-old girl to be my daughter's nanny. And I think …" My momentum runs to the edge of a cliff and skids to a stop an inch before being airborne. It's funny how limitless the mind is, but such a small fraction of thoughts materialize into spoken words. Somewhere between the mind and mouth exists a sticky web of fear and self-doubt.

Hazel nods while humming. "It's truly amazing, isn't it?"

"I didn't finish."

"You didn't have to. Someone special to you resides inside this young girl. You've found a familiar soul."

"I don't know." Elbows on my knees, I drop my head and run my hands through my hair.

"Then you didn't read my books very thoroughly."

I read them years ago, when I was her student, and I've re-read them since Swayze broke down in tears three days ago in my garage.

Canting her head to the side, she taps her chin. "Then again, you're here. The door to my office is shut. And you look like you haven't slept in days. Who is it? Your wife? A parent?"

"A childhood friend. I named my daughter after her."

"When did she tell you?"

"Who? What?" I look up.

"Your nanny. When did she tell you who she was?"

"That's why I'm here. She doesn't know."

Hazel straightens in her chair, interlacing her fingers and resting them on her desk. "Then how do you know?"

"She knows things about me that only my friend knew. She talks like she's known me forever. But when I tell her stories about my time with Morgan—my friend—there's no recognition of anything about her."

"How does she explain her knowledge of you?"

"She can't. And ... I think it scares her. The other night she said it's because she's reading my mind, but only stuff from the past."

"Have you tried to connect the dots for her?"

On a laugh, my fingertips dig into my temples. "I can't connect the dots myself."

"I disagree. I think you have connected them, and they've led you to me."

"I can't say the words. It's too ..."

"It's beautiful and miraculous. Surely as someone who has studied the human body you have to be awed by the division of cells that make life. We are all energy in many forms. Who's to say we aren't energy in a spiritual form too?"

I'm not this guy. Words like fate, serendipity, and *reincarnation* have not passed my lips that often—except with Daisy. "The timing ... what are the chances of her coming back to me after Jenna dies?"

"Oh dear ..." Hazel presses her hand to her chest. "Reread my books."

"I did."

"Then do it again. Focus on the part where I talk about the anatomy of the soul. My beliefs are a little different than traditional beliefs on reincarnation."

She chuckles. "The western world doesn't really acknowledge it at all. We tend to get caught up in the belief of one birth, one God, one Heaven, and judgment day. Other cultures acknowledge reincarnation as a way of life. It's a fact, not a theory to them. And they openly discuss their previous lives.

"I have my own theories based on my personal experiences and memories of past lives. I believe the soul loses parts of itself and picks up pieces of other released souls before settling into human form again. Your nanny is not Morgan. And not 'yours.' She may have a part of her woven into who she is in this life, but I don't believe two souls are ever the same. Just like two snowflakes are never the same. Everything is part of something bigger, small threads of infinity, ever changing."

She shrugs. "Are we in search of something greater? Does each journey lead to an ultimate goal of spiritual oneness? I don't know. I guess I'll know if and when I get there."

She blows me away. She always has. My father took me to church while my mother cheated on him. His faith gave him the ability to forgive her indiscretions. I believed in God until Daisy died, then I questioned his existence. Jenna gave me back my faith—until she died. Now … I just don't know what to believe. My father would go into cardiac arrest if he knew where I am at this moment and what I'm discussing with Dr. Albright.

"What should I say to her? She had a moment … a bit of a breakdown the other day, and I didn't have much to offer except a friendly hug. All words failed me because this young woman had me scared out of my mind with her knowledge of my past."

"Good question." She jabs her index finger in my direction. "If she claimed to be your childhood friend, then a simple validation of her claims would make moving forward easier but still awkward because she isn't exactly the same person. But..." Hazel drums her fingers on her desk "...if she can't make that connection, then the burden of proof falls upon you."

"She's miserable. I feel like telling her might put her out of her misery."

"Don't be so sure." She shakes her head while bringing the teacup toward her lips. "If it doesn't trigger her memory, which it clearly hasn't so far, then it could serve as more frustration like someone suffering from amnesia." Hazel's lips dip into a slight frown when I release a long sigh. "You miss your wife."

I nod, focusing on her teacup. Jenna drank hot tea every day. She was a tea connoisseur.

"You miss your friend too."

I nod.

"You miss you."

I glance up. Hazel gives me a sad smile. "The people in our lives give color to our existence. When we love, we choose to let part of our heart—part of our soul—live inside of another person. Their happiness is our happiness. Their grief is our grief. And when they die ... part of us dies too."

"If I can find Morgan in Swayze, then I can find that part of myself that died with her?"

With a soft, endearing chuckle she shakes her head. "Wouldn't that be something? Unfortunately, I can't answer that. We're discussing something that a lot of experts won't even acknowledge as a possibility. It seems we've forgotten that the greatest discoveries in the history of mankind have come from bold minds who dared to believe the unbelievable and venture to do the impossible. I guarantee you most of my colleagues think my published works on reincarnation are a disgrace to this department."

I try to hide my grin. Everyone thinks she's crazy. At one time I thought so too. Now ... I don't know what to think.

"Thank you for seeing me." I stand. "I think you're bold and daring—not crazy at all."

"Shh ..." She winks. "I like crazy. And let me know what happens. I'm awfully intrigued."

THREE NIGHTS AGO Nate dismissed me with a "chin up, we'll figure this out." The *we'll* meant a lot to me. Since then we've exchanged minimal words in passing. I don't know what he's supposed to figure out. This is my problem, not his.

Griffin's avoidance of this subject has been disheartening too. I try to see this from their viewpoints. It's asking a lot for them to say they believe me.

"That's a lot of ginger." Griffin sweeps my ponytail off my shoulder and kisses my neck as I stir and season the Alfredo sauce.

My thoughts return to the present. I've been making dinner on autopilot while Griffin's been glued to NASCAR. "It's garlic. And yeah, I may have put a little too much in. But can you really have too much garlic in Alfredo sauce?"

He chuckles while lifting the spice bottle I just set on the counter. "No. I don't think you can have too much garlic in

Alfredo sauce. However, I do think too much *ginger* might mask the Alfredo taste."

"Shit." My nose wrinkles as I focus on the label. "Dang it! I've ruined dinner."

"I love ginger ... and adventure." Griffin ladles the sauce over our two bowls of fettuccine. "Stop frowning." With a bowl in each hand, he bends down and traps my lower lip between his teeth, holding it there until I relinquish a grin that tugs it from his grip. "There's my girl. I'm not sure I've seen you smile for days."

My gaze moves up his face. "I'm sorry."

"Don't apologize." He jerks his head toward the sliding doors to my balcony as I grab our drinks.

We ease back into the two red-padded chairs separated by a round table. The side street below and old park across from it is a five-dollar view at best, but it faces east so we can enjoy dinner without the blinding sun.

"Tell me about your day or that perpetual frown you've been brushing off as nothing."

"I'm sorry."

"Stop. Apologizing." He grins while shaking his head as he twirls the pasta around his fork. "I'm not mad. I just don't understand. Have I done something wrong?"

"No." I poke at my food, but I'm not feeling hungry. "I have something to tell you, that's all."

Griffin coughs, and coughs, and grabs his water, gulping the whole thing down. My nose wrinkles as I make a guess as to what has him so choked up. Tapping his fist to his chest, he clears his throat. I take a tentative bite of my pasta.

"Ew ... yuck!" I spit it back into my bowl. "I love ginger too, but this is nasty and *not* an adventure."

Griffin laughs while digging his phone out of the pocket of his jeans. "I'll order pizza."

I take our bowls to the kitchen and return with the pitcher of ice tea to refill our glasses. Griffin loves blueberry rooibos ice tea. I love that this amazing man beside me doesn't need a constant buzz to enjoy life—to enjoy me.

"Forty minutes." He slides his phone onto the round table and holds out his hand.

I take it, letting him pull me onto his lap. Griffin nuzzles the back of my neck under my ponytail.

"Are you dumping me?" he mumbles as his arms hug my back to his chest, fingertips slipping under the hem of my blue tank top to tease my skin. "Is that what you need to tell me?"

I giggle because his touch tickles and his words are ridiculous. "No, I'm not dumping you. I'm never dumping you. And if you try to dump me I will hunt you down, tie you up, and take away your bike until you come to your senses."

Laughter rumbles from his chest. "What if I cheat on you?"

"I'll cut off your dick, but you're still mine."

"Oh … that's wrong, baby." His body stiffens beneath me like he's trying to protect said dick from my evil threat. "You'd miss my dick."

I cover his hands with mine and interlace our fingers to keep him from tickling me. "I would, but you'd still have your tongue." Propping my legs up onto the railing, I let go of a long sigh. "I called the school and told them I had to regretfully withdraw my acceptance for the temporary teaching position this fall."

"What? Why did you do that?"

"Nate asked me to watch Morgan full time."

"And you said no because you have your very first teaching

job. *Right?*"

I shake my head. "It was just for maternity leave."

"It's a job, Swayze." Griffin's voice escalates.

"So is watching Morgan. Nate pays me."

"So it's Nate now? I thought he liked to be called Na-thaniel."

My feet drop to the ground, and I scoot sideways on his lap to look at him, but before I am turned I already know there's a hard scowl affixed to his face. I can tell from the sharpness of his words and the way his hands grip mine harder when I say Nate's name. "He's Nate to me."

"What does that mean?"

"You know what that means."

Griffin shakes his head with caution. "No. I don't think I do."

"Stop acting like we didn't have this conversation even though you haven't said a word since then. Ignoring it won't make it go away. I know because I've tried."

He scratches the back of his head. On instinct my eyes go straight to the flex of his bicep and the tightening of his inked skin covering it. But now is not the time to get distracted.

"The mind reading thing?"

My head falls to the side. "That's what we're calling it?"

He grunts a laugh, holding his hands out, palms up, before letting them flop back down to the arms of the chair. "Do you have a better explanation for it yet?"

My eyes narrow while my insides knot into a hundred little angry fists ready to fight, ready to defend. "You think I'm crazy." I stand and distance us until my back touches the railing. "I knew it. Why didn't you just say it? Why pretend to be supportive? Did you really think it was nothing more than wacky hormones or lack of sleep?"

"You know damn well I never said that. But I did say you should look for another job, *not* accept a full-time position in the very environment that brings about these episodes."

"Episodes?" My head juts forward as I grab the rail. "I'm not having seizures or breakdowns or feelings of dizziness. This doesn't go away. I know what I know and it's real, not some illusion or dream."

"Okay, calm down." He reaches for me.

I let him grab my wrist, but I don't submit to his pull. Hugging me, nuzzling my neck, and touching my skin may turn me on, but it won't change what's in my mind. He scoots to the edge of his seat when I resist his silent command to surrender to him.

"You can read the professor's mind ... or see into his past. Whatever it is ... I'm just saying nothing good can come from immersing yourself in the very environment that's causing you this stress. The answer isn't spending *more* time with him and Morgan. You have a life, a degree waiting to be used, and a boyfriend who wants to spend the rest of his life with you."

Tears sting my eyes. I don't like having my future—my dreams—laid before me like all I have to do is grab it. I can't grab it. Whatever is going on in my head feels bigger, like I'd be living a lie if I didn't figure it out before letting it go.

"Are you asking me to marry you?" I rub the tears from my eyes before they escape.

Griffin leans back, interlacing his hands behind his head, eyeing me with the intensity of the sun. "It wasn't a proposal. I may be a jerk sometimes, but I'm not the guy who uses a marriage proposal as a distraction or to win an argument. I just meant that I love you more than any man will ever love you.

And your happiness means everything to me. But you don't seem happy right now. When you accepted the teaching job you were happy. Before you met the professor you were happy."

That's my dream. As much as I want to be a modern, practical woman who sees how ridiculous it is to spend thousands of dollars on a white gown, expensive floral arrangements, and a sit-down dinner for two hundred people, I'm still the twenty-one-year-old girl who hears love songs on the radio and imagines waltzing around a dance floor in a wedding dress as Mrs. Griffin Calloway.

"I *am* happy. But I'm also scared. It's not just Nate. I told you, before I saw him at Dr. Greyson's office, there were times that I'd see people at the store or a movie or wherever and I *knew* them. But it was always a brief thing that I shook from my mind like crazy déjà vu moments."

He shrugs. "That's normal. I see people who look familiar to me and it drives me crazy because I know I know them, but I can't remember their name or how I know them."

I laugh, shaking off his efforts to empathize. "You see someone familiar and it drives you crazy because you can't remember anything about them, but they *look* familiar and that's the only connection your brain makes. I see certain people and I know their name is Craig Hall, homecoming king, ACL injury in the season-opening football game. He vaguely looks familiar because my memory of him is of a time before his black hair peppered to gray and his waist was a thirty not a thirty-four."

Griffin looks at me with an unreadable expression. I've been avoiding a psychiatrist who has years of education and experience. He's probably heard everything, yet I expect my twenty-three-year-old boyfriend to grasp something beyond comprehension like a great Renaissance philosopher might do? I don't think Griffin's soul is quite that old.

This is impossible to explain, but I try anyway. "If you told me you saw the ghost of your great grandma Annabelle and her poodle Corky, I would think you're crazy. If you told me you levitated six feet off the ground while listening to Slipknot after an intense workout, I wouldn't believe you."

Griffin takes several large gulps of his tea and watches it as he circles the glass, rattling the ice. "You're giving me permission to not believe you?"

"Yes."

"So if I say I think you're losing it, will you be mad at me?"

"Yes."

His head snaps up, brow drawn tight. "But you just said—"

"I know. I'm asking you to lie to me if the truth hurts. I'm asking you to love me even when you don't understand me. It's selfish and immature. *I'm* selfish and immature. But I'm also alone and scared and going through something that has derailed my life. So maybe you think I'm crazy now, but if I don't figure this out I will most certainly go crazy beyond anything I am right now."

Griffin studies me for a few seconds. "Okay."

"Okay?"

"Yeah. Okay. But I want you to go see a doctor."

"Dr. Greyson?"

"No. A doctor who will make sure you're ..." He clears his throat and takes a hard swallow while rubbing his hand over his mouth and looking at the floor between us.

It's heartbreaking to see him struggle to say what he wants to say.

Big brown eyes look up at me. "I want … I need to know that you're okay. Physically."

"I've had a physical."

"Jett's wife died of a brain tumor two years ago."

My perpetual frown returns. A tumor has crossed my mind, but I don't see how a brain tumor could explain this. "Sorry, I didn't realize your boss had a wife that died."

He nods.

"I'm not sure how a brain tumor could do this. I've had scans before—when I was younger and too smart for my own good. They came out clear."

"Jesus, Swayze! Can you just do this for me?" He bolts to standing.

I freeze. This is not Griffin. He's calculated … controlled.

Caging me in with his hands resting on the railing, his brooding eyes trap me in his gaze. "Please," he whispers while lowering his brow to mine.

The gravity of the pain on his face elicits chills along my skin and sends my heart into my throat—thick and pulsing. "I love you so fucking much." His voice breaks as he brushes his lips over mine. "And I'm scared too."

CHAPTER THIRTEEN

THE FOLLOWING WEEK I start my full-time position as Morgan's nanny. Nate asks me to bring her to the university so some of his colleagues can meet her. I never saw that request coming, but I don't hesitate to pack her up so Nate can show her off.

Jenna's car.

Nate's entire world in the backseat.

Heavy noon-hour traffic.

My heart doesn't beat until I'm parked in the lot outside of Nate's building. "We made it, baby girl." I unlatch her seat from the base and hook it onto the stroller. "Are you going to sleep all afternoon?"

As if she feels the need to answer me, she wrinkles her nose and fists at her squinted eyes and mouth before relaxing back into lullaby land. I slide down the seat's visor to protect her from the sun shining brightly in a cloudless sky. It's perfect today. After a long stretch of stifling heat and humidity, there's a nice breeze delivering low eighty-degree temperatures.

"Knock knock." I wait for Nate to glance up from his computer.

He smiles so big it steals my next breath because I've seen that smile a million times before in some unknown way. It's familiar, comforting, and unforgettable. Those wavy ginger locks, mesmerizing blue eyes, and strong jaw framing his perfect smile is nothing short of gorgeous. There's no way his female students aren't gaga over the handsome Professor Hunt.

"Come in. How was the drive?"

I hold up my hands. "My knuckles are still white."

He makes his way around his desk and takes Morgan out of her seat. "You don't like to drive?"

"I'm fine driving my car with no one's life in my hands."

"I trust you."

The cutest rolls have filled out on her arms and legs, but in Mr. Hockey Player's arms, she still looks tiny.

"What?" he asks, holding her with the confidence of a seasoned dad. She nestles into his neck like it's her favorite place in the world.

"I didn't say anything."

"But you have a funny grin on your face." He eases into his desk chair and rocks her.

Trapping my lips between my teeth, I shrug.

"Tell me." Nate eyes me playfully. Who is this guy? It's like every day he's a little more of the Nate I remember.

"The truth?"

He nods, a pleasant smile still holding his lips as he gives me his full attention.

"You won't freak out?"

"Spill."

"You're a great dad, just like your dad. I know he couldn't give you the world in a tangible way, but ..." I've gone too far. My heart won't stop racing like something bad is about to happen.

"But?" Nate's head cants to the side.

Taking a slow, deep breath, I let my mouth narrate the pictures in my head. "He tried. When you were thirteen he sold a watch his father gave him so he could send you to that hockey camp in Minneapolis."

Nate's smile fades and his eyes divert to something on his desk—or maybe the past, the camp, the watch. "Are you sure?"

I nod several times, walking the parameter of his office lined with bookshelves and a wall of diplomas and other certificates. His gaze returns to mine when I make a quick glance back over my shoulder.

"I didn't know that."

"Ask him."

Pressing his lips to the top of Morgan's head, he mumbles, "I don't need to."

"Because you think I'm making it up?" I slide my purse off my shoulder and onto the floor by the stroller and sit in one of the two chairs opposite his desk.

"I believe you."

"You do?" Those two words shoot from my mouth like confetti.

He chuckles. "I cheated on that Spanish test. The answers were written on my leg, just above the large hole in the knee of my jeans. I never did learn Spanish and the risks of getting caught were too high, so I switched to French."

"You did?"

He nods.

"Funny. I didn't know that."

His expression goes slack, and he blinks quickly a few times as he looks around the room like he's avoiding my comment.

"So ... can you be home by two this Friday? I have a doctor's appointment."

Nate returns his attention to me as Morgan squirms and fusses. I fish her bottle out of the diaper bag, it's still warm from heating it up just before we left. I knew she'd want to eat soon. Like we've been doing it forever, I hand him the bottle as soon as he shifts her into a cradled position, and I drape a burp cloth over his shoulder.

"Is everything okay? Just routine stuff, I hope." His eyes narrow.

"Not routine. But I don't think they'll find anything." I sit back down in the chair. "Griffin asked me to get my brain checked out." I laugh.

Nate doesn't.

"His boss's wife died of a brain tumor. He's just worried that my special ability to see into your past and those of random other people might be caused by some brain issue. I'm doing it for him." I shrug. "That's what you do for the people you love."

"I'm sure you're fine."

"Thanks, Dr. Hunt." I smirk and he does too.

"Oh my gosh!"

My head whips around toward the high-pitched voice. A brunette, maybe in her fifties, holds her hands over her mouth, hiding part of her gasping expression.

"She's here." Her voice could crack the windows.

Without a single glance in my direction, she breezes past me toward Nate and Morgan. "Nathaniel, she's the most precious thing I have ever seen."

"Thanks, Donna. I won't tell your four kids that you said that." Nate winks at her. He's always been such a flirt.

For the love of God, I think. Again, I just *know* this about him.

"Can I steal her for a bit? Thea, Madeline, and Grace are down the hall. They'll want to see her too."

I love that he doesn't instantly pass her off. A flash of conflict ghosts across his face as he stares at his daughter. So protective.

"We're all moms, Nathaniel. She'll be in good hands. I'll guard her with my life."

"I can take her to see them."

"No, no. You have a student waiting for you." She finally gives me a quick glance and polite smile.

Nate's gaze shifts to me. The introduction, the correction to her incorrect assumption, never comes. After a pregnant pause, he looks up at Donna. "Don't touch her hands unless you wash yours. Don't let her suck in air from her bottle. And if Marietta shows up, don't let her hold Morgan because I don't want my daughter smelling like cigarette smoke."

Before he gets the last few words out, Donna nabs Morgan, the bottle, and the burp cloth from his shoulder. "Don't fret, Nathaniel. I'll take good care of little Miss Morgan," she says in a baby-talking voice while walking out of his office.

I want to chase after her and make sure they do in fact wash their hands before touching Morgan's hands, and tip her bottle at the right angle so she doesn't suck in air, and guard her from chain-smoking Marietta. It's scary how much I love that little girl who isn't mine. I have lots of experience watching children, but I've never felt so attached to one as fast as I have with Morgan.

"She'll be fine." I smile at Nate.

The wrinkles lining his forehead ease a bit.

"So, Professor Hunt, maybe you should teach your student something." My fingers drum on the arms of the chair.

His shoulders relax as the last bit of worry drains from his posture and his mouth forms that handsome smile.

"I want to know if you still eat purple popsicles." I grin. Knowing so much yet so little about Nate at the same time thrills me like a child opening gifts on Christmas—pure wonder and anticipation.

He reclines back and props his jean-clad legs up on his desk, crossed at the ankles. His black and white Vans look brand new. I have no recollection of him wearing new shoes, and that makes me sad for the young boy I see in my head.

"You want to talk about Daisy?" Nate's eyebrow lifts a fraction.

"It's the part of your childhood I don't know."

He scratches his chin, twisting his lips to the side. "Doesn't that seem odd since she was such a big part of my childhood?"

"Really? *That's* the part that stands out to you as odd? Not the fact that I'm basically a stranger to you, fifteen years younger than you, and I've managed to channel or see into your past with vivid detail?"

Nodding slowly several times, gaze affixed to me with a glassy-eyed, almost contemplative expression, he wets his lips and speaks the words I've been dying to hear. "Purple popsicles it is."

My brain does a happy dance while every part of my body on the outside remains cool like it's no big deal. *It's a huge deal!*

Nathaniel Hunt Age 14

I FOUND MY forever at fourteen. Of course I never told anyone that, not even Daisy. Fourteen-year-old boys who looked seventeen in size, played hockey with older kids, and settled disputes with their fists didn't fall in love. Having Daisy as my best friend garnered me enough crap to last a lifetime.

"I wish you had cable." Daisy tossed a fast-food bag on my notebook then shoved my backpack off the foot of my twin bed and plopped down in its spot.

"Why is that?" I steadied my geometry book to keep it from falling onto the ground.

"Because he's always sleeping in his recliner with the TV on when I come over, and he never hears me. If you had cable, I'd change the channel to porn so when he woke up he'd wig out about the idea of us seeing it."

I laughed, shoving greasy fries into my mouth. It was my first meal of the day, which sucked since it was eight o'clock at night. Daisy spending her allowance on food for me was not a highlight of my childhood, but hunger came before pride.

"It might give him a heart attack since our food fairy only brings us fast food." I held up my cheeseburger before shoving half of it into my mouth.

"I put his in the fridge." Her nose wrinkled. "The cold fries will taste disgusting."

"He won't care," I mumbled with a mouthful of greasy goodness. "It's food. He hasn't found a job yet, and we'll probably be on the street in a week."

"Don't say that." The downward turn of her full lips made me want to kiss them. I loved kissing Daisy. And she liked kissing me. It was something I could give her. My shit lot in life made it hard to feel like a man, which was crazy since I was only fourteen, but I wanted to be a man for the girl who was my forever. Instead, I was a charity case along with my dad.

"I'll bring some apples and bananas tomorrow. I just worry they won't be enough calories."

"Stop wasting your money on feeding the poor." I tossed

the bag on my already cluttered nightstand, pitched my notebook and geometry book onto the floor, and grabbed her by the waist, pulling her up to straddle my lap.

"Don't call yourself that." She wrapped her arms around my neck.

I chuckled. "Don't worry. Mom will show up to save the day." My hands slid into her jeans' pockets. That was the extent of my bravery. My friends were copping feels up girls' shirts. A few had been the lucky recipients of hand-jobs. And my older hockey buddies were going all the way. I respected Daisy too much to cross those lines. I respected her parents too much to take advantage of their daughter, especially when I knew they turned a blind eye to her charity—the charity that kept my stomach from eating itself.

"What do you mean save the day?" She played with my hair, threading her fingers through the wayward curls.

"Dad thinks she starts to feel guilty about abandoning me and that's when she shows up for a few weeks, uses money from her rich boyfriend to fill the fridge and pantry, cooks a few meals, makes an appearance at one of my hockey games, and then leaves again."

Daisy smelled good, better than the cheeseburger, which meant a lot coming from the mind of a hungry teenager. She'd gone from wearing unisex clothes and no makeup to girly clothes that hugged her newly formed curves, shimmery lip glosses, and flowery lotions that shot my own side effects of puberty into overdrive.

"Why does he let her come home? She's cheating on him. I don't understand why they're still married."

"My dad says he loves her no matter what. I think he's worried God will be upset if they get divorced. She's always on the prayer request list at church. It's kinda embarrassing. Like … everyone already thinks the worst about our situation, why does he have to announce it to the world?"

She giggled. "What's the prayer? 'Dear God, we ask that David Hunt's wife stop cheating on him and return home to feed her family and catch up on laundry?'"

"Nah…" my teeth dug into my lower lip as I tried to hide my grin "…just the ironing. I do the laundry, but I've never ironed before. I'd probably set my dad's shirts on fire."

More giggles ensued.

"Stop. No. You're not—" I grabbed her wrist.

She batted it away. "It's cool." With the hair tie she fished out of her pocket, she pulled my hair into a ponytail. It was just long enough to work.

"It's girly. Knock it off." I pretended to struggle against her as she pushed my arms down and hooked her legs over them to keep me from pulling out the ponytail.

She weighed nothing, and I had recently started lifting weights to keep up with my older teammates. We played the game that she was really restraining me, but we both knew better. I liked her squirming and bouncing around on top of me for reasons any teenage boy liked it, and she liked to pretend she was in control.

"I need a haircut." I grumbled as she leaned back and grinned at her work.

"What if you're like Mason and you cut your hair and lose all your strength?"

"Who's Mason?"

Daisy rolled her eyes. "From the Bible."

I barked a hearty laugh. "You haven't been to church a day in your life. And I know you've never read a word from the

Bible because if you had done either, you would know that it's Samson not Mason."

Her eyes narrowed. "Don't be a smart-ass. No one likes a smart-ass. It's not my fault I don't go to church, it's God's fault." She crossed her arms over her chest.

"It's not God's fault. It's your parents' fault for being atheists."

"What do you mean atheists?"

"They don't believe in God."

Her head jerked back. "That's not true. They're just mad at God."

"For what?"

She yanked my ponytail in opposite directions to keep it from slipping out from the hair tie.

I gave her a twisted frown.

"Can you keep a secret?"

It was the most ridiculous question ever. We were best friends. Whether she knew it or not, I was going to marry her some day and have three kids and a nice but modest house paid for by my sizable paycheck from the NHL. I was the only one who knew that. And that right there was proof of my secret-keeping abilities. "That's a stupid question, Daisy."

"If you don't stop calling me Daisy, I'm not going to tell you anything ever again. This is exactly why I need a real boyfriend who calls me Morgan or babe or … princess."

"Princess? Really? What are you? A poodle?"

Every single day, for four years, she'd been threatening me with the "real boyfriend" thing. I no longer cared. I had her attention.

Her smiles.

Her kisses.

Her spare minutes.

Her fears.

Her dreams.

That was as real as real got.

"Shut up." She put her hand over my mouth.

I licked it.

"Ew …" She pulled it away.

Before her sour face set into anything permanent, I kissed her. She kissed me back. It was clumsy at first, but then we found our rhythm. Her head moved in one direction and mine moved in the opposite as our lips figured the rest out on their own. My tongue grazed hers, and after a quick second, hers retreated like I'd tempted it with the forbidden.

"Gross, jerk," she said after pulling away with a breathless voice and flushed cheeks, but her smile robbed all anger from her words.

"Tell me your secret."

"Promise not to—"

"Yeah, yeah … I'm not going to tell anyone."

"Fine. You better not." Her gaze sank to just below my mouth. It was an odd moment, a nervous side to my best friend that I didn't see very often. "Two years before I was born, my mom had a baby boy. He was born dead—stillborn or something like that."

"Oh that's … terrible. I can't believe you never told me this. That's really sad."

She nodded, risking a glance. "They've been mad at God ever since."

"I suppose I would be too. That sucks."

"Yeah." She shrugged. "My grandma thinks we're all going to Hell now."

"What do you think?"

"Well, I don't know. It's not like I don't believe in God. I may not know the difference between Samson and Mason..." she grinned "...but I like the idea of God. And sometimes when I'm scared or need something really bad, I pray to him. I'm not sure I'm doing it right."

"What do you ask God for? My dad says we should spend more time giving thanks than asking for stuff. Like with my mom ... he says he thanks God for the days she is here more than he asks God to bring her back. That's kinda cool, right?"

Daisy shrugged. "He's probably right. I should say thank you. Maybe that will make him more likely to say yes when I do ask for stuff."

"Like?"

Her hands slid back around my neck and her lips brushed along my ear as she whispered, "I always ask God to remember to feed you and to make sure you don't end up homeless."

CHAPTER FOURTEEN

S WAYZE'S SMILE BREAKS my heart. When I tell her about my past, she doesn't move, doesn't blink, just ... grins. If my best friend lives inside of her soul, I wish we could talk about it. How can she remember everything but the one person who made my childhood truly special?

"I'm scared..." Swayze's smile fades "...because you're adding beautiful color to everything in my head that's black and white. But it's like watching a movie based on actual events. You know what's going to happen. I can't unsink the Titanic. And Daisy ..."

"Died," I mutter, wanting so much to connect with the memories in her mind.

"Yeah." She mirrors my sad smile.

It's impossible to not stare at her, waiting for something more than curiosity to shine in those blue eyes. A glimmer of recognition would probably stop my heart.

"You haven't asked me how she died," I say, but what I think is: *You haven't asked me how you died.*

If I'm honest with myself, I'm not sure I could tell her that and keep my shit together.

"No." She shakes her head. "I don't want to know. Not yet ... maybe not ever."

"Why?"

A tense concern mars her face. "I don't know. Is that

weird?"

I chuckle in spite of my chasm of emotions.

Hope.

Grief.

Confusion.

Clarity.

"You're asking the wrong person. I cleared Jenna's clothes out of our closet, but her overnight bag that we took to the hospital is still in the back of my vehicle. My daughter bears the name of the first girl I ever loved, and I've accepted the fact that you're ... someone connected to my past. So..." I shake my head "...I'm not the best judge of 'weird.'"

One side of her mouth slants into a half smile. "My whole life, I've known stuff that hasn't made sense for me to know. It stole my childhood, but I never *felt* truly different until you."

Her words make it hard to breathe. I want to whisper, *Daisy.* I want her to acknowledge us. I want to ask her why she was alone the night she died.

All these years later, I feel that hole in my heart, in my soul, like no matter what happens in my life there will always be part of who I am that's incomplete. These are the words I would tell my best friend, Daisy.

"Well, I hope I don't disappoint. I hope I can help you find answers."

"Me too."

"Blowout! Huge blowout! Oh goodness ..." Donna holds Morgan out at arm's length.

I jump up and take her, also keeping her at arm's length. "Oh no. Sorry, Donna."

Donna looks down at her poop-stained shirt. "It's fine. I should have known when her face turned bright red that something explosive was about to happen. I'll go get her bottle and burp cloth before I head home for a change of clothes."

"Sorry ..." I bite my lips together. I don't know what else to say.

"Hush, it's fine." She waves off my comment while walking out of my office.

"Here." Swayze takes Morgan and lays her on my desk that she's already covered with a changing pad. "And you were worried about her. Clearly, Morgan can take care of herself when strangers run off with her." She giggles, peeling off the soiled onesie.

"Like a skunk spraying its predator?" I laugh.

"Exactly." Swayze folds up the onesie and sets it aside while I ease off Morgan's diaper.

Squirt!

"Shit!" I shove the dirty diaper back down over her, but not before the front of my shirt looks like a Dijon mustard bottle exploded onto it.

Swayze's hand flies to cover her mouth and the huge grin I know she's hiding, eyes wide and unblinking as they flit between Morgan and me. "Language, Professor," she mumbles behind her hand.

She's right. I roll my eyes. "A little help?" My attempt to sound upset is spoiled by a stupid grin crawling up my face. And it feels so damn good even if just inches below it there's poop splattered all over my shirt and my daughter now has it up the front of her too because I instinctively shoved the dirty diaper over her to protect me.

Swayze turns and snorts a stifled laugh as she grabs several wipes from the diaper bag. She turns back to me with tears in her eyes. "I'm sorry ..." She erupts into laughter until the tears in her eyes stream down her cheeks. "Oh my gosh." She cringes, making a quick assessment of the situation. "This is too big of a mess for baby wipes. We need a sink."

"The restroom is just down the hall." I nod toward the door.

"Okay. Um …" Her nose wrinkles.

I try not to move, but Morgan kicks and coos with delight. I'm sure she feels pretty great right now after getting rid of so much crap.

"You're already a mess, so I say you carry her to the bathroom and hold her while I wash her off."

"Fine. Let's go before this mess gets any bigger."

Swayze nods, grabbing the diaper bag.

"And stop laughing," I say while picking up Morgan, letting the diaper fall to the changing pad.

"I'm not laughing." A giggle escapes before she can get the last word out.

It's a single bathroom, which is nice since no one else needs to see this mess. We manage to avoid running into anyone on our way.

"Hurry up before she goes again." I hold Morgan over the sink.

"I have to let the water warm up a little." Swayze shoots me a quick glance, still trying and failing at containing her amusement.

She wets a wad of paper towels and quickly cleans the poop off Morgan.

"I'll bathe her as soon as I get her back home, but this is good for now." She takes her from me.

"Careful. She might not be done." I stare at Morgan's naked backside as Swayze hugs her to her chest.

Swayze eyes my shirt. "I think it's safe to say she's on empty right now. I'll go get a diaper on her and a new outfit. You should do…" she frowns "… something with that shirt."

"Ya think?" I smirk.

When the door closes behind her, I unbutton my shirt and shrug it off. There's no way this shirt will ever get worn again, but I spend the next five minutes scrubbing the hell out of it anyway. Since I don't have a change of clothes, I attempt to dry it a little under the hand dryer so it's not soaking wet when I put it back on.

"We're going to—" Swayze pushes open the door and freezes.

It takes me a few seconds to figure out what has her in such shock. But when I follow the line of her gaze to my bared abdomen, I know.

"Nate," she says my name like I just broke her heart.

I don't move. Maybe I should cover up what's caught her attention, but I don't because I'd give anything to know what I believe is true.

"Nate," she whispers again like a desperate plea while inching toward me, letting the door close behind her, eyes focused on only one thing.

I can't blink. If the slightest bit of realization flashes in her eyes, I don't want to miss it.

Maybe I should put on my shirt, but I don't.

Maybe I should back away as her hand reaches out to touch me, but I don't.

Maybe I should say something—fucking anything—as her fingertips brush the heart-shaped birthmark on my abdomen, eliciting goose bumps along my skin, muscles hardening beneath her touch.

But ... I don't.

Her fingers don't move from my skin as she closes her eyes.

Remember ... please ... just remember ...

Her touch. Professor Albright said this girl is not my Morgan, but ... what if she is? With one touch, I'm that young boy in love with his best friend. I'm that young boy standing in front of Daisy, watching her push back my unbuttoned shirt and tracing her fingertips over my birthmark.

One touch has just erased twenty-one years.

One touch has just erased everything my analytical mind can comprehend.

"You feel it?" She opens her eyes and meets my gaze, but all I can see is pain and confusion.

I can't speak, so I give her a slight nod.

"Why?" she says on a breathless exhale.

Because you're my best friend. Because not even death could separate us.

"I don't know." It's all I can say because I don't understand it, so I can't explain it. I can name every part of the body, recite the stages of human development, DNA, the life-saving abilities of stem cells ... so many miraculous things that make up the human species. But this I can't explain. Nor can I deny the existence or truth of whatever *this* is.

There's a knock on the door.

Swayze jumps back. "Donna is watching Morgan." She shakes her head like she's trying to clear her mind. "I-I just came to tell you we're leaving."

I slip on my damp shirt and start to button it. "Thank you for bringing her."

We don't look at each other.

"We'll see you later."

I nod, staring at my hands as I button the button next to my birthmark.

The door clicks shut behind her.

"Fuck …"

I MESSAGE SWAYZE to tell her that I'm going to be later than expected. After two solid hours of watching live video feed of her and Morgan, I click out of the screen and actually get some work done. It occurs to me that by this point it's not necessary to monitor them. I'm not. Now I'm just being creepy as fuck and watching *her*. Wondering what she's thinking. Waiting for her to light up with some grand ah-ha moment.

By the time I arrive home, silence fills the house. Swayze has dozed off in the recliner chair with a sleeping Morgan nestled on her chest. I take a seat on the sofa and watch them some more. It's crazy how for years every girl with blond hair and brown eyes reminded me of Daisy, but when I met Swayze at Dr. Greyson's office, I didn't think of Daisy. Now all I see is *her*.

Some days I swear her eyes are brown instead of blue.

"Watching me sleep is kinda creepy." She opens her eyes and grins. "I'm supposed to be the creepy one, not you, Professor."

Professor. She calls me Nate when she's vulnerable, Nathaniel when she's nervous, and Professor when she wants to pretend we're nothing more than employer and employee. I knew everything there was to know about her then … and I'm going to know this new version of my best friend. She's the distraction I need. A gift.

"Tell me about your family."

I hold her gaze even as her eyes narrow. I may be a different person to her, depending on her desire to deal with the past, but she's so much more than a nanny. And now that I know that, I can't pretend it's anything but a fucking miracle.

"My family?"

I nod.

"Well, you know my dad died of a heart attack. He was a CPA for almost thirty years. My mom is a product photographer. She's worked for several large companies over the years while trying to balance her career with raising me. I'm not sure she's taken her camera out of its bag since my dad died."

Swayze shakes her head. "She said she needs to decide 'what's next' in her life. But I think she's afraid she'll see him through the lens of her camera. He was the one who convinced her to pursue her passion. He bought her first camera. She took a gazillion rolls of film, all of him, before digital. It's crazy how many photo albums she has, all of my dad. He was handsome, even when he started to lose his hair. She was—*is* beautiful. I like to imagine they had a passionate relationship before they had me. I just never saw that kind of love."

"Grandparents?"

"Yes. All four are still alive. My mom's parents live just outside of Chicago and my dad's parents live here in Madison." She presses the home button on her phone on the arm of her chair. "I have to go."

"Of course." I take Morgan from her; she doesn't even make a noise. The outing to my office and big blowout must have exhausted her. "Thanks again for bringing her to see me at work today. My colleagues really enjoyed seeing her."

"Even Donna?" Swayze gives me a suspicious grin as she

grabs her bag and walks toward the front door.

"Even Donna." I chuckle. "I should give her some money for a new shirt. It's probably ruined ... like mine."

Swayze's gaze drops to my shirt, but I know she's not thinking about the shirt; she's thinking about my birthmark.

"It's not shaped like a heart. More like a banana."

Her eyes shoot up to mine, confusion all over her face.

"My birthmark. The only person who thought it was shaped like a heart was Daisy."

She nods slowly, but I don't detect any real understanding.

"Just like Daisy was the only one who knew about me cheating on that Spanish test."

Swayze twists her lips and continues to bob her head, but I have no clue what she's thinking. It's like watching the rainbow wheel spin on my computer with no results.

"Well, don't forget I have my doctor's appointment Friday."

That's it—nothing more than a spinning rainbow wheel. What would she do if I just told her? The words make their way to my mouth, but I can't force them out. Instead, I smile and nod. "I can work from home Friday. If you need all day, that's fine too."

"Okay. I'll let you know. See you tomorrow."

"Goodnight."

I watch her until she gets to her car. When she turns to give me a final wave, I return a quick wave and close the door. She may be right. My staring is getting a little creepy. After laying Morgan in her crib, I collapse onto my own bed, rubbing the tension from my temples as my thoughts drift back to twenty-one years earlier.

Nathaniel Age 15

"DAISY," I WHISPERED while my shaky fingers unbuttoned my wrinkled dress shirt.

The cracked window let in a soft breeze, but the humidity hung heavily in our house that had been without air-conditioning for over a week. Crickets sang in the distance, but the pounding of my heart nearly drowned them out.

"I'm so sorry about your uncle." A tear splattered on my hand, but it wasn't mine. It was hers.

The man who inspired me to play hockey died, and I hadn't shed a single tear. Daisy had enough emotion for the both of us. She eased my shirt off my shoulders. It fell just below my waist, holding onto my wrists.

"Don't cry."

She shook her head and swatted at the emotions before they got away again.

"I don't want to do this if you're not ready."

Her lips pressed to my neck as her hands ghosted down my stomach. Dropping her chin, she watched her finger trace my birthmark. "I love this heart. I think it's where cupid hit you with his arrow just as I stepped on the school bus that fateful day."

I chuckled. "Except I've had it forever."

She traced it again and the promise of what was to come, mixed with her warm hands on my naked skin, had me harder than I had ever been in my life.

"I guess you were always meant to be with me," she murmured with a voice as shaky as my hands.

"We don't have to do this." I kissed the top of her head and closed my eyes. "It feels like grief sex—sympathy sex."

She shook her head with her chin still dipped toward her chest. I wondered if she was looking at my birthmark or my erection tenting my dress pants.

"Maybe you should save this for your real boyfriend." Only an idiot in love with a girl who was too good for him would try to talk said girl out of having sex with him for the first time. An untimely case of the nerves left me babbling because I respected Daisy and her parents, but I also wanted to give her everything she wanted. Not having a dime to my name left very little for me to offer her, but when she asked me to take her virginity, I said yes.

Young.

Stupid.

Impulsive.

Completely in love.

She giggled and looked up at me while her hands worked on removing my belt. "My real boyfriend will want to be with a girl who knows what she's doing. And since I suspect you're a virgin too, I bet your real girlfriend someday will be happy that you figured stuff out with me first."

The words that came out of her mouth were a hundred times more confident than the nervous hands trying to unfasten my pants. We were nothing more than jittery teenagers attempting to act like grownups.

"I love you." My hands framed her face. I honestly can't remember if that was the first time I said those three words to her. My mind had thought them a million times. But I wasn't going to take something that I couldn't return without her knowing that she wasn't a conquest or a way to get rid of my virginity.

She wet her lips then bit them together, but I could still see them quivering. "I love you too."

"We don't have to do this," I said as she got my belt loose and moved to the button of my pants. We had explored each other's bodies, but never completely naked. It was easy to make out with her, slide my hands up her shirt or rub between her legs on the outside of her panties. Boundaries make it easier to relax and be in the moment, led by desire and curiosity.

Taking away those boundaries made things pretty damn scary.

"Do you have a condom?"

I nodded as we both looked down at her hand inching down my zipper. If she didn't hurry up, we weren't going to need the condom.

"Are you sure your parents won't be back before we're done?"

Thirty seconds. A minute tops if I didn't breathe and if I could get my mind to focus on death instead of the anticipation of seeing Daisy naked.

"Yeah."

She glanced up. "Yeah they will or yeah they won't?"

I kissed her hard, not like two kids making out. I kissed her with purpose and urgency. My hands touched her over the material of the black dress she wore to my uncle's funeral that day. We were too young to know what we were doing. Self-doubt crept in in a way it hadn't done before.

Was I touching her the right way?

Was I touching her in the right spot?

Was she scared?

Would she like it?

Would it hurt?

Would there be blood?

The most pressing question that danced in my head at that moment was would I come before I ever got inside of her?

I unzipped the back of her dress. She stiffened.

"What's wrong?" I whispered after breaking our kiss.

"Nothing." She kissed my neck to cover up the lie.

Nothing didn't shake like a leaf.

Nothing didn't hold its arms close to its body to keep the dress from falling off.

"We don't have to do this."

She shook her head. "I want to. It's just …"

I pulled back to see her face. We were half committed to doing it. My shirt still hung from my arms and my pants clung to my hips, but just barely. Her dress made an attempt to fall off, but she hugged her arms to her chest to keep it in place. I imagined impatient hands tearing off clothes and naked bodies crashing together in a frenzy of desire. Apparently that only happened in movies or with adults who knew what they were doing.

"It's just what?"

Daisy grimaced. "What if your parents do come home early? Or what if the condom breaks? Or what if I bleed and it gets on your sheets and your mom sees it? Or what if—"

"Or what if we just don't do it tonight." I wanted it. Boy did I ever want it in the most painfully-aroused, heart-pounding, dick-ready-to-explode way.

"Maybe we should think it through some more."

I nodded. Thinking it through wasn't going to change anything. I was certain none of my friends had thought it through before losing their virginity. There was no intelligent, well-thought-out reason for two fifteen-year-olds to have sex. If we didn't do it out of stupidity and out-of-control hormones, then we weren't going to do it for a very long time.

"Another night?" she said with a vulnerable smile.

"Another night." I nodded while trying to give her a reassuring expression.

We put our clothes back on in awkward silence, sneaking the occasional peek which accompanied a guilty grin. And to prove God did exist and he was looking out for us, just as I buttoned the last button of my shirt, my newly-reconciled parents came home *early*.

CHAPTER FIFTEEN

I T'S BEEN FIVE days since I've seen Griffin, a record for our relationship. This is not the kind of record I'm trying to set. He's been busy. I've been busy. His late-night invites to come stay with him or for him to come stay with me have been rejected by me. My head is all over the place. This obsession with Nate and his past requires nonstop thought. I haven't slept well in weeks.

My appointment with my doctor goes well. He doesn't find any urgency to have a CT scan or MRI, but given my symptoms and Griffin's concerns, he agrees to order some more tests for next week. The money my mom shared from my dad's life insurance is dwindling, thanks to counseling and other medical expenses.

After my appointment, I accept Nate's offer to give me the whole day off. My apartment needs deep cleaning, my fridge needs restocking, and I could use a night out with someone who doesn't know anything about my messed-up brain. So I invite Erica out for drinks.

As I finish applying my makeup, my phone rings.

"Hey, Griff."

"Hey, stranger."

I chuckle, but deep down I feel guilty for avoiding him this past week.

"I've been waiting for you to call, but I'm running out of

patience."

"Sorry, Griff, but you'd be proud of me. I went to the doctor today and he's set up some more tests for next week, but he didn't seem too concerned. He actually suggested I go back to seeing Dr. Greyson. And … I took the rest of the day off, cleaned my apartment, and went grocery shopping."

"Sounds exciting. So where are we going tonight? My mom wants us to stop by later, but we don't have to stay long."

I hold still and talk slowly with him on speakerphone while I apply my mascara. "Can't tonight. But I don't work tomorrow so we can do whatever you want."

He laughs. It's an odd laugh, a little disbelieving. "What do you mean you can't?"

"I'm going out with Erica tonight. I think I need some girl time to just get out of my head for a few hours. You know what I mean?"

"Are you fucking kidding me?"

I frown at my phone and the agitated voice speaking from it. "Wow, nice attitude. What crawled up your butt and died today?"

Silence fills the bathroom, I glance down to see if we've been disconnected. "Griff?"

He clears his throat. "Have fun with Erica. Don't worry about tomorrow. I'm busy. In fact … I'm going to be busy for quite some time."

"What's that supposed to mean?"

No answer.

When I look down again at my phone on the vanity, the call has been disconnected. I try calling him back. He doesn't answer.

After tossing my makeup back in its bag, I shoot off a quick text to Griffin. Erica should be knocking on my door any minute, so I don't have time to get into a big argument over his bruised ego.

Swayze: *Don't be this way. It's one night. I don't see the big deal. I'll call you tomorrow.*

After pressing send, I stare at my phone. The message changes from *delivered* to *read,* but no three dots appear on my screen. He's not responding. With two soft knocks at my door, I don't have time to fret over it.

We call for a car instead of driving. Three bars later, I have a nice buzz going. It's the best I've felt all week.

"Has he texted back yet?" Erica asks as I check my phone for the hundredth time.

"No." I frown.

"Men are such babies." She shakes her head while bringing her wine glass to her mouth. "Even the hot ones."

"I just don't understand it. I mean … yeah, I've been a little distant this week, but it's one freakin' night. I promised him all day tomorrow, which he knows will turn into all day on Sunday."

She eyes some guy a few tables over. He's giving her the same look. With one look, I feel like an outsider.

"Maybe you should make a bootie call. Guys like that," Erica says while eye-fucking the dude behind me.

"Why do I get the impression you're trying to ditch me?"

Her gaze meets mine again. "I would never do that unless it had been a long time since I'd had really good sex."

"The blind date?" I ask.

"I faked an illness to get out of the date before the end of dinner."

I laugh. "So basically you're saying it's been a really long time?"

Erica nods, returning her attention to Mr. Neatly-Trimmed Beard behind me.

"Fine then. I'll just check my notifications since I've lost your attention."

She doesn't respond.

I click on my phone. There's still no text or calls from Griffin, but I have a dozen different social media notifications, most of them are from Griffin's sisters from a couple of hours earlier. I click on Instagram.

"Oh my god …" I can't even breathe as a million emotions course through my body and sting my eyes.

"What's wrong?" Erica acknowledges me this time.

"Oh my god …"

"Jeez, Swayze, what is it?"

I am the worst person on the face of the earth, and the cringe on Erica's face when I show her my phone confirms it. Griffin's sisters have pictures posted of him blowing out candles on a birthday cake at his parents' house.

"You forgot his birthday?"

What little buzz I had a few seconds ago is gone. I'm feeling everything right now, and it's so fucking painful I can't even speak.

"How is that possible?" Erica continues to prod.

She doesn't know anything about my memories of Nate. She doesn't know how little sleep I've had. So I go with the only truth I can find that might work as some sort of explanation. "My life has been crazy. And we haven't been together for that long. I just didn't have his birthday in my mind or…" I shake my head "…I don't know, I just didn't pay attention to the date today."

"Your phone. How did you not have it in your phone?"

I have nothing. Not. One. Good. Excuse.

"Hey…" she reaches across the table and squeezes my hand "…don't cry. It's not the end of the world."

"But what if it's the end of us?" I grab the cocktail napkin from under my drink and use it to blot my eyes.

"You think he's going to break up with you because you forgot his birthday?"

"No, I …" Oh god, I can't even say it, but I try anyway. "I think he could break up with me because when he seemed upset about me going out with you tonight I asked him what crawled up his butt and died."

"Oh …" Erica wrinkles her nose. "That's not good. You should go. You're just wasting time." She glances at her phone. "It's already eleven. You have one hour to make sure he gets the best birthday blowjob ever. Go. I'll order you a ride."

I can't stop the tears. It's not just Griffin. It's his whole family. I feel like I've failed all of them today. What kind of girlfriend forgets her boyfriend's birthday? What kind of girlfriend says what I said to him earlier?

Nausea twists my stomach. How could I do this?

"What's his address?" Erica asks while tapping the screen of her phone. "You do know his address, right?"

I nod, wiping more tears away while mumbling his address.

"Okay. Five minutes. Blue Camry out front."

I stand, wobbling a bit on my heels. "Thank you."

"No problem. Good luck. Let me know how it goes. I work all day tomorrow, but I have a few breaks if you need a shoulder to cry on."

I hope I don't need a shoulder to cry on, but I'm not sure

this will end well.

I TEXT HIM on the way.

He doesn't reply—doesn't even read it.

I call.

No answer.

The knot in my stomach pushes more acid up my throat, and I can't stop the slow leak of tears. The driver lets me off in front of his house. I've had too much to drink. My eyes are swollen and surely streaked with mascara. No explanation. No gift. Not even a card.

Nothing.

I'm here with nothing to offer him on his birthday—what little is left of it. The front door is locked so I knock. A few seconds later I ring the doorbell. The porch light flips on and he opens the door. I've never felt anything but love from this man—until now.

"I'm a terrible person."

He stares at me with a cold, dark gaze, holding a blanket around his waist. I know he's not wearing anything beneath it because he sleeps in the nude.

It's been a long week and all I want to do is let him strip me down and collide into each other with the insatiable desire we've always had between us.

"I know sorry won't make up for what I've done."

It's like I don't even exist. His expression holds no emotion. It's numbing and heartbreaking.

"But I am ... I'm so sorry." Another tear manages to escape when I blink.

His gaze roams along the entire length of my body. He's getting a rare glimpse of me in a short black dress with high heels and my hair pulled into a high ponytail. I need it to be enough for him to step back and let me inside.

It's not. I can see that when his icy glare returns to my face. "Say something."

"Like what?"

"Can I come inside?"

He gives a firm snap of his neck to the side and back again.

"Your mom reminded me of your birthday a few weeks ago. I just forgot because of everything that's been going on. And then I went to the doctor today because you asked me to, and I cleaned my apartment because deep down I know you hate how messy it is most of the time, and I just ..."

I've never had a love like this to lose before now. How am I supposed to know what this is? Feelings of stupidity and inexperience mix with fear. Are we breaking up? Is that what this is? It doesn't feel like a fight. If I turn and walk away, I don't think he'll chase after me. And that's why I can't walk away. I have to plead my case until there's nothing left to plead.

He steps back and my heart surges with hope because he's going to let me in, but then—

Clank!

The door shuts in my face and my heart shatters right here on his front porch.

"Griffin!" I bang the door and try to turn the handle, but it's locked.

The light above me goes out and it feels so final.

"I'm sorry! I love you!" I continue to bang on the door. A few dogs bark in the distance as I wake up the neighborhood in my desperation. "Please let me in! I don't want us to be over!"

Sobs rip from my throat. This hurts. *Nothing* has ever hurt this bad. Not even when my father died.

"I'm so … incredibly … sorry …" I whisper while resting my forehead and fisted hands on the door.

THE NEXT MORNING I order him a fruit bouquet since he's not a flowers or a cookie bouquet kind of guy. I text. I call.

Nothing.

I spend the day mourning and hating myself for being so insensitive. Every time I hear a noise in the hallway, I rush to look out my peephole, but it's never my grocery store guy. Desperation gobbles up all sense of self-worth and dignity. I'm ready to trade my soul to the devil to get my guy back.

By the next morning, I'm at the very bottom. After taking a shower, I check my pulse to see if I still have one. There is no life in me right now. I can't think about Nate and every finite detail I know about his past. I don't have Griffin and … Fuck. Me. It hurts everywhere.

Something pulls me to my car. I'm pretty sure it's desperation. I'm drowning in it. That same pathetic force leads me to his neighborhood, but I don't pull down his street. Instead, I park a block away and worm my way toward his house, staying one street over so he can't see me if he's outside mowing the lawn or working in his garage. This is a new pathetic low, even for me.

I squint to see through the trees between two houses. He's mowing his lawn, a usual Sunday chore. Instead of confronting him again, I make the short walk to his parents' house. If I'm going to make this right, I need his parents' forgiveness too.

"Swayze! What a lovely surprise." Sherri answers the door, all smiles. "Come in."

Words fail me. I wasn't expecting this kind of reception. "Where's Griffin?"

Surely my wide eyes and slack mouth says it all. "Um ..."

"How's your friend?"

I follow her to the kitchen where she pours me a glass of ice tea.

"My friend?"

"Yes. Griffin told us something really important came up with your friend. We missed you at the birthday party."

He lied for me ... or for him. I'm not sure what this means.

"She's ... uh ... fine."

"Good to hear. So what are you up to today?" She gestures to the deck.

We go outside and sit in the glider chairs. Scott's running the weed eater in the backyard. It must be the Calloway yard day.

I have an out. Griffin's lie gives me one. But I don't know how this will end if I don't confess. And I can't let this go on any longer.

"Griffin lied."

Sherri gives me a confused look. "About what?"

"I forgot his birthday." My eyes burn. It's a race to say what I need to say before I break down. "And I could list all the reasons why I forgot it, but they don't matter. I love him and I should not have forgotten his birthday. And I made it even worse by saying something I should not have said when he seemed upset about my other plans on Friday. Then ..." My emotions tighten around my neck like a noose. I can't get another word out.

"Oh, sweetie…" Sherri reaches over and rests her hand on my arm "…you made a mistake. It'll be fine. Griffin loves you."

I try to swallow, but the emotions are too thick so I just shake my head.

"Yes, he will. Have you tried talking to him?"

I nod several times and wipe the tears before they make it down my face. "H-he's so mad." Biting my lips together, I try to regain my composure.

"I'm sure he's just disappointed. That's all I saw in him on Friday. Just give him some time to get past it. I know he'll be ready to patch things up. Scott used to be the same way when we were first married. He'd shut down. I learned to let him have his space. The good news is they grow out of it as they mature. Griffin is still learning how to navigate a serious relationship. He's going to make a few mistakes along the way—overreact. You both will."

I nod again and before I can get it together, Sherri comes over and pulls me into her arms and I fall apart. When I manage to piece my emotions back together, I apologize to her. She quickly waves off my attempts to make amends like I have no reason to apologize. We spend the next hour chatting about Griffin's sisters, their boy issues, and my turning down the temporary teaching job to watch Morgan full time.

Griffin hadn't even shared that with her. I want to believe it's to make sure I always look good in their eyes, but after Friday, I'm not sure what to believe.

"I should go. Thanks for letting me cry on your shoulder. It wasn't my intention when I came over here."

"We love you, Swayze. You're family to us, so don't ever hesitate to come see us."

I give her one last hug. Just as I open the door, the loud rumble of a Harley draws near sending my heart back into my throat.

"See, he's already looking for you," Sherri says as I step outside.

"He doesn't know I'm here," I murmur to myself.

When he takes off his helmet, I'm certain Sherri sees he's surprised to see me too. And the downward turn of his lips proves I'm not a good surprise.

"I'll be inside if you need me," she whispers in my ear before retreating to the house.

I want him so bad right now. It's the strangest feeling. My attraction to him has never waned, but right now I want to devour him. Not being able to have him magnifies my desire for him, so does that tight black T-shirt and his jeans hugging his muscular legs. He looks rough and sexy and so forbidden at this very moment.

"Hey ..." My weak voice sounds like the insecure book nerd talking to the captain of the football team for the first time. "Did you get the fruit arrangement?"

"I gave it to my neighbor."

I flinch, but it doesn't soften his expression one bit.

"Why are you here?"

"I wanted to apologize to your parents for Friday."

He narrows his eyes a fraction like I've overstepped some line. "Is that so? Did they forgive you?"

"Yes," I say with zero confidence.

"Well, lucky you." He brushes past me.

Taking a courageous breath, I turn. "I want *you* to forgive me."

He stops, keeping his back to me.

"What if you ignore my birthday and Christmas and … Valentine's Day? And I don't say anything because I deserve to not have you acknowledge me on any special occasion. But on every other day we're still us … together."

He blows out a long breath. I cross my fingers that it's a sign of him surrendering.

"What if you find someone else to jerk around?" He continues to walk toward the house, carrying my heart crumpled in his hand.

Just as he opens the door, Sherri greets him with a disapproving look.

"For fuck's sake." He shakes his head and storms past me again to his motorcycle. Before I can try to stop him, he peels out.

"Here." Sherri dangles a keychain in front of me as I watch my world drive off.

"Eventually, he'll go home."

I take the keychain.

"One is to his house. The other is to his garage. Don't take no for an answer. He may be two hundred and thirty pounds of muscle and intimidation, but I know my boy … he won't hurt you. Get in his face until he surrenders. He wants to … he's just too stubborn to see it right now."

CHAPTER SIXTEEN

I LEAVE MY car parked a block away for fear he won't come home if he sees it in his driveway or across the street.

Two hours later the rumble of his bike pulling into the driveway sets my pulse racing out of control. The hard part is I still don't know what to say to make this right. When he comes in the side door, I stand up from my spot on the couch.

He doesn't see me as he shrugs off his sweaty shirt, but then he stops when he catches me out of the corner of his eye.

"The answer was no on Friday. No yesterday. It's no today. And it will be no tomorrow."

"It was a birthday. Our whole relationship is over because of a forgotten *birthday*?" I chase him down the hallway. "Would you just listen to me!"

He turns so fast, I bump into his chest. My eyes widen and and I open my mouth to speak, but … nothing.

"Good talk." Griffin turns into the bathroom and removes his jeans. "Now get the fuck out." He turns on the water to the shower.

Sherri's words run through my head. We're young and immature at relationships. He won't hurt me. Don't take no for an answer. But nothing I say matters. "I love you." "I'm sorry." They are meaningless to him right now.

Fine. No more words.

I slip off my sundress. Griffin glances over his naked shoulder just as he slides open the shower curtain. His eyes make a quick assessment of me.

"No," he says then steps into the shower and closes the curtain.

My fingers unhook my bra, and I slide off my panties. "Yes." I whip open the shower curtain and step into his tiny shower before shutting it.

He glares down at me, the dim light and water running down his body only make him that much more intimidating. Taking a step forward, he backs me into the wall of the shower, sucking up all the oxygen in this tiny space.

I can't find a single breath, but I keep my chin tipped up in defiance.

"I'll fuck you, but it won't be gentle and it won't change anything."

I swallow hard. "It was a birthday. One day."

"It's not just my fucking birthday!"

My heart stops. I'm not sure what I expected, but it wasn't this.

He won't hurt me. I keep reminding myself of this very important fact because Griffin is a beast towering over me with every muscle in his body flexed and quivering like he could snap something—possibly me—in half.

"You've blown me off all fucking week like the whole goddamn world revolves around you. I got a job promotion. Did you know that? No. Because you haven't given me the time of day. Friday was just the icing on my fucking birthday cake. So if you want to know what 'crawled up my butt and died' … it's you."

There are no tears. Where are my tears? He's throwing verbal punch after punch. The pain is real, but I can't move. I can't blink. I can't even find a single emotion because he's destroyed me.

"Dry off. Get dressed. And go home. Or I'm going to fuck you and it won't mean—"

My hand covers his mouth. His jaw clenches and his eyes redden, but he doesn't push me away.

"It will mean *everything*," I say calmly, but with an equal edge to my own voice. "Because what we have is so much more than a missed birthday, a bad week, a good week, a string of misspoken words, a few bad decisions, or the whole goddamn world coming to an end." With my other hand, I shove his chest, but my brick of a man doesn't budge. And he doesn't look pleased that I just tried to shove him.

"So you don't have to forgive me right now. And you don't have to be gentle with me. But don't you *ever* try to tell me that *you* inside of *me* won't mean something."

I think I've waited my whole life for *this* girl to come out of my body and speak her mind.

The second I move my hand from his mouth, he grabs my legs and lifts me up. Before I can find a breath, he buries his cock in me while releasing a low growl. He lifts me up again and slams me back down onto him while keeping his gaze affixed to mine.

Again and again … he fucks me while doing nothing else but pinning me to the wall of the shower with his heavy body and piercing gaze. I need his mouth. I need something to make this moment intimate. I need an emotional connection. So I lean in to kiss him, but he pulls back, eyes dark, each thrust unforgiving.

My eyes drift shut. I let him have this, whatever he needs this to be. Loving him means trusting him to love me back in his darkest moments.

"God …" He grunts on a final thrust, warmth spilling into me.

I open my eyes to his neck straining back, eyes pinched shut, fingers digging into my legs as he finds a release that seems to reach beyond the sex.

Blinking the shower water out of his eyes, he drops his chin and looks at me.

Now a million emotions come to the surface. I bite my lips together and will them away. For the first time in days, Griffin's face softens into something reminiscent of my grocery store guy.

"I need you to love me," I whisper, baring every ounce of my vulnerability to him. "More than anything."

He flinches like what just happened has seeped through a crack in his anger and settled into his conscience—his heart. His grip on my legs loosens, but he keeps me pinned with his body.

"I do love you," he says with raw pain, surrendering to his emotionally strangled words. "More than anything." His mouth covers mine. It's gentle at first, then it builds into something demanding as his hand slides between us. My eyes roll back under heavy eyelids as I let him take me to another dimension, one that's seductive, erotic, beautiful, and heartbreaking … and I don't want it—I don't want *us*—to ever end.

WE LIE TANGLED in Griffin's bedsheets with moonlight filtering in through his blinds. I turn onto my side and trace the lines of his tattoos and perfectly-cut body as he sleeps in his usual position on his stomach with an arm draped possessively over my waist. It's crazy to think of the big things that couples weather together and the little things that can undermine everything over time. These little things multiply like cancer and ruin even the strongest relationships.

Since we got out of the shower several hours ago, we haven't said more than a handful of words to each other. There's still too much pain that words can't fix yet. Every time I try to say something, Griff silences me with his mouth on mine, his hands possessing my skin, his body claiming me completely. Maybe words can't fix some things.

Maybe everything there is to say can be said in the silence of this room.

In the dark of night.

Between the space of two sheets.

Griffin's head turns toward me and his sleepy eyes blink open. I continue to feather my fingers over his back and the sexy curve of his ass—defined, firm, and inked.

"What time is it?" he mumbles.

I glance at his alarm clock. "Almost two o'clock. Go back to sleep."

"Why aren't you sleeping?" He rubs his face into his pillow and rests his cheek on it, blinking heavily.

"I can't sleep. I still feel terrible about—"

"Shh …" He palms my ass and pulls me closer.

"Don't you think we should talk?"

Griffin rolls onto his back while sliding me onto his stomach. "No talking yet."

"Why not?" I whisper.

He sits up until we're nose to nose, my legs straddling his lap, his erection sliding against my clit. "Because I'm not done *taking*." Guiding my hips up a few inches, he lines himself up and slides me down onto him. We both let out a slow moan and close our eyes.

Demanding lips silence the pain.

Possessive hands soothe it.

The rock of our hips push it away.

And when we fall apart—sweaty, breathless, and exhausted—we are a little bit better. A single touch can say things twenty-six letters can't even begin to say.

I WAKE TO an unfamiliar beeping. "Griff … your alarm," I mumble, burying my head under the pillow.

When the beeping continues, I notice there's not a warm arm draped over my body or a muscular leg entwined with mine. I don't like the emptiness. My hand slaps at the nightstand until the beeping stops. Easing to sitting, I rub my eyes. Next to the alarm there's a note.

Good morning.

Working all day.

The only words that matter are these: your grocery store guy loves you. And …

You owe me a birthday blowjob.

~Grif

"Totally sex-crazed." I roll my eyes, but my face hurts from grinning so big. It feels like I went to Hell and back in three days. I had no idea that Hell is simply my life without Griffin Calloway.

After a quick trip home to shower and grab breakfast, I text Nate to let him know I may be a few minutes late, but I jump out of my car and jog to the door with thirty seconds to spare.

"Good morning." Nate smiles while screwing on the lid to his stainless steel coffee mug.

Morgan's dressed and kicking around in her swing, which he has in the middle of the great room. Some kind of classical music plays from the TV while pictures of nature drift across the screen.

"Good morning." I set my bag down and give him an appreciative grin when he hands me a cup of coffee. "How was your weekend?"

Nate slips his laptop into his computer bag and latches it. "Good. My parents came over for dinner on Saturday night."

"How are your parents?"

He slings his bag over his shoulder. "They're good. My mom has been struggling with fibromyalgia, but she's managing the pain. I'm sure my parents are much different than you remember."

I shrug. "Your memories, not mine. But it's good that they're good, right?"

Nate gives me a concentrated look for a few seconds before nodding. "Yes. They reconciled years ago. Counseling. Church every Sunday. At one time I thought I was the only reason they decided to give it a real second chance, but twenty-one years later … they're still together, and it's not for my sake."

"That's pretty rare. I don't think most couples try that hard to make things work."

"True." He sips his coffee. "How was your weekend? Did everything go well Friday?"

"Friday …" I chuckle, the kind that hides the pain. "Friday's appointment went well. I have another appointment this week, but it's early. I should be done before you need me here."

"That's fine." He walks toward the back door and stops. "And for the record, I always need you here. Morgan still likes you better than me. It's such a sad truth." Glancing back over his shoulder, he winks.

I giggle and shake my head. "Go to work, Professor. I have to snoop around your house before you get there and can see me on your spy cameras."

"I can rewind the footage." He quirks a cocky brow. "But snoop away. I have nothing to hide."

Who is this guy? It's all I can think when he shuts the door behind him. I like playful Nate. He's proving to be everything I imagine the boy in my mind would have grown up to be.

Kind.

Fun.

Strong.

Sexy.

I laugh. In another life I would have crushed on Professor Hunt pretty hard. But that life would have been one where we didn't have a fifteen year age difference, and that would have been a life without Griffin. That's not my life nor is it one I ever want to imagine again after the events of the previous days.

Last night … my mouth turns up into a giddy grin thinking of Griffin's body over me, beneath me, inside of me. I grab my phone to shoot off a text in response to his note this morning.

Swayze: *Hope you're working "hard" knowing that my mouth will be wrapped around your cock later. xo*

Trapping my lower lip between my teeth, I press send.

"Lazy Daisy, how are you this morning, sweet baby?" I take her out of her swing. "Let's get you some floor time. Whatcha think about that?" I spread out a blanket and lay her on it.

After she gets tired of floor time, I warm up a bottle and sit in the recliner to feed her. My phone chimes with a text from Nate. I glance up at the camera. "Yes, Professor?" Resting the bottle against my chest to keep it tipped up for Morgan, I open my messages because all that showed up on my home screen was:

Professor: *Um …*

"Um what?" I give the camera another quick glance while tapping the message icon.

It's just "um." I don't get it. Until … I glance at the previous message I sent *HIM* instead of Griffin.

"Oh my god!" I whisper, panic sending my heart nosediving to the pit of my stomach. The only part of my body that moves is my eyes blinking over and over. This cannot be right. I'm not seeing this correctly. There's no way I sent that text to the wrong person.

It hits me that I just clicked on my messenger, forgetting that the last person I texted this morning before the cock text was Nate about possibly running a few minutes late.

I can't look up.

I can't move.

I can't breathe.

And I definitely cannot ever come back from this. It's like accidentally seeing someone naked. You can't unsee that. Nate will never be able to unread this text.

"Oh god …" I whisper again. What if he thinks it wasn't an accident? What if he thinks I meant to send him the text?

Morgan fusses as the bottle drops to my lap. I grab it and tip it back up for her. My chest aches and my skin burns with searing embarrassment. I didn't think I could possibly hate these cameras more. Wrong. I hate them so much more right now. He's watching me die from the inside out, right here—live.

By the time Morgan finishes her bottle and drifts off to sleep, my shirt is soaked in sweat. I still have not given the camera a single glance. With my chin down, I take Morgan to her room and lay her in the crib. Keeping my gaze affixed to my feet, I snag my phone and go into the bathroom away from his creepy cameras.

I take off my shirt and splash cold water onto my face and chest. "You stupid idiot, Swayze," I scold the overheated, messy blonde in the mirror.

To text or not to text, that is the question. I can't have him thinking it was meant for him, so I make the digital walk of shame.

> **Swayze:** *Kill me now! I'm so monumentally sorry. That text was not meant for you. I hope you know that.*

I press send and decide I should say more.

> **Swayze:** *I'm embarrassed beyond words, even though I seem to be finding plenty to text you. If you don't fire me, can we pretend this never happened?*

I press send again. Maybe I should also say …

> **Swayze:** *I'm not that person. I don't usually send those texts to anyone, even the right person. I had a fight with Griffin and we made up last night, and he left me a note and the text was in reference to the note.*

I press send and I reread the messages. "What the hell? Why did you say all of that?"

Swayze: *Ignore the last text. It was TMI.*

Send.

Swayze: *I'm just nervous.*

Send.

Swayze: *And really scared for you to come home. It's going to be awkward.*

Send.

I wait. He's not responding. Why is he not saying anything?

Swayze: *Are you getting my messages? Why aren't you saying something?*

Send.

Swayze: *I suppose you're busy. You are at work.*

Send.

Swayze: *Last text. I promise. Just at least send me a quick emoji or even just a "K" so I know you know what I need you to know.*

Send.

"So I know you know what I need you to know? What is wrong with me?" I shove my phone into my pocket to prevent my fingers from typing every single thought that pops into my head.

My phone buzzes. I grab it like it's a bomb and I have three seconds to disarm it.

Professor: K

K? That's it? That's all the reassurance he has for me? K? Men are stupid. They take everything so literally.

IT'S ONLY BEEN a few months since Jenna died. I've mastered the "I'm good" on the outside, but having a miniature reminder of her makes healing on the inside nearly impossible. My sexual urges are rare and easily *handled* in the shower once or twice a week. The last time being the night after I thought about Daisy touching me after my uncle's funeral.

Until … Swayze sent the text this morning. An accident? Yes. I knew it the second it popped up on my screen. I should have been able to laugh it off, and I tried. But then I thought about it *all the damn day*.

I considered walking across campus to talk to Professor Albright about it since she knows the Swayze/Daisy connection. Then I *really* thought about telling an eighty-four-year-old woman about my inappropriate thoughts toward a twenty-one-year-old girl, and I decided to make an emergency appointment with Dr. Greyson instead.

I skip the reincarnation part. Maybe Swayze has already told him, but there's no way he would tell me that. I hope he does know about it because I think it gives merit to why I might have these thoughts about Swayze after her text. At least, that's what I tell myself to keep from feeling like a terrible father, terrible husband, and terrible boss.

"Nathaniel, what you're feeling is normal. The desire. The

guilt. The conflict. There's no right or wrong timeline when it comes to grieving the loss of a spouse. Your thoughts about this young woman don't diminish the love you had with Jenna. Happily married people have thoughts about people who are not their spouse. Thinking something and acting on it are two different things."

"What do I say to her when I get home?"

"From what you've told me about her texting you back, I think less is best. If it's awkward, just reassure her you know it was an embarrassing mistake and there's no need to discuss it beyond that."

"And how do I stop thinking about it?"

Dr. Greyson chuckles. I appreciate the rare occasions when he lets his professionalism slip a bit. Sometimes I need an unbiased guy's advice more than I need to be analyzed and have every emotion redirected back at me in the form of another question.

"I can give you some exercises to focus on other things. Visualization tools for when you want to think about something else. Not a fix. Time might be the only true fix. Maybe you'll find someone else to fill those kinds of thoughts."

"When I *want* to think about something else? Are you implying there will be times that I *don't* want to think about something else?"

Dr. Greyson steeples his fingers at his chin. "Again, they are thoughts. Unless you get the impulse to act on them or they keep you from doing your job or attending to your daughter, I don't see any reason to berate yourself if your mind occasionally goes there."

I sigh. "Are you giving me an out to 'be a man?'"

"I'm giving you an out to be human."

"Easier said than done."

"Are you attracted to her?"

I shrug. "She's attractive ... and *young*."

"And your employee."

"Yes."

"Think of her as a student. I'm sure you have plenty of attractive students every year."

I nod slowly. But none of my students are Daisy. I don't know how I would have reacted to the text if Swayze were just a nanny I'd known for a couple of months.

Feeling a little less guilty, I make my way home. I don't know how I'm going to ease Swayze's mind when I can't ease my own. *"Hey, I know you're really embarrassed and I'm horny as fuck, but let's just forget it ever happened."* Yeah, that'll work.

I ease open the door and muster some confidence as I walk into the great room. "Hi."

"Hey," Swayze says with her back to me as she washes up the bottles at the kitchen sink while Morgan swings.

"Did you two have a good day?"

"Yeah." Her answer comes out like a squeak, but she still doesn't look at me.

"I'll wash the rest of those so you can head home. I'm sure you have stuff to..." I can't back up the train "...do," I whisper the final word. She has a boyfriend waiting for her to wrap her lips around his cock. Why didn't I simply tell her thanks and that I'd see her tomorrow?

"Okay, thanks." She wipes her hands and takes the long way around the kitchen island to avoid passing by me. "Bye, sweetie." After pressing a kiss to the top of Morgan's head, Swayze grabs her bag and speed walks to the front door. "Goodnight."

I should let her go. Lord knows I'm just as embarrassed as her, but I can't. We're both adults. I'm the older adult. The boss. It's up to me to make this right.

"Wait."

She stops at the door. Her shoulders deflate. "Uh, yeah?"

"Turn around."

She doesn't.

"Swayze, look at me."

Like tightening a screw that's already tight, she turns a tiny fraction at a time.

"Look. At. Me."

Just as slowly, she brings her eyes to meet my gaze. Her face wrinkles like looking at me causes her physical pain.

I remind myself that I am fifteen years older. I have a doctorate degree. I have weathered the loss of people that I love. I have survived brutal fistfights, broken bones, hockey stick jabs to my ribs, and pucks to my face. I have reprimanded students for cheating on tests and plagiarizing reports. I can handle a text.

"It was a mistake. I'm not upset. You are a grown woman. I need you to be the responsible adult who takes care of Morgan while I'm at work, and you can't do your job if you're focused on something as trivial as a text sent to the wrong person. You have to pretend it didn't happen. Okay?"

She nods, but her grimace stays cemented to her face. "It's just … I don't want you to think that I'm …" Her brow draws even tighter as she seems to look for the right word.

"I think you're great with Morgan. Clearly I'm intrigued by your knowledge of my past. I enjoy your company when we find time to talk. But what you do when you're not here is not my business or my concern."

"Thank you." She blinks and averts her eyes to the floor.

I don't push her any further. If she asked me what I thought when she sent the text, I too would focus on anything in the room but her.

"You're welcome. Drive safely. I'll see you tomorrow."

CHAPTER SEVENTEEN

E MOTIONALLY DRAINED FROM the past week, I drag my
tired ass to the door of my apartment building as thunder
echoes in the distance.

"After you, lovely."

I cringe at the creepy, gravelly voice of Doug "Dougly"
Mann, Erica's strange neighbor who entertains a slew of
women. He has to be paying them. It's the only explanation.

"Thanks." I give him a quick glance as I step into the
building while he holds the door for me. It's the first time I've
seen him up close, but even now, sunglasses cover part of his
face and a gray fedora hides his clown orange hair.

"Everything okay?" he asks as I stop to stare at his face for a
brief second.

I never noticed the raised, pearly scar stretching from the
right corner of his mouth to the top of his cheekbone. It's
clearly an old scar, but it's also familiar. I don't want to feel an
ounce of familiarity toward this cringe-worthy man, but I do.

"Cold?" He chuckles.

"What?" I duck my head and hustle the rest of the way inside the building.

"Your whole body just shook like you're shivering."

"Oh, did it?" I take the stairs two at a time hoping if I
physically distance myself from him, the familiarity will fade as
well.

"Would you like to come up to my place for a drink? Maybe something to warm you up."

Skin-crawling.

Vomit-inducing.

Stranger-danger alert.

"Can't."

I fumble my keys to find the right one.

"Can't?" He towers behind me.

I drop my keys. Before I can retrieve them, they're in his hand, dangling in front of me.

"Or won't?"

I should scream. But why? Because I'm scared. Again, why?

My eyes don't move from the scar, even with my keys dangling in my peripheral vision. I know that scar. "How did you get that scar?" I mutter with what little air is left in my lungs.

Doug traces it slowly with his finger. "Just a misunderstanding. Why? Do you like it? I've got other scars if you'd like to see them."

I shake my head, still mesmerized by the familiarity of that scar. Squinting, I try to see his eyes through his dark sunglasses, but I can't.

"Sweetie? Is everything okay?"

My head snaps toward the stairs. "Mom."

Doug steps back. "You dropped your keys, Miss."

I snatch them and he pivots, climbing up the next flight of stairs.

"We'll have that drink another time," he says.

I watch him, feeling frozen in place and even more chilled than I was when he opened the door for me.

"Who's that?" Mom asks.

"Uh ..." I shake my head and work to unlock the door

without dropping the keys again. "Guy who lives upstairs."

"Do you know him well?"

The door opens and a bit of relief washes over me as I step inside and lock it behind us.

"No." I toss my bag on the counter and wash my hands. After Doug's close proximity, I feel like I need a shower to wash the essence of his creepiness off my whole body. "With the exception of Erica, I don't really know anyone in my building. So what brings you by?"

She pulls out a chair to my small round kitchen table and takes a seat while releasing a long sigh. "Sherri called me."

"Sherri? As in Griffin's mom?" I lean back against my kitchen counter and cross my arms over my chest.

"Yes. She's worried about you. And now I am too. Why didn't you come to me last week when you and Griffin were having trouble?" Her words are laced with as much pain as is shown on her face.

"I wanted to. It's just …" I love my mom. And after I graduated high school and started college, we were friends. The pressure of being something extraordinary was gone, and we were able to have a normal mother-daughter relationship. But then my dad died.

"It's about your father?"

I nod.

"I'm still your mother. I'm always here for you. Do you know how it made me feel to have Sherri be the one to tell me what happened?"

"I'm sorry." I cringe. "I feel like you're still struggling with dad's death. I don't want to be another burden on you."

"I'm fine, Swayze."

"You're not fine. It's been over a year and you haven't

picked up a camera. You haven't worked. You haven't cleaned out his closet. And when we have dinner together, all we do is talk about dad."

"He's my husband and your father. What's wrong with remembering him?"

"He *was* your husband."

"Swayze ..." Her lips tilt downward.

"I loved him too. I miss him too. But it's like our relationship is nothing but memories of the past. If you showed any interest in my life now, my job, my relationship with Griffin, basically anything, then maybe I would have felt like your shoulder was the one I needed to cry on last week."

The woman before me breaks my heart. She's not even fifty and she's acting like an eighty-year-old widow waiting out the rest of her life. My mom is beautiful. Guys have always looked at her. I may not have seen my parents all over each other with grand displays of public affection, but I saw my father stare down more than one guy who dared to look too long at her.

"You don't understand." Her head drops, eyes cast to the floor.

"Then make me understand. Let me help you."

"I have a psychiatrist."

I laugh. "I know. And clearly he's doing a great job."

"Swayze ..." Her eyes cut to mine.

"I'm sorry I didn't call you last week. Griffin and I made up. But there's a lot going on in my life right now that I want to share with my mom. Not the grieving woman who meets me for dinner once a week, but my *mom*. The one who used to roll her eyes at me picking out sexy bras and panties when I got my first boyfriend in college. You bought me a box of condoms and a tube of lubricant for my nineteenth birthday. For two years between my second year of college and dad dying … you were the coolest mom—the coolest friend—ever."

"I'm not trying to be this way. I just feel like I can't find my direction."

I nod. "I know. But you'll never find it if you spend all of your time looking back. You don't have to forget him. You just …" I shake my head. "I don't know. I guess you need to find a way to embrace the living a little more."

A sad smile tugs at her lips. "I'm sorry. I'm going to try to be better."

"Okay." I match her sad smile.

"I was cool." Her face lights up. "Wasn't I?"

I chuckle. "The coolest. The kind of cool that would have embraced Griffin instead of losing her shit over his tattoos and 'steroid' muscles when we first started dating. The cool version of you would have whipped out your camera and snapped a million images of his body to the point of completely embarrassing me."

She laughs a little. "I miss that mom of yours too." As I walk toward her, she stands and we hug it out.

I had no idea how much I really missed and needed my mom until this moment.

"This Thursday we talk about you. That's it." She pulls back and presses her palms to my cheeks.

"We talk about us."

She nods. "Deal." After kissing me on the forehead, she grabs her purse and opens the door. "I love you. That much has never changed. You know that, right?"

"I know."

"Whoa … Krista …" Griffin's voice sounds from the stairwell. "It's not Thursday."

"Very funny, young man. I'm allowed to see my daughter on other days too."

He chuckles, pulling her in for a hug that makes me giggle because I know she didn't see it coming.

"I'm glad you two are good." She gives him an awkward smile as he releases her.

Griffin glances at me.

I shake my head. "Your mom told her. Not me."

A wrinkle of pain pulls at his brow when his gaze returns to my mom. "It was a bump. We're good."

She heads down the stairs. "I'm glad. Call me anytime, Swayze. Even if it's not a Thursday."

"Bye, Mom."

Griffin steps inside my apartment and closes the door, leaning back against it with his head turned to the side.

"I wondered if—"

"Shh." He holds a finger to his lips and presses his ear to the door. "Okay. She's gone."

I giggle. "What are you doing?"

He tugs at the button to his jeans, giving me a heated look as he pulls down the zipper. "On your knees."

I shoot him the hairy eyeball. "Really? You just embraced my mom. It was a special moment. I had tears in my eyes."

"It was special. I had tears in my eyes too. Now ... on your knees." He releases himself from his briefs and strokes his cock, but it seems plenty hard without him needing to stroke it anymore.

"You did not have tears in your eyes." My gaze stays glued to his hand fisted around his cock. And because I want to ... I kneel in front of him.

"Happy ... fucking ... birthday to me." He moans as my

tongue circles the head of his erection. His fingers thread through my hair.

I take him partway into my mouth and look up at him.

Griffin smirks. "Tell me about your day, babe." He really wants to know. That's indisputable. However, this is also his way of dragging out this blowjob for the next fifteen minutes. But one of the most endearing things about him—his genuine interest in my day—is the reason I can't do this. He should have just tilted his head back and enjoyed my mouth wrapped around him.

I sit back on my heels and laugh, covering my face with my hands. It's a long, hearty laugh that seems to last forever. When I finally catch my breath and peek up, Griffin has something between a smirk and a scowl affixed to his beautiful face. He's tucked himself back into his briefs, but his jeans are still unfastened and his sinewy, tattooed arms cross his chest.

"I'm sorry." My hand flies to my mouth to cover up my giggles that negate the apology I just gave him.

"You look it." His eyes narrow as he zips and buttons his jeans.

I feel badly. I really do. Every inch of Griffin is perfection. There's not too many women who wouldn't give their right nipple to have what's right in front of me. My craving for his body is real, but so is the embarrassing day I've had.

He holds out his hand. A look of aggravation still clings to his face. I take it and he helps me up. Curling my hair behind my ears, I suck in a deep breath to chase away the giggles.

"I thought I texted you this morning about a blowjob."

Shaking his head, his perturbed expression intensifies. "You didn't text me."

"I know, I said I *thought* I did. I accidentally sent it to Nate instead."

His head cocks to the side. "This better be a joke, and it's not a funny one."

"It's fine." I laugh. "He's not upset. It was just really embarrassing." I grab his shirt and lean up for a kiss, but he pulls back.

"You sent a suggestive text to another man. It's not fine."

"What is your problem?"

He brushes past me, resting his hands on his hips, while he looks up at the ceiling. The frustration rolling off him almost suffocates the room. "Why do you think if my opinion differs from yours that it means I have a problem?"

"This is about your birthday again. Maybe we should talk about it now."

"No." He turns. "This is about the text you sent your boss. What did it say?"

"I don't remember."

"Where's your phone?"

I roll my eyes and grab my phone, clicking onto my message screen. "Do you want to see it?"

"No. I trust you. Just read it."

"Hope you're working *hard* knowing that my mouth will be wrapped around your cock later. xo"

"That'll do it." He closes his eyes and pinches the bridge of his nose.

"That'll do what?"

"Paint an image in his mind that he won't forget anytime soon."

"What? No. There's no image to paint. He knew it wasn't meant for him."

"Did you write my name?"

"What do you mean?"

"Did you say, 'Griff, hope you're working 'hard' knowing my mouth will be wrapped around your cock later?'"

"No."

"Then for at least a brief moment, he thought about your mouth wrapped around his cock. And he's not going to stop thinking about it anytime soon." Griffin shakes his head. "Not gonna lie ... that doesn't make me too happy."

My head whips back. "Well, I'm so sorry that doesn't make you happy. It thrills me to have my boss thinking I rock his baby all day and suck cock all night."

He rubs his mouth.

"Are you grinning?" I move closer as he steps back and shakes his head. "Yes, you are."

The back of his legs hit the sofa, and I lunge at him. His hand falls from his face to catch me as we tumble onto the cushions. Sure enough, he's grinning.

"Not funny." I straddle him, fisting his shirt as he shakes with laughter.

"Baby ... you've never sucked my cock *all* night."

"Stop it." I surrender, burying my face in his neck while he wraps his arms around me. "It was meant for you. It was meant to be sexy. But it turned into the most embarrassing moment of my life."

"You're a mess." Griffin rests his hand on the back of my head and rubs my back with his other hand.

"I know."

"But you're my mess."

I lift my head, searching his eyes for a glimpse of the man who tried to kick me out of his life a few days ago. "But I think you've known that I'm a mess since the day I didn't have money to pay for tampons, wine, and my junk food cravings."

He nods, stroking the back of my hair.

"So why was forgetting your birthday—having a bad week—the end for us?"

Discomfort flashes in his eyes that squint a fraction. "I was going to ask you to move in with me."

Ouch. The wounds on my heart start to tear open again.

"I thought we'd go to dinner, take a long ride on my bike, and find a spot to watch the sunset. I wanted to tell you about my promotion. I wanted to hear about your week because I knew you were not yourself. Then I wanted to tell you how crazy it was for us to live apart when I spend most of my waking hours thinking about the next time I'll get to see you."

"I'm sorry." I hate the way those words sound. Every fiber in my being means them, but they still sound like hollow words filling space and quickly evaporating.

Meaningless.

Forgotten.

Invisible.

"I know you're sorry."

"But you don't forgive me?"

He rubs his lips together and shakes his head. "It's not that. I forgive you. It was just a moment that gave me pause. You weren't the girl I wanted to ask to live with me. You weren't the girl I'd been missing all week. I feel like I'm losing you to another man's past. It's a fucking awful feeling to see you suffer and not know how to fix things for you."

"I don't need you to fix anything for me. I just need you to hold my hand sometimes as I try to figure this out for myself."

He sits up a little, and I slide off his lap onto the cushion next to him.

"How can I hold your hand when I can't reach it? That's my point. On Friday I realized your answer to a shitty week was distancing yourself from me. What happened to the girl who said I made her feel safe? What happened to the girl who fell into my arms after a long day and said one hug righted all the wrongs?"

This love thing hurts. "I guess I didn't look at it like that. You have been my pillar of strength. You still are."

"And you're my greatest weakness because I let you into the part of me that's unguarded." He takes my hand and presses it to his chest.

Griffin has defined love for me in ways I never imagined. I'm not sure I realized his real role in my life until I was faced with the possibility of not having him in my life at all. The day I chased him down the hall to his bathroom, I was chasing the part of my heart that broke off and gave me the middle finger while saying, "I belong to him, not you."

My hand curls, fisting his shirt. "This messy girl is going to mess up—a lot—because I'm young and stupid. You weren't supposed to come into my life until I had it together. You're the guy who is supposed to appear after a string of bad decisions. But here you are, watching me stumble around the craziest self-discovery. If I don't lose you, it will be a miracle."

"Swayz ..." His hand cups my cheek.

"Griff," I whisper, covering his hand with mine. "I need a miracle."

CHAPTER EIGHTEEN

J ENNA USED TO lay out my clothes. Today she would have
had a tie draped over my suit jacket. The right tie. The color
or pattern would be symbolic of my day, and she would know
what that symbol needed to be.

The night I asked her to marry me, we discussed children
over her birthday dinner at our favorite steakhouse. She asked
me how many I wanted to have someday. I shook my head,
afraid to tell her. Jenna rolled her eyes and grabbed a pen out of
her purse and an old receipt. She tore it in half and wrote a
number on it without showing me. She handed me the other
half and the pen.

"Write your number," she said.

"My number?"

*"How many kids you want to have. And if our number is the
same, you get down on one knee right here, right now, and ask me
to marry you."*

I wanted to marry Jenna, but I knew there wouldn't be any
kneeling that night. Growing up without much money gave me
the drive to make sure my family would always have food on
the table. Growing up with no siblings gave me the desire to
have a table full of mouths to feed.

She showed me her number first and asked me not to run
away or pass out.

Five.

Jenna wanted five kids. Career-oriented people like us did not have five kids. One was a luxury.

I didn't run or pass out. Pushing my chair away from the table, I got down on one knee. There was no speech. There was no ring. All I had was half a receipt in my hand that I unfolded to reveal my number—five.

Life didn't care about our desires or dreams. We realized it after seven years of trying to conceive a child. That one child of ours isn't a luxury. She's a gift and a symbol.

Today there's no tie draped over the suit jacket on my bed, symbolizing success, courage, or prosperity. Instead, there's a little girl grabbing and kicking at the mobile of toys dangling above her play mat on the floor of my bedroom. Morgan is symbolic of life. When I look at her, I see everything I ever wanted, everything I've lost, my greatest love, my deepest sorrow, my darkest moment, and the promise that love never dies.

"Professor?"

I smile. It's "Professor" today. I'm glad. Yesterday's text derailed my afternoon and made it impossible to sleep last night. An average day without incident is exactly what I need.

"In the bedroom."

"Are you dressed?"

I finish buttoning my dress shirt. "I am now."

"Wow. What's the occasion?" Blue eyes inspect me from head to toe.

"I have an orientation and I'm speaking at a luncheon for our department. But ..." I frown at the ties hanging in my closet. "I need the right tie."

Swayze steps in front of me and sifts through the ties. "This one." She grabs a blue and white striped tie.

"Can't."

She chuckles. "Why not? It goes with your pants and it brings out the blue in your eyes."

"I'm sure it does, but I have to choose between these three ties."

"Boring. And…" she grabs one of the *boring* ties "…you need to untie them when you're not wearing them or else—"

"Stop!"

She freezes. But it's too late. The unknotted tie hangs from her finger.

"Um … I don't understand."

I shake my head and sigh while adding that tie to the others I will not be wearing.

"Wait." Her jaw drops. "Oh my gosh. You *still* don't know how to tie a tie? Nate, how can that be? You're thirty-six. You have a *PhD*."

There's my Daisy. Professor is now Nate. And she's giving me that look. The one that says she knows the most intimate details about my childhood.

"I hate ties."

"I know." She looks up at me and wrinkles her nose.

"It's okay." I smirk. "I know you know."

With a slow nod, one that looks equal parts relief and regret, she returns her attention to the ties. "So why do you have all these ties that require you to *tie* them? Why not buy clip-ons?"

"Because thirty-six-year-old men with PhDs don't wear clip-on ties."

She laughs. "Who tied your ties? Your wife? Please don't tell me your dad is still tying your ties."

"Jenna did. She liked to do it. She should have been a stylist or a personal shopper."

"That explains the walk-in closet full of clothes for Morgan."

I nod.

"Sorry. I didn't mean to bring that up."

"It's fine. We found out we were having a girl a month before Morgan was born. Jenna's nesting involved nonstop shopping."

"You said she should have been a stylist or personal shopper. I've never asked, what was her job? I'm sure you make good money, but I feel like this house exceeds the salary of a professor your age."

"Her grandfather—her mother's father—invested in cheap real estate years ago. When he finally decided to sell it, the land was worth millions. Like every other millionaire who wants to feel like they're giving back, he started a foundation. When he died, Jenna took over running the foundation and the hefty salary that came with the job."

"Foundation for what?"

"Botanical research."

"Are you talking about Strauss Botanical Gardens and Research Center?"

I nod.

"Wow. I've attended several weddings there."

Morgan fusses. Floor time is about over.

"This one." Swayze holds up the blue and white tie she originally suggested.

"Can you tie it?"

"Maybe." She gives me the just-a-minute finger and fishes her phone out of her pocket. "Everything you could ever need to know is on the internet. Here." She plays a YouTube video.

"You think I'm supposed to learn how to tie my tie from a video?"

"No." She hooks the tie around my neck and gives it a playful tug. "I'm going to tie it for you while watching the tutorial. And if you're lucky, someday I may teach you how to tie it on your own like a big boy."

"If you tie it well, I can simply loosen it and slip it on and off like I do with my other ties."

"They'll get all wrinkled. That was my original point. If you're going to leave them knotted, then you might as well buy clip-ons."

Swayze's eyes flit between her hands working the tie around my neck and the screen of her phone on the bed. I'm impressed she's able to talk, tie, and follow the instructional video at the same time.

"Boom! Perfect." She takes a step back and grins.

I go to grab it, feeling the natural need to adjust it because I hate wearing the damn thing.

"Don't touch it." Shooting me a warning glare, she picks up Morgan. "Look at your daddy. Isn't he handsome?"

Swayze looks at Morgan, but I look at Swayze. How can she not see the obvious explanation for this?

"What's the grin for, Professor?"

"Nothing." I slip on my suit jacket.

"You've had a lot of nothing smiles lately."

I head toward the kitchen. "It's you."

"Me? You find me amusing, do you?"

Filling my stainless steel coffee mug, I search for the right response. I wish it could be how much I love reminiscing about the past with my best friend. It's better therapy for coping with the loss of Jenna than anything I've received from my time with Dr. Greyson.

"I find you to be a good distraction."

"Oh ..." she says, like the *oh* someone might say before running to the bathroom to vomit.

I turn, screwing on the lid to my mug. "That's a good thing. In case you didn't catch my meaning."

"I think I understand your meaning, and I'm not comfortable with being *that* kind of distraction. I don't think it's appropriate."

Where do I go with this? Has she made the connection? Or maybe she's just made the connection that *I* think she's Daisy even if she still can't recognize it.

"I need you to be more specific about what you find inappropriate."

"Really?" She narrows her eyes on a sidelong glance as she heats up Morgan's bottle. "And I thought we were done talking about this. What happened to the 'forget it ever happened?' Gah! I can't believe Griffin was right about this."

With one arm crossed over my chest and the other bringing my coffee mug to my mouth, I let her words play in my mind. They don't make sense.

Shit!

Now they do.

"No." I shake my head. "You've got this all wrong. I wasn't referring to the text. I meant your knowledge of my past. Talking about Daisy. *That's* the good distraction."

"Oh, oops. Well, thank God." She sits in the recliner and gives Morgan her bottle.

"You thought thinking about your text was my good distraction?" I made an emergency trip to Dr. Greyson's office yesterday. My voice shouldn't hold such an offended tone.

"Maybe." She cringes. "It's my boyfriend's fault. When I told Griffin what happened, he tried to convince me that you ... well ..." Her teeth chomp down on her lower lip while her nose scrunches.

"I what?" My head juts forward.

"He insisted that, for at least a split second, your mind imagined I was talking about you in the text. You know, like I *didn't* accidentally send it to the wrong person. So ..." She shrugs. "Griffin thinks you won't be able to easily forget the image that first popped into your mind."

My jaw relaxes to say something, but I'm at a loss for words so I clamp it shut again.

"*I'm* not the one who thinks it. It would be really wrong for your brain to go there. And he doesn't know you like I do. He wasn't there last night when you said those things to me before I left. Those weren't the words of a man who had inappropriate images in his mind. Right?"

I nod several times.

"That's what I thought."

Good. She read my nod as "you're correct" instead of "yes, it *was* really wrong of my mind to go there."

"I'm sorry. I don't know why *my* brain went there just now—making absurd assumptions about the meaning behind your smiles. It really makes me feel good to know that something positive has come from my unusual knowledge of you. I can deal with the crazy if it gives you a sense of peace—a needed distraction."

Grabbing my bag, I give her a tightlipped smile. "Very kind of you. Well, I have a long day ahead. You two have fun."

NATE'S THINKING ABOUT me giving him a blowjob. This isn't good. Griffin was right. Why does he have to be right about this? Personal fact number 6742 that I know about Nate Hunt: he flaps his jaw like a puppet when he's contemplating telling a lie. He didn't exactly lie, but he also didn't exactly tell me the truth. I'm surprised he didn't slip on the puddle of guilt beneath him as he made his way to the garage. I could see it dripping from him as he lost his battle to find a single good response to my accusation—Griffin's accusation.

I won't confront Nate. That's just wrong. What if he can't control his thoughts? I'm not telling Griffin either. He'll lose his shit and refuse to ever let me step foot in this house again. But the worst part is now that I know Nate has thought or is thinking about it, I can't stop thinking about *him* thinking about it, which means *I'm* thinking about it.

My mind won't stop creating an image of my mouth around Nate's cock. The mind isn't simply a dangerous place, it's the most dangerous place. All that's wrong, sinful, and evil starts in the mind. It's ironic how the part of the human body that controls everything is also the most out of control part of the body.

When Morgan goes down for her morning nap, I put her in her crib because I'm feeling a little snoopy today. Nate already confessed his busy day, so I feel fairly certain monitoring the nanny cam is not top priority. Besides, he gave me permission to snoop yesterday, citing that he has nothing to hide.

I start in his office. Boring anatomy books and other textbooks clutter his shelves. He never was one for reading novels. I move his rook and knight on the chessboard just to mess with him. There's no doubt in my mind that he's in the middle of a grueling chess match with himself. A picture of Jenna sits on the corner of his desk. She's looking down at her hands folded on her baby belly. It's painful to look at it.

After exploring all that's in plain sight, I wander down the hall to his bedroom. There's a camera in the corner of the room. I noticed it the first time I came in here. It's a good idea to monitor most of the rooms, but I can't stop my thoughts from stretching to the obvious possibility that on Nate's computer there's footage of Jenna and him having sex.

I can't think of them having sex without thinking about the text. And there's no way to think about the text without thinking about my mouth around his cock. That sends my brain in the direction of Nate's thoughts. Does the idea arouse him? How often does he think about it? Where does he think about it? Is that really the reason for his grins that seem to come out of nowhere but always when he's staring at me?

Twenty-one feels too young to contemplate fate, big goals, or even a grand purpose in life. Since meeting Griffin and his family, I've found the place I want to be. I'll take a small house, a couple of kids, maybe a dog, and our vacations will be wherever we can go with four wheels and a rooftop cargo carrier. We can pack a loaf of bread, peanut butter and jelly, and a bag of chips to eat at roadside picnic stops. It won't be a four-star hotel, but when Griffin and I sit beneath a tree, hold hands, and watch our kids chase butterflies while the wind carries their laughter, we'll feel certain no one has it better than we do.

I want the Calloway life, where everything is measured in love, and time together is the ultimate gift.

This is the confusing part for me. If that's my life, then why am I here snooping around another man's bedroom? If fate exists, then I know that's the reason I forgot my wallet the day I met Griffin. Yet, none of that explains how I ended up here in Nate's house, watching his daughter and reminiscing about a past that happened before I took my first breath.

I walk around his bedroom, but I don't touch anything. What am I looking for?

A sign?

An explanation?

A missing puzzle piece?

The other end of this wormhole?

There are two sinks in the en suite bathroom. An electric toothbrush, a bottle of foam soap, a beard trimmer, and several bottles of cologne surround one of the sinks. The other sink is naked.

One hand towel.

A single bottle of shampoo and a bar of soap in the shower.

The toilet seat is up.

Several dozen empty hangers occupy one side of the closet.

Not one pair of high-heel shoes.

Half of this room is a ghost. It's lonely. It's heartbreaking.

I berate my mom for clinging to the past, but maybe it's something. Something feels less empty than nothing. If Griffin died, would I be able to purge my life of every reminder of him? How did Nate do it? Less than three months after losing Jenna, he let her go with the exception of a few photos.

Sitting on the edge of the bed, I stare at the digital alarm clock next to a coaster holding a partially-filled glass of water. After a few moments of drumming my fingers on my legs, I make my boldest move yet and slide open the drawer to his nightstand.

There are two books.

"Reincarnation. Really, Nate?" I chuckle as I take the top book out and open it. At least a half dozen sticky notes mark different sections of the book. He's written on the sticky notes.

Calls Morgan "Daisy"
Birthmark
Snoopy and Charlie Brown
Spanish test
Hockey camp
The time period

"What are you doing?" I whisper. He what? Thinks I've been reincarnated? That's crazy. Reading minds falls under crazy as well, but reincarnated people remember their past life, not other people's past lives.

"Wow." I shake my head. "What am *I* thinking?" Without a second of hesitation, my mind jumps to my own imaginary rules of reincarnation, an unconscious acknowledgment that it exists. I've never given it much thought, but Nate certainly has given it a lot of thought and research.

"Jesus …" He has half the book highlighted. I flip to the end, a photo falls out of the back of the book onto the floor. I bend down to pick it up. A grin tugs at my mouth. It's the Nate I remember. He's rolling his eyes at the blond girl standing next to him on a dock. She's sticking her tongue out at him.

"Morgan Daisy?" I grin even more. I have a true face to put with the name. She's so close to how I pictured her in Nate's stories. I shiver, holding out my arm to see the goose bumps pebbled along my skin. I'm not sure I've ever listened to Nate talk about his memories of Daisy without it giving me goose bumps.

With my back to the spy cam, I slip my phone out of my pocket and take a picture of the photo. I can't stop staring at it. I can't imagine finding love at such a young age. And I definitely can't imagine losing a first love—a best friend.

The more I think about it, I agree with Daisy's parents. What kind of God takes away such beautiful innocence? They lost two children. If there is a God, he can't blame them for losing faith. It's easy to give thanks and praise for blessings. It's easy to feel loved when life bestows happiness upon us. But blind faith in the face of such tragedy is a jagged pill that not everyone can swallow.

Making sure all the sticky notes and the photo are in their original spots, I close the book.

Threads of the Soul – A Case for Reincarnation by Dr. Hazel Albright

"I'm not Daisy," I whisper, running my hand over the glossy-finished cover. Sometimes I wish I were her. She'd know all the right things to say to Nate, where I fumble words and do stupid stuff like sending him inappropriate texts and untying his ties.

I laugh, putting the book back in the drawer. Professor Hunt can't tie a tie.

CHAPTER NINETEEN

"COME IN. OH my, you look handsome, Nathaniel. I love that tie." Professor Albright winks over her shoulder, reaching for a book on the top shelf behind her desk.

"This one?" I point to the faded leather-bound book.

"Please."

I hand it to her.

"I've been waiting for you." Her grin shines with mischief.

"I had a feeling you needed help getting a book down. That's all. Have a good day." I walk toward her door.

"Shut the door and sit down."

I grin. Her curiosity amuses me. It's the reason I'm here.

"I'm not going to be around forever. You need to tell me about the girl. I won't sleep well in the afterlife with that unknown weighing heavily on my mind."

"I thought this is the afterlife." I shut her door and turn.

"Aw ..." She points a finger at me as we both take a seat. "You've gone beyond reading my books; you've studied them."

"I have. But I still don't have a clear understanding of everything."

"No one does. My words are nothing more than my own studies, observations, and theories. That's the best explanation anyone has for the future or what happens when we die. Can you prove a Heaven or Hell? Or the existence of a higher power? No. Of course not. No one can."

"Then what do I believe?"

Dr. Albright laughs. It's warm and comforting. She's never condescending. That's what I remember loving most about her class. She acts like a student with her students. Her style of teaching embraced how to think, not what to think. While my classes are more fact-based than hers, I've always tried to maintain that same group-learning mentality versus teaching to the masses.

The mind functions with memory, but flourishes from discovery.

"I'm sure you've heard it many times, but you have to discover your own truth."

"And those books are your truth?"

"Yes."

"You remember other lives?"

She nods. "I do. But I had help."

"That's why I'm here. Your books don't go into that much detail, but you mention hypnosis."

"My mentor helped me find the details buried in my unconscious mind by using hypnosis. Your heart is, and always has been, a part of your body. Sometimes you can feel or hear it, but how many people get to see their hearts? Well, some patients who have had open-heart surgery or transplants have been shown pictures or even video of their hearts. It's incredible, like the first time you see an x-ray of part of your body."

"Deeper meaning."

She smiles. "Yes. Involving more senses during the discovery process makes our understanding of something more vivid."

"Your mentor. Can I meet him?"

"Maybe in another life." She smiles.

"He died?"

"Three years ago."

"Can you do hypnosis?"

"What's this about, Nathaniel?" She leans forward, resting her arms on the desk. "Does your nanny want to be hypnotized?"

"I don't know."

"Ah, you're stuck. She's told you all she can and *you* want more."

"I want her to recognize who she was over twenty years ago, not just who I was at the time. I have questions for her."

"And by her you're referring to your friend?"

"Yes. Her death left me with a lot of unanswered questions."

"Do you not know how she died?"

"She drowned."

"So what are your questions?"

"I want to know why she was at the lake by herself."

"You want to bring forth her memory of how she died? Sounds cruel to me."

I didn't think of it like that. "She would relive her death?"

"It's possible. I remembered dying in two other lifetimes. One was quick. The only thing I have from it are a few brief flashes. The other time was a slow death, and I suffered a lot."

"Do you have nightmares about it?"

"Not anymore. It haunted me for months. So we used hypnosis to suppress those memories. Now I only know what I've told you. No details. No pictures in my mind. No *feelings*."

My gaze shifts to the humming bird feeder outside of her window. This isn't what I wanted to hear.

"Some things are best left alone. I learned that the hard way. My curiosity and need to discover more led to unnecessary suffering. Early scientists sacrificed their bodies and sometimes their lives to make new discoveries. I sacrificed my mind, my emotional well-being, because my desire for more took over my natural instinct for self-preservation."

"Hypnosis is not the answer?"

"I didn't say that. A tool can create or destroy, depending on the hand that holds it. But we're not talking about you. We're talking about a young girl who doesn't suspect she's your childhood friend. If she figures this out and wants to go deeper, that's her choice not yours."

"Would you hypnotize her if it were her choice? If she asked you?"

"A moot point, young man."

"Why do you say that?"

"I think it's unlikely she will make the connection without being hypnotized first, which means someone else would have to convince her that she should do it."

"And if someone did?"

Hazel wrings her hands and her eyes narrow a fraction. "Enjoy what she can freely give you. I told you before, she's not your friend—just like your daughter is not you or her mother, no matter how much she looks or acts like you."

I nod with understanding, but I don't know if I can accept it yet. "When I got here you thought I was going to tell you Swayze remembered who she was in my life. Am I right?"

A sad smile steals her mouth. "I knew it was unlikely, but … yes, the explorer and the scientist in me hoped for it."

"Thank you." I return a similar sad smile as I stand to leave.

PHARRELL WILLIAMS' "HAPPY" greets me when I open the door. A few steps more reveal Swayze's shaking hips and flailing arms. Her back is to me, so I don't think this greeting is meant for me—like the text I can't get out of my head.

Just beyond her animated dance performance, there's a sound that's ... unfamiliar, but I like it. No, I love it.

"She's giggling."

"Oh!" Swayze whips around with her hand over her chest. "You scared the living daylights out of me. You can't sneak up on people like that."

Morgan, kicking in her swing, giggles some more. Without taking my eyes off my happy baby, I wash my hands and take her out of the swing.

"Are you giggling, sweetie?" I kiss her cheek and neck. She giggles again. I can't remember the last time my heart felt joy this pure.

Swayze shuts off the music.

"Sorry." I grin. "I didn't mean to startle you."

I don't know if her flushed face is from the dancing, the startling, or embarrassment, but it looks good on her. Daisy used to race me to the treehouse or the lake on the abandoned property. I'd press my hands to her warm cheeks and kiss her before she could catch her next breath.

"I'm going to put a bell on you. For such a big guy, you possess some stealth moves."

"I can set the security alarm to chime." Easing to my knees, I lay Morgan on her play mat to expend some more of her energy.

"Good idea. I'd like to know when you're home."

"In case you're snooping around?" With a sly grin, I glance at her over my shoulder, expecting her to return an eye roll.

Instead, her eyes widen and her lips part.

"Were you snooping?" I'm not mad, but maybe a little surprised.

"I don't know, Inspector, was I? Did you skip your luncheon and speech to monitor the nanny cam?"

Clever girl. Was she snooping? Or is she offended that I asked?

"No." I chuckle. "I wasn't watching you today."

"Besides, you told me to snoop away."

"This is true. Did you find anything exciting? Spare change in the sofa? The code to my safe? My watch ... yeah, did you find my watch? It's a gray sports watch. I lost it about six months ago. I have no idea what happened to it."

Swayze laughs. It's not Morgan's giggle, but it makes me feel close to the women I have loved and lost. Daisy laughed like laughing was her hobby. Jenna laughed all the time too—usually at me. She also asked me about my day, and in the same breath she said, "Did you make someone smile today?" It was her positivity that shined. I needed to chase that sunrise, the hope for something beyond the love that I'd lost.

"No watch. But I see you still keep nudie girl magazines under your mattress."

I don't.

"Your recollection of my past isn't one hundred percent accurate. The magazines under my bed weren't nudie girls, they were *Sports Illustrated* swimsuit editions."

Morgan giggles. I love this. A smiley, giggling baby brings out the buffoon in even the manliest of men—of which I like to consider myself. I rub my nose on her belly, baby-talking, "No they weren't. Your daddy did not have nudie girl pictures under his bed. No he did not."

"Then why hide them under your bed?"

"I didn't want my dad to see them."

"But if the women weren't naked, then why hide them?"

"So he didn't give me grief for having them." I give her a look, the one that says, "*Do you get it?*"

Her eyes narrow a fraction and widen again. "Oh … because you used them to—"

"Thanks for watching Morgan. Drive safely home."

Laughter bubbles from her chest as she nods several times. "Yeah, let's not go there."

There. I've made Morgan and Swayze smile today. It eases the frustration that I've felt since leaving Dr. Albright's office. The long list of what ifs makes me uneasy.

What if Swayze never makes the connection on her own?

What if my chance to understand Daisy's death slips away?

What if Swayze finds a different job?

What if she moves away?

What if I can't handle losing Daisy a second time?

What if I can't raise Morgan on my own?

What if I tell her she's Daisy?

That's the biggest what if. I want to tell her. It physically hurts to keep this to myself, especially when I see Swayze struggle with her knowledge of me, wondering where it stems from.

What if telling her makes everything better?

What if it doesn't?

"Where are you?"

I glance up at Swayze as she slips the strap of her bag onto her shoulder.

"You look distracted."

I shake my head. "Just a long day. That's all."

"You should give her a bottle and put her to bed. Maybe relax by reading a book or something."

"Books don't relax me. They never have."

"I know."

Of course she does. Daisy inhaled two to three books a week. I read on a need-to basis.

"But I thought maybe the gazillion years of school you've had may have given you a love for reading or at least a hunger for knowledge. What's the last book you read that didn't have anything to do with your job?"

"The instruction manual to the hanging bike rack I assembled last weekend."

"Really?" She cocks her head to the side.

I sense a bit of disbelief in her tone.

"Huh. Okay."

"Don't forget about my conference this weekend. You get her all night."

"Wait. No." She shakes her head. "I'm going to a motorcycle rally with Griffin. I told you this ... way back."

"Me or Rachael?"

"You. I think. I don't know. What does it matter? I requested the time off. Can't Rachael watch her?"

"She left for school yesterday."

Her nose wrinkles. "Sorry ... what about your parents?"

I don't mean to sigh so heavily. I feel bad. It's not my intention to guilt her.

"Can you skip the conference? Or take her with you?"

"I can't skip it. I'll figure it out. How long will you be gone?"

"A week."

"A week?" Again, my emotions slip. "I have classes starting

next week."

"I'm sorry. But what about your parents?"

"They leave for vacation Monday."

"There has to be someone."

I shake my head. "There's not." Morgan coos. I hate the small percent of me that's feeling the burden of being a single parent. "But it's not your problem. I'll figure it out."

"Nate, I'm really sorry. But I promised Griffin and—"

"It's fine. Not your fault."

Her slow nod accompanies a somber expression. "I'll see you in the morning."

"Goodnight."

"Are you mad?"

I grunt a laugh. "Not at you. It's fine."

"You sound upset. I feel really bad."

"Swayze, I said it's not your problem. Goodnight."

"I care for Morgan, so it feels like my problem too. Maybe I could ask my mom if she could watch her."

"I'm not having a stranger stay overnight with her, no offense to your mother. I'll see if my parents will stay the night."

"Do you not trust them?"

"Swayze ..." I roll my eyes up at her. "Not. Your. Problem."

She frowns. "Goodnight."

I should say something. Stop her from leaving. Reassure her that I'm not upset with her—but I don't. We've had plenty of conversations lately. I'm surprised and a little disappointed she didn't mention or remind me of this before now.

The front door closes.

"We're in a real pickle, baby girl."

Morgan grins again, destined to spend most of her childhood laughing at my mistakes. Her mom sure did.

NATE IS UPSET with me. I want to help him, but that would make Griffin mad at me. Every day it gets harder to treat my time with Morgan as just a job. My worry about who will watch Morgan may not be the same as Nate's, but it's close.

She's not just a job. And that little fact could be very bad for me.

"Griff?"

"In the bedroom."

His house smells like pot roast. My stomach growls in response.

"Hey."

"Swayz." He turns from the small pile of neatly folded clothes on his bed, giving me the once-over.

"Griff." My eyes make the same quick inspection of him.

We both grin. It's sexy. It's just … us.

"Tell me about your day." He turns back to his bed and fills a bag with his folded clothes.

"They scanned my brain early this morning."

"And?" He glances over his shoulder, concern marring his beautiful face.

"Preliminary results looked good. My doctor called this afternoon to confirm it."

Griffin's body melts into relief. I suppose it's a relief, but it still doesn't explain how I know Nate so well.

"Morgan giggled for the first time. I felt bad that the professor missed her first giggle, but I think parents who work full time have to expect they'll miss a lot of firsts. I haven't decided yet if I'll shove her down when she takes her first steps or if I'll let it happen and gloat."

"You'll gloat." He chuckles.

"You think? I don't know. If Jenna were still alive and they were both working full time to maintain their high standard of living, I might gloat. But Nate's just trying to survive as a single parent. You know?"

"I suppose. Have you started packing?"

"You could say that." I plop down on his bed next to his bag.

He eyes me. "And how would you say it?"

"I have my dirty clothes by the door to take down to wash when I get home."

"You're dragging your feet. Do you not want to go?" His lips pull into a tight line like the ones next to his eyes as he focuses on packing.

"I want to go with *you*."

"With me?"

"Yes. Anywhere with you."

"It's not a cabin in the woods for a romantic weekend. I asked you to ride on the back of a motorcycle for a twelve hour trip to a motorcycle rally."

"True. You need to work on your romantic getaway ideas."

"If you don't want to go—"

"I'm going. What do you want me to say?" Flopping back on his pillow, I cover my face and laugh. "I realize you're— we're—going because these guys you met through work invited you. But they are in their forties and fifties. You're twenty-four."

"I like riding with them. Age shouldn't matter."

"True. But you said you haven't been to this rally before.

So I searched it up online and read some blogs from people who have attended it."

"You can't believe everything you read online."

Lacing my fingers behind my head, I grunt. "I hope not because it sounds like a mix of vulgarity, old people mourning their youth, beer chugging, loud noise, and pole dancing."

"Then don't go."

I sit up. "I'm going even if it's not my crowd."

He stills his hands, studying me for a few seconds. "It could be fun."

It could be, if you're into pot-bellied men acting like chauvinistic assholes, making crude comments to women in body paint and pasties.

"It could be." Biting my lips together, I nod. "I smell pot roast."

"In the oven. My mom dropped off leftovers."

I leap off the bed. "Did you eat?"

"Yeah."

"Good, so the rest is mine. Do you have bread?"

"In the freezer."

"Ugh … that sprouted grain crap?" I grumble on the way to the kitchen.

"It's pot roast. Why do you need bread?"

I shove a knife through the frozen pieces of sprouted grain crap to break them apart.

"Here. You're going to cut off a finger or ram the knife into my counter." He separates two slices and puts them in the toaster.

"I like pot roast on bread, lots of ketchup." I pull the pot roast out of the oven and toss the hot pads aside."

He pins me to the counter. "I like you in my bed, lots of

begging."

"Don't distract me. I'm starving."

"Me too." His head dips to my neck.

I close my eyes as his tongue trails up to my ear. "Griff …" Everything south of my stomach wants sex right here, right now. But my stomach craves pot roast on bread, dripping with ketchup.

My toast pops up.

"Five minutes. Just let me eat first." I rest my hands on his chest to push him away.

He adjusts himself, taking a step back. "I can't compete with pot roast."

"You know I would choose you over pot roast." I fork the tender meat onto the toast and squeeze a moderate to heavy amount of ketchup on it. "But why would you make me choose?"

Ketchup drips onto the plate as I take a huge bite.

"You can sit at the table." He chuckles.

I shake my head. "This is fine."

"I'll throw some clothes in a bag. We should go back to your place and get your laundry going first." He heads down the hall toward the bedroom.

I inhale the rest of the sandwich, mopping up every drip of ketchup with the crappy sprouted grain bread. "Make sure to tell your mom she makes the best pot roast ever. Then make sure to never say those same words to my mom."

"Got it."

As I wash off the plate, my phone rings. It's probably my mom. She has creepy timing. I retrieve the phone from my bag. It's not my mom.

"Hey, Professor."

A shrill scream sounds, clenching my heart. It's Morgan.

"Sorry to bother you, but she's..." distress bleeds from his voice "...colicky or something. It's never been this bad. I don't want to be the overreacting parent that calls the pediatrician, but I'm ..."

"Okay, just ... I don't know. Maybe she's teething?"

"I looked that up. It seems a bit early, but ... shh ..." He tries to soothe her. "It's like something is hurting her."

"It could be gas pains. I really don't know. There's no shame in calling her doctor."

The line goes silent for a few seconds, but then another scream pierces my ear.

"Did you call your mom?"

"Yeah, she ... she said it was probably colic. Stupid catch-all. But she won't stop crying. She was just fine an hour ago. God ... I don't know what to do."

"How long has she been crying?"

"I ... I don't know. Ten minutes. Thirty. An hour. I don't know. It feels like forever."

"Do you need me to come over?" I hate offering. It's not going to sit well with Griffin.

"No. Yes. I don't know. I can't think."

"I'll be over in a bit."

"Thanks." The defeat in his voice tugs at my heart.

"Who's that?" Griffin carries his overnight bag into the living room.

I cringe. "It was Nate. Morgan won't stop crying. He's a little distressed."

"Did you tell him to call a doctor?"

"Yes. I think he's afraid to call the doctor. His mom thinks it's colic and it probably is, but he's just ... not able to think straight."

Griffin shakes his head, flipping off the lights. "Did you tell him you're off duty right now?" He opens the back door as I grab my purse.

"I uh … told him I'd be over in a bit."

Thunk.

He drops his bag to the floor and flips back on the light. "You're fucking kidding me."

"Griff, I won't be long."

"How do you know that? Do you have some magical pill to give her? Is that all you're doing? Driving over there to deliver the magic pill and then coming right back home?"

I don't know what I'm going to do. But I need to go because I won't be able to think about anything else except the shrill cries and distressed pleas.

"Don't be mad."

"You're choosing him over me."

"Knock it off!"

His eyes narrow with my outburst.

"It's not a competition—not between you and a sandwich and not between you and Nate. I'm going over there because it feels like the right thing to do. This isn't any different than the time you skipped out on me to help a friend whose bike broke down an hour north of town. I didn't accuse you of choosing him over me. He needed your help more. That's it."

"Go."

I shake my head. "Tell me it's okay to go, not because I need your permission, because I need you. And if leaving now lands me locked out of your house on your front doorstep later, then I won't go. I choose you. Always. But it pisses me off that there has to be a choice."

Griffin closes his eyes and pushes out a long breath. "It's okay to go."

My fingers lace around the back of his neck, waiting for him to open his eyes. "I love you, Grocery Store Guy."

His eyes open. I kiss him. He barely kisses me back, but I feel a small pull and that's enough.

"You might not always be first in line, but you're always first with my heart. Okay?"

He nods.

"Meet me at my place?"

He nods.

I give him one more peck on the lips and leave before one of us says something we shouldn't.

CHAPTER TWENTY

THE CRIES RATTLE my bones as I open the front door. The man standing in the doorway to his bedroom, gently bouncing the arched-back baby, shares no resemblance to the confident professor. He's the young boy in my head—feigning confidence while drowning in desperation.

"Sorry. I would have been here sooner, but I stopped to pick up a few things." I hold up the bag in my hand. "Teething gel, homeopathy pills for teething and colic, calming baby massage oil with lavender."

"Hold her. I'm going to call the doctor." He takes the bag from me with one hand while passing Morgan to me with his other hand.

Kissing her warm head, I take in his disheveled hair, wrinkled white tee, and black jogging pants. Nope. No sign of Professor Hunt anywhere.

"I know. I'm a disaster." He looks in the bag. "How can I know so much but feel like I know nothing at the moment?"

There's nothing I can say. I'm twenty-one with no true parenting experience and way too inexperienced at life to give sage advice.

"Call the doctor."

He glances up from the bag. "So you think so too?"

Bouncing his screaming daughter, I nod several times. Nate lost his wife in an unexpected blink. I don't want my gut instinct to be wrong; I'm not going to suggest rubbing gel on her gums or dissolving pills in a teaspoon of water until a doctor rules out anything serious.

A few minutes later, Nate jogs down the hall. "He's meeting me at his office." He grabs a pair of running shoes from his closet.

I put Morgan into a football hold with her tummy pressed to my arm and swing her back and forth. Her cries ease a fraction.

"You have a pediatrician willing to meet you at his office instead of sending you to urgent care?"

"He's a friend of mine."

"So why were you afraid to call him?"

Nate looks up.

"Really? You're worried he's going to think you don't know what you're doing?"

"Do I?" He finishes tying his shoes. "For the love of God! Listen to her. She won't stop. Something is wrong."

Desperation. He's killing me.

"Let me know what you find out." I start to hand her to him.

"You're not coming?"

"I ... I don't know. Do you need me to come with you?"

"If you want to, that would be great."

Morgan shakes in my arms as her cry hits a peak. A few seconds of silence follow before she gets her second wind.

"I'll go." I don't know if I *want* to go, but the slight relief on Nate's face says he needs me to go.

"Thank you. Let's go."

We arrive at the pediatrician's office after the loudest fifteen minutes of my life. Nate falls short of keeping his shit together, but I applaud him for his attempt. The agony etched into his brow is too deep to fool anyone.

"Nathaniel." The tall blond with green-framed glasses shakes *Nathaniel's* hand.

Kids must love his fun glasses and huge smile. Moms must love everything else about him. He's hot. A different kind of hot than Griffin, but still … hot.

"John, this is Swayze." Nate unfastens Morgan from her car seat.

"Nice to meet you." John shakes my hand before washing his hands at the sink.

"You too."

He examines Morgan. I watch Nate. Are his thoughts on Jenna? Or is he asking God why? Why take the mother of his child and leave him lost without a sense of what to do?

We go through a few questions, and I say *we* because I have more waking-hours knowledge of Morgan. The doctor concurs that it's nothing serious. He prescribes a change in her formula and gives Nate a few samples to try when he gets home along with the things I picked up for gas and teething pain.

I put Morgan in her car seat. Before I get the harness latched, she's asleep. She wore herself out.

"I apologize for calling after hours. I was just—"

John shakes his head. "Hey, man, don't ever apologize. First-time dad. On your own. I'd be a mess too. Don't tell Bella I said this, but no amount of schooling can replace motherly intuition. She's better with our kids than I am."

"Thanks."

"Let me know how the change in formula works. And…" he gives me a quick smile before returning his attention to Nate "…I'm glad you've found someone. It's good for you and

Morgan."

"Oh…" Nate shakes his head and chuckles "…Swayze isn't … I mean, she's Morgan's nanny. That's all."

I return a shy grin and shrug.

John's eyebrows lift a fraction. "You found a nanny that comes with you to after-hours doctor's visits. She's quite the find. Sounds like she's a keeper."

"Yeah, well…" Nate redirects his focus to the car seat, refusing to look in my direction or John's "…again, thanks. I'll call you."

I'm not sure which is worse, the screaming or the awkward silence. For Morgan's sake, I'll say the screaming is worse. But the ride home isn't fun.

"I shouldn't have called you," Nate says as we go in the house. "I had a weak moment, and I overstepped a line."

What do I say? In my years of being a nanny, I've never had anyone call me to accompany them to a doctor's visit outside of my normal working hours. But maybe other nannies have had it happen. I've also never been a nanny for a single parent.

"I wanted to help you out, even if my help was in the form of moral support."

"Still …" He sighs, setting the car seat on the floor.

Morgan hasn't made a sound since we left the doctor's office.

"I'll pay you overtime for this." He rubs the back of his neck, eyes filled with regret.

"You don't have to pay me anything extra. Technically, you didn't ask me to come over here. I offered because I, too, was concerned about Morgan."

He steps closer, too close for the silence surrounding us.

The last time we were this close I had my hand on his bare abdomen, and the time before that, he hugged me in the garage to comfort me during my breakdown.

"John thought we were ... together," he says.

Definitely too close. Yet, I feel no urge to step back. Standing this close to him feels familiar and a slew of other crazy emotions.

I look up. He's so close I have to strain my neck a little. "Crazy." My voice trembles. "Since I'm so young."

That's it? That's my best response? Yes, I'm fifteen years younger than Nate. *But ...* he just lost his wife a few months ago and I have a boyfriend. *That* should be why it's crazy.

He grins. "True. Sometimes I forget how young you are because of everything you know about me that happened before you were born."

Why are we having this conversation an inch from our toes touching?

"Do you have a few minutes?"

Do I have a few minutes to stand this close to a man who is not Griffin? No. His name is all it takes to force my feet to distance us.

"A few minutes for what?" I glance at Morgan.

"I want to show you some photos."

"Of Morgan?" I return my attention to him.

"No." He jerks his head toward the bedroom and lifts the car seat. "I don't think I should take her out of here until she wakes up on her own."

I follow him down the hallway. "You mean you're afraid to take her out of it."

"Exactly."

Griffin is at my apartment. I should be there. Why am I

following Nate when I need to find my way home to my boyfriend?

He retrieves a shoebox from his closet and sits on the bed. I take a seat next to him, but not too close.

"Where was this taken?" He holds up a photo. It's young Nate dressed like a pirate.

"Outside of the bowling alley."

"How can you tell? There's no sign, I'm facing the street, and the background is blurred and black because it was night."

"You know how I know. Are we back to this?"

He doesn't respond. Instead he grabs another photo. "What about this one?" It's Nate and the girl from the photo in the back of the book in his nightstand. Morgan—Daisy. They're eating cotton candy.

"Circus."

He grins and nods.

We go through five more photos. I know the location of all of them.

"I have to go," I say as he reaches for another one. "It's late. Griffin's at my apartment waiting for me, and I have laundry to do before my trip."

He nods. I see the you-just-popped-my-balloon disappointment on his face.

"Yeah, sorry, you're right. I thought you might like seeing things that could validate what's in your mind."

I do like looking at these photos. Tomorrow I plan on doing nothing but looking at them when Morgan takes a nap. "If it weren't so late—"

"I get it." He puts the lid on the box and returns it to the top shelf in the closet. "Another time."

Tomorrow.

"Yeah, another time."

"Thank you." He runs a hand through his wayward hair. "I'll act my age next time and not send you a SOS before calling John."

I chuckle. "It's fine. Really. Hopefully the new formula works. I'll see you in the morning."

"Goodnight."

IT'S ELEVEN BY the time I get home.

NASCAR's on TV.

Lights turned off.

Griffin's asleep on the sofa. No shirt. Bare feet. Taut inked skin begging to be licked.

Several piles of neatly-folded clothes cover my coffee table. I don't deserve my grocery store guy. After removing my clothes—all of them—I grab his hand. Sable eyes blink open and make a slow inspection of my naked body.

"Come to bed." I tug on his hand.

He grips my hand but doesn't budge. Shadows from the TV dance across his face, making his expression indiscernible. If I could choose a mind to read, it would be his. I want to know what makes him tick. I want to know what he thinks when he looks at me for long minutes. Even when I'm not looking at him, I feel his eyes on me. I don't know how ... I just do.

Easing to sitting, still holding my hand, he ghosts his other hand up the inside of my leg, stopping an inch from the top. My pulse jumps up a notch.

"I know every curve of your body." His gaze works its way

up to mine.

My lips part, letting my breath fall out in a heavy pant.

"I know what each curve feels like under my hands." He bypasses the apex of my legs, skating his hand along my skin— over my hip, dipping down to my ass, up my back, and around to my breast. It's agonizing—striking a match in slow motion.

My eyes close, teeth digging into my lower lip as he squeezes my breast. I love the controlled strength in his touch and the calloused pad of his thumb brushing over my nipple.

"I know how you taste." He teases his lips and tongue across my belly. "I know what you want before you say the words."

"Griff..." I release his hand, moving both of mine to his head.

"Shh ... I know."

He does know. Griffin knows me more intimately than I know myself. With the slide of two fingers and the flick of his tongue, I let go of the thoughts in my head and give myself to him.

"Griff..." I claw at his head, holding my breath, praying this need and the pleasure it promises will last forever. This is my favorite part.

Teasing the edge.

Wanting it to last.

Needing it to end.

The anticipation breeds addiction.

"Don't come yet." He bites the inside of my leg and slides his fingers out of me.

A nervous chuckle squeezes past the thick pulse in my throat. "Then you better walk out that door. If you put your mouth on me one more time or touch me again ... I'm gone."

He stands, towering over me like Nate did, but Nate confuses me. Griffin commands me without saying a word.

It's protective.

It's possessive.

It's lust.

It's love.

It's everything.

Cradling my face in his hands, he kisses me. It's the slow start of a love song. I'm certain every time he kisses me like this I fall in love all over again. This is the kiss I dreamed of from the moment I turned over the receipt and read his phone number under *Grocery Store Guy*.

My hands slide up his chest, wrapping around his neck as his hands feather down my sides, wrapping around my waist. Lifting me a few inches off the ground, he continues to feast on my mouth, carrying me to the bedroom.

As he releases me to the floor, I keep my hands wrapped around his neck, whispering over his lips, "You did my laundry."

He smiles and it's incredibly sexy. "I did your laundry."

Inching my head side to side, I match his grin. "I'm in deep. So. Very. Deep."

"Yeah?"

I nod and my fingers find the button to his jeans.

"How does that make you feel?" he murmurs, both of our chins tipped down, watching my hands ease down the zipper.

"Scared ... intoxicated ..." I squat, pulling down his jeans and briefs. My mouth voyages up his body, eliciting each muscle they touch to contract.

"Swayz ..." He closes his eyes as I kiss his neck while sliding my hand along his erection.

"But mostly…" I whisper, brushing my lips across his ear "…it makes me feel … enraptured."

My back meets the bed as he pins my hands above my head and crashes his mouth to mine. Our love song picks up its tempo—each emotion building toward the climax. Two entangled bodies move with more need … more urgency.

Since we ended our fight in the shower, sex has felt more desperate—more meaningful. It's not just a physical need, it's an emotional connection that demands nurturing.

After the bed's a tangled mess of sheets and blankets and the only sounds in the room are my name on his lips and his on mine as we fall … fall … fall … playing out our love song until the final note, we find serenity.

"DON'T MOVE. FIVE more minutes."

I giggle. "Did you skip your workout for me this morning?"

"Mmm…" his chest vibrates against my cheek "…yes I did." He rolls onto me, wedging himself between my legs.

My skin wakes up under the touch of his tongue trailing from my neck to my nipple. "Mr. Calloway, I don't want to be responsible for you falling off the exercise wagon." I arch my back.

His hand snakes under my backside, adjusting me so the head of his cock nudges my entrance. On a soft moan, he slides inside of me. "Are you sure?"

My breath hitches. "I … I might be okay with you slipping off the wagon this morning."

Griffin moves inside of me, slowly waking up my body. "I want you to move in with me."

My hands grip his ass, letting him know that I'm awake and needing more. But Griffin sets the pace, and right now his pace is conversational. He's a damn tease.

"Faster ..."

"My thoughts too. I don't see any reason for you to wait to move in with me."

"That's not what I mean." My nails dig into him a little more. "We'll..." I try to move against him faster and harder, but it's wasted effort. "...talk when we're done."

He sucks and bites the skin along my shoulder; muscular arms hold his upper body a few inches above mine. "Now." He rocks into me a little harder, making sure I feel his point. "Just say yes and we'll be done talking."

I release something between a laugh and a frustrated groan. "Griff ..."

"Griff what?" He circles his hips.

Fucking tease.

"You like this?" He speeds up.

"Yes ..." I stretch my neck up to kiss him. He indulges me then pulls away, pumping into me faster.

"Does this feel good?"

"Yes ..."

Faster. Harder.

"Do you love me?"

My eyes close as my muscles tighten. "Yes."

"Do you want me to make you come?"

"Yes ..."

"Are you sure?"

"Yes!"

There it is ... it's close ... right ... there ...

Stars ...

"Move in with me."

"Yes … yes … oh my god yes!" Morning sex is the best.

Griffin's tongue invades my mouth and two seconds later his head strains back and my name falls from his lips after two "fucks" followed by three more.

He must like morning sex too.

After another long kiss, he rolls out of bed, grabs his overnight bag, and looks over his shoulder. "We'll move your stuff when we get back in town."

"We should talk—"

"Swayz, we just did. I said, 'move in with me' and you said, 'yes, yes, oh my god yes.'"

I throw a pillow at him. "You're such a caveman. I would have said yes without you pounding it out of me."

"Maybe. But what fun would that have been?" He struts off to the bathroom.

I'm moving in with Griffin after one fight that nearly broke us up. I'm moving in with the guy I want to marry, but he hasn't proposed. I'm moving in with Griffin, and I still don't understand the visions of Nate in my head.

The average life I settled into after my dad died has tumbled into something unexpected, amazing, and scary as hell. I'm so afraid of losing him in the process of finding myself. And then there's Nate who stands too close, pulls at my heartstrings with his adorable daughter and single-dad role. But he thinks I'm the reincarnation of Daisy—I'm not.

CHAPTER TWENTY-ONE

"GOOD MORNING. HOW'S my favorite baby?"

Nate carries Morgan down the hall in one hand and his messenger bag in his other hand, passing her to me with a huge grin on his face.

"She's your favorite baby?"

I kiss her chubby cheek. Her mouth opens into a big smile. "Yes. I have no children of my own yet, no nieces or nephews, no friends who have named me Godmother to their children. So … how did the rest of the night go?"

He grabs his usual to-go cup of coffee. "Perfect. She didn't wake up once. I think it must be the formula. There's enough to last the day. I'll pick up more on my way home."

"Have you found someone to watch her when I'm gone?"

Nate eyes me over the black lid to his cup, taking a cautious sip. "My parents will watch her until Monday. My mom can be physically limited, but hopefully her knowledge mixed with my dad's physical abilities will be the equivalent of one capable adult."

Why do I feel so guilty?

"And next week?"

He shrugs. "I don't know what I'm going to do yet."

"You have class."

He nods. "I do."

"You can't take her."

"This is true." He sticks an apple in his messenger bag and latches it.

"I'm sorry. I really wish there was something I could do."

"Not your child. Not your problem." The tight smile on his face doesn't help my guilt.

"Still …" My lips twist into a painful frown.

"Not. Your. Problem." Nate kisses Morgan on the head.

"It feels like my problem." I follow him to the back door.

He shakes his head and chuckles. "She's not your—"

"I know, I know … stop saying she's not my child. I get it. But I care about her, and I don't want some stranger watching her or you losing your job because you're trying to teach a class with a baby attached to your chest."

"What do you want me to say?" He turns.

I cradle Morgan to me. This little girl needs me. I feel it in a way that's hard to explain. "I don't know," I whisper, the guilt bearing down until my chest aches.

"Do you want me to ask you to stay home to watch her?"

My gaze falls to Morgan. I can't look at him, not when he's looking at me with those eyes that feel as familiar as my own. "Do you want to ask me to stay home to watch her?"

"Yes."

My heart pauses for a breath—a silent gasp. I asked the question, but I didn't expect a one-word answer delivered with such raw honesty.

And when our eyes meet, there's not a flash of regret.

"But I won't."

Dear heart, you can start beating again.

"And I won't tell you that it's unnerving to think of you on the back of a motorcycle for hundreds of miles or surrounded by a bunch of beer-chugging men who get off on objectifying women."

"Nate …" I need to respond, but he's robbed every thought that makes any sense.

"I guess…" his eyes avert away from mine as his teeth trap the corner of his lower lip "…it's just what I think your father—any good father—would say to his daughter."

Would my father approve of me going to a motorcycle rally with Griffin? Absolutely not. But he's not here. I'm an adult. And Griffin loves me. I trust him with my heart and my life. He makes me feel safe, even when I don't know why I have this desperate *need* to feel safe. Yet, I do.

"Griffin would never let anything happen to me."

Nate studies me. "A man on a bike amid SUVs and semi-trucks doesn't have a lot of control. He's at fate's mercy."

"Aren't we all at fate's mercy?"

Nate flinches. It's slight, but I see it. And the regret grips my heart.

"That was terrible. I didn't mean—"

"It's fine." He opens the back door.

Nate is a single father because fate lacked any sort of mercy the day Morgan came into this world and Jenna left it. Why did I have to remind him of that?

"Have a good day."

My lips pull into a tiny, painful grin. "You too."

The door closes. My familiar stranger breaks my heart every day. When I'm home, all I want is to fall into the world of Griffin Calloway—love's muse. But when I'm here, with Morgan gazing up at me, so innocent and helpless, I feel like something incomprehensible has led me to her.

I can't risk losing Griffin, searching for something that may never be found, but I also can't let this go. Part of me belongs to this unknown.

"Let's get some floor time ... in your daddy's room."

Morgan's arms flail. She's excited about it too. My bare feet pad down the shiny wood floor toward the open door at the end of the hall. Nate used to keep his door closed; now he leaves it open. It feels like an invitation. He wanted me to see those photos last night. He gave me permission to snoop. Maybe this is his way of helping me figure this out.

The camera no longer phases me. I lay Morgan on her mobile play mat and retrieve the box of photos from Nate's closet.

"My god ..." I pull out picture after picture and arrange them on the floor beside Morgan's mat. They're so vivid in my mind—holidays, hockey games, the tree house, the lake. My hands move them in order; I'm not sure how they know—how I know—but I do. When I'm done, there are six pictures that I don't recognize, but they are of Nate. He's older than my memory recalls, maybe in his twenties.

"Nate ..." I stop on a black and white portrait of him with his shirt off, maybe on a beach. He's looking off into the distance like he's lost or even a little broken. There's a darker tint to his wavy hair, maybe from the water, and a trimmed beard shadows his jaw. A smattering of hair covers his defined chest. He's ... beautiful.

"Were you thinking of Daisy?" I whisper. This photo ... I can't stop staring at it. I've never seen such a deep expression on the face of another human. "I'm not her."

But I wish I were. I can only imagine how incredible it must have been to be loved by Nate. Will I ever make a mark on Griffin like the one Daisy made on Nate? If I died today, would Griffin mourn me for the rest of his life? Would he find another to love and name his daughter after me?

I chuckle. "I hope not." One Swayze is enough.

Morgan starts to fuss.

"Are you hungry? Or just tired of floor time?" I set the beach photo aside and gather the other pictures, returning them to the box, but my gaze returns to that photo. I want to be there on that beach with him. I want to run my hands through those windblown locks and look into those soulful eyes until I feel exactly what he was feeling in that moment. With my back to the camera in the corner, I slip the photo into my pocket. I will return it—eventually.

"This is so messed-up," I mumble, returning the box to the closet shelf. "Okay, fussy pants, let's get you fed." She feels warm when I press my lips to her forehead. "What's going on? Do you not feel well?"

Morgan drinks less than half of her bottle before she falls asleep, warm—too warm. I take her temperature. 102 degrees.

Swayze: Morgan has a 102 temp.

Professor: Eating?

Swayze: Not quite half her bottle.

Professor: Crying?

Swayze: Sleeping.

Professor: I'll call John.

Five or so minutes later I get another text.

Professor: Let her sleep. See if she eats when she wakes. Retake her temp and let me know. I can come home if you need me.

Swayze: We're good for now. I'm not worried. I just wanted you to know.

Professor: Thank you.

"HEY." NATE DROPS his messenger bag on the counter.

I look up from my book, hot as hell from a small heater sleeping on my chest most of the day. "Hi."

"How's she doing?"

"Still 102. But she took the rest of her bottle and part of another one."

He nods, resting his hand on the top of her head. I can't look at him without seeing the Nate in the photo stashed away in my pocket.

"Are you okay?" he asks.

I blink and avert my gaze from his eyes. It's impossible not to look into his eyes and wonder what he was thinking when that picture was taken. "Yeah. Just … hot."

"I'm sure." He eases her from my chest, and she fusses a bit before falling back to sleep in his arms. "Thank you."

I lift my stiff body out of the chair. "No apology necessary. Rocking sick babies is part of the job. I've done it many times before."

He rests his cheek on top of her head. It's precious and heartbreaking. She needs her mom and he needs his wife.

"Still …" Those soulful eyes find my gaze and a sad smile tugs at his mouth. "I feel bad that I wasn't here."

"You can't be everywhere and everything to her always."

"Well…" he rubs circles on her back "…I'm glad you were here. In fact, I have an offer for you."

Sliding my bag over my shoulder, my head tilts to the side. "What's that?"

"I'm in a bind. A big one with school starting next week and my parents leaving town. Would you consider staying home if I offered you a five thousand dollar bonus?"

"Excuse me?"

"If I had another option, I wouldn't ask. I feel like a dick. This isn't a finer moment for me, but I'm imploring you to stay. Take the money and use it for another trip when I'm not in such a desperate predicament."

"Nate, I ..."

"I know I said it's not your problem. And if you say no, then I'll have to ... I don't know ... figure something out. This isn't an attempt to make it your problem. I'm just offering you a lot of money—on top of your regular salary—to stay. Think of it as a business offer."

Five grand. That's a lot of money considering the inheritance from my father has dwindled since paying Dr. Greyson, paying off my car, and the new computer I purchased six months ago. Five grand in savings. Five grand to help do some more renovations around Griffin's house. Maybe a new sofa. His is an old hand-me-down like mine.

Griffin. I don't know how he would feel about this. He's been looking forward to this trip all summer. But ... five grand.

"I'd have to talk with Griffin. We're supposed to leave tomorrow. Five thousand dollars isn't worth my relationship. If I talk to him and he's not on board, I just ..."

Nate shakes his head. "I understand. I'm not asking you to ruin your relationship to bail me out of this mess. Call me after you talk to him."

"I will." I rock forward onto my toes and press a kiss to Morgan's rosy cheek. "Feel better, baby." My eyes shift upward, meeting his gaze. *Fuck.* This is the look. He's giving me the same look that's on his face in the photo. My spine prickles, turning to ice. "I looked at the photos," I mutter, my mouth just inches from his, separated by Morgan's tiny head.

He blinks several times. The depth to his eyes go on forever. It engulfs me. I can barely breathe.

"I know." He wets his lips while his gaze drops a mere inch, settling on my mouth.

I step back with such a jerk, my feet stumble to keep me upright. Nate can't look at my mouth. It's not his to look at like that.

"You okay?" A smile curls his lips.

I misread that. He wasn't looking at my mouth. He wasn't thinking of kissing me. Gah! I'm an idiot. "Yeah. I'm good. I'll uh … call you." My hand comes up in a nervous wave. Who waves to someone standing two feet in front of them?

"Okay." His eyes narrow but his grin remains.

GRIFFIN LOOKS UP from his motorcycle, giving it a final wipe down. The chrome shines like it's brand new. But nothing shines quite like his smile.

"You should be home packing." He flips the rag over his shoulder and gives me his sexy once-over.

"About that …"

"Yes?" He prowls toward me, backing me into his workbench.

The look in his eyes says *take off your clothes*. I've seen it many times. I usually like that look. But the garage door is open, and he's right, I should be home packing. Maybe I'm off today. I misread Nate's look, perhaps I'm misreading Griffin's.

Taking off my clothes might be the right idea. Soften him

up with sex. He used it to make me agreeable this morning; maybe I can work my own manipulative magic.

"Shut the garage door." I give him my sexiest expression while my right hand teases his denim just below the button to his jeans.

He peaks a single brow then glances down at my hand. "You hungry, Swayz?"

I bite my bottom lip and nod.

"You want me to shut the garage door?" His eyes pull into a slight squint.

I nod, rubbing him more.

"Are you going to get on your knees for me?"

I nod, tugging on the button to his jeans.

"Right here?"

"Uh-huh."

Griffin steps back, fastening the button I just undid. "Spill."

"Spill?"

"You have never seduced me in my garage ... in the daylight. We're leaving for a week where I'll spend every night buried inside of you. Clean clothes wait for you to pack them. Your mom's expecting you to stop by her house to say goodbye before you go to bed tonight. I'm not questioning you craving my cock." He smirks. "I'm just calling you out. This isn't how you go about it."

"Maybe it is." I make a last ditch effort to make my lion purr before dropping the news. Stepping toward him, I reach for his jeans again.

With a headshake, he steps back, denying me. "You like to tease, but you're not the girl who does *this* without me telling you to do it. Control is not your thing. So just cut the fake seduction crap and tell me."

I blow out a long breath and step back to lean against the workbench. "Fine. But let me finish before you lose your shit."

His posture stiffens.

Great.

"Nate didn't realize we had this trip. I told Rachael, but she must have forgotten to tell him, assuming she would still be here to cover in my absence. His parents leave for vacation Monday and his mom's not in the best health anyway. And classes start Monday for Nate. He's the professor, he can't miss the first week of school. He has no one else."

"Swayze—"

"Let me finish." I'm breathless. Anticipating his reaction has my heart in an arrhythmia. "I told him earlier this week, I couldn't stay. He knows it's not my problem to solve. I'm not going to lose my job if I go with you. But ..." Dang! I'm sweating.

Griffin plants his hands on his hips and leans toward me with a scowl that could freeze the sun. "But what?"

"He's desperate. Today he offered me a five grand bonus if I stay home to watch Morgan." I hold up a flat hand. "I didn't say yes."

"So you said no?"

"I said I needed to talk to you first."

"Well, then let's talk."

I wring my hands together, chewing on the inside of my cheek. "If you want me to go—"

He barks out a laugh. "I invited you. That means I want you to go. But here we are *talking* about you not going, so the real question is do you want to go?"

"You know I do."

"Then what's there to talk about?"

"Did you hear me say he offered me five thousand dollars to stay?"

Griffin rubs his hand over his face, keeping the other one planted on his hip. "So I need to come in with a better offer for you to go?"

"No! Jeez …" My fingers thread through my hair, tugging at it while I take a deep breath. "It's a lot of money. We could buy some new furniture for your—*our* place. We could take another trip. Go to Hawaii or something."

"I can't believe this has come down to money." He looks up at the ceiling, shaking his head.

"It's not just the money. Nate has no one else. And Morgan's running a temperature. And—"

"Just stay." Griffin turns and continues polishing his bike.

"If you want me to go—"

"For the love of God, woman!" He wads up the rag and tosses it aside. "What do you want from me?"

I flinch. "If I stay, will you be mad?"

He huffs out a sigh. "I'll be bummed."

"Is that mad?"

"Don't do this shit to me, Swayz."

"I don't want to lose you over this."

"It's not an ultimatum. In fact, you're uninvited. There. Happy? Now you don't have to make the choice."

"I'm uninvited?"

"Yes." He stalks toward the house.

"So if I decide to go, you're no longer going to take me?"

"That's correct."

"You can't be serious." I catch the screen door before it shuts behind him.

"Dead serious." Griffin grabs a bottle of green juice out of the fridge and tosses the cap in the garbage can.

Watching Morgan gives me a sense of maturity. When I'm with her I feel ten years older. I become who I need to be for her, like I sucked it up and channeled the mature Swayze to give Nate support last night at the pediatrician's office. But right now, I don't feel a day over my actual age. The urge to stomp my feet and argue just for the sake of arguing is almost too strong to deny.

"Speak. Don't just stand there digging your nails into your palms." Griffin taunts me with his aloof but arrogant attitude.

I relax my hands. "I know it's unfair and immature, but I want you to want me to stay. I wish you knew Nate and Morgan like I do. If you did, I think you would see how much they need me right now. You're a compassionate guy."

"Well, I don't know them. But I do want you to stay. Lord knows you'd be a fucked-up case of doom and gloom the whole trip worrying about them."

"I don't want you to be mad at me."

He chugs the rest of the juice and tosses the bottle in the recycling bin. "Well..." he chuckles "...that's just too damn bad. I'm human. You can't expect me to act like I'm not just because you think I'm a 'compassionate guy.' I'm not going to give you my blessing to stay home."

I nod. There's nothing more to say. He's right. I'm asking too much. "I should get home."

Griffin stares at me with no response.

"Unless you want me to stay tonight ... but if you're mad, then maybe you don't want me to stay."

"Shit..." he shakes his head "...you sound so fucking insecure right now."

The hair on the back of my neck bristles. "Don't be such a jerk. If I sound insecure it's because I love you. And loving someone the way I love you is kind of scary, and scared people can sound insecure because nothing makes you feel more vulnerable than putting your heart on the line."

He studies me, every piece of my heart stripped raw, bared to him in a bed of insecurities. I've never pretended to be something I'm not with Griffin. It's all of me or nothing at all. We both know it without needing to say the words.

Griffin steps closer. His hand slides behind my head. "I love you for staying. I hate you for not going. But your heart isn't on the line. Your heart's just … mine. And I take care of what's mine."

Chocolate. Wine. Tampons. Chips.

I could have been anywhere the day I met my grocery store guy. Ten minutes later. Five minutes earlier. A different line. A million other tweaks of fate could have changed the course of my life.

Fate.

God.

A higher power.

Or maybe just damn good luck.

After calling Nate to let him know I'm not going, I stay the night with Griffin. If I'm going to move in with him, I can't run away every time we have an argument.

"I'm leaving, baby." He kisses me on the head.

My eyes fight the need for more sleep. It's four in the morning.

"Go back to sleep. I'll call you when we stop for breakfast in a few hours."

"No." I grab his hand. "I want to see you off."

"Everyone's waiting outside for me."

"I'm up." My head feels like a bowling ball atop my shoulders as I stand.

Griffin grabs one of his sweatshirts and shoves it over my head, leaving the hoodie covering my matted hair. My arms swim in the long sleeves, but it covers my panties enough to keep his friends from seeing more than they should.

"I'm sure your neighbors love the four a.m. rumble of six Harley engines revving up."

Griffin chuckles. "I'm sure." He takes my hand as we step outside.

"Swayze …" One of the guys whistles.

I give him the middle finger and a small smile.

"Feisty." He winks and blows me a kiss.

"Shut it, Frank." Griffin glares at his long-haired friend with a creepy smirk.

"Brave girl." Meg, his boss's new girlfriend, shakes her head from the back of Jett's bike. "No way in hell I'd let Jett go without me. Too many skanks ready to jump anything that moves. And your boy Griffin will draw a lot of attention. Lots of willing bodies ready to keep him warm at night. Lots of booze. Lots of—"

"Meg, no disrespect, but shut the fuck up." Griffin slides on his gloves and pulls me into his chest. "Stop, Swayz."

I think I might vomit. This is a bad idea. I should go too. "I lied." I stare at his chest because I can't keep my composure looking into his eyes. "If you cheat on me, I won't cut your dick off. I'll hate you forever. I don't want to hate you forever."

He tips my chin up.

Don't cry.

"I'm not cheating on you."

"But you're mad that I'm not going. And there will be lots of alcohol. And women with big boobs, and they're going to want you. Look at you ... of course they're going to do everything they can do to get into your—"

He silences me with a deep kiss, framing my face with his hands, pulling me to him so that I have to stand on my tippy toes, bracing myself with his arms. God ... if he kisses another woman like he's kissing me, I'll die. My heart will self-combust into nothing but ash.

His buddies whistle and hoot like the idiots they are.

"I can't breathe," I whisper past the lump in my throat. It's not just the women. It's the long trip on a motorcycle. Nate was right. Griffin is at the mercy of every other vehicle on the road. Stupid people texting, driving under the influence, sleep-deprived truckers, and rain-slick roads.

"I'll call you every night as long as I have a signal."

I nod slowly, blinking away my fears.

"And if I don't call, it means I don't have a good connection. That's all it means. Nothing more. Okay?"

"I love you." My voice dies on the last syllable.

"Love you too." He gives me one last kiss and mounts his bike.

Without me.

I think of Morgan and Nate, but it doesn't help. There's too much fear strangling my heart. Maybe later my altruism will ease my worry, but right now, I hurt all over.

Engines rumble. Lights beam. My world rolls onto the street, shifts gears, and takes off with a final wave.

CHAPTER TWENTY-TWO

G RIFFIN CALLS ME three times. It's a long day of riding. They get caught in rain an hour before stopping for dinner. I still question if I made the right decision, but I'm not sorry I missed the downpour.

Morgan's fever broke late this morning. She's still not quite her jovial self, but at least she's eating. Nate should be home soon with dinner. I keep glancing at my overnight bag on the floor. He leaves for his conference early in the morning, so I'm spending the next two nights here. It's going to feel weird.

I pull the stolen photo out of my pocket. It's an odd need I have to carry it around with me. I can't stop staring at him. It's the Nate I didn't know then and I don't know now. There's this line where it all comes to a stop. Years of blank space haunt me. Hell … everything about this haunts me.

The door chimes when he opens it. I took him up on his offer to use the chime because I don't like people sneaking up on me. It might be because I'm snooping around, but it's also this stolen photo. I shove it back into my pocket.

"Hi." He sets a pizza box on the counter and a paper grocery bag.

"Hey." I slide my hand in my pocket to make sure I didn't bend the photo in my rush to hide it.

"Swing time." He smiles at Morgan in her swing.

"Yes. She just ate."

"I picked up some groceries so you have food to eat while I'm gone. I'll leave cash as well in case you decide to order something to be delivered."

"Thanks. But you don't need to leave cash. If I weren't here, I'd still have to buy food to eat."

He washes his hands, giving me a boyish grin. "True. But you're doing me a huge favor. I can't thank you enough."

"It's fine." I shrug.

Nate's smile fades. "Are you having second thoughts about staying?"

Easing onto the barstool, I flip open the pizza box. It's plain cheese. "Griffin's boss's girlfriend made this comment ..." I sigh, still seeing the you-stupid-girl look on her face.

Nate hands me a plate.

I slide a piece of pizza onto it. "She thinks I'm crazy for letting him go without me. Apparently there are lots of girls there. Drinking. Crazy stuff that I don't like to think about."

"You don't trust him?" He takes a bite as he sits next to me.

"Trust." I laugh. "It's always about trust. When I talked to him about staying here, he admitted he was mad. Then he proceeded to tell me that it wasn't fair to expect him to not be mad, after all, he's *human*."

"That's fair."

Shifting my body toward him, I roll my eyes. "It is fair. He is human. *That's* what makes this trust thing so hard. I'm sure, when I'm in his arms, he can't imagine cheating on me. But what if he has a few drinks and thinks about me not being there. Resentment builds, judgment blurs, and some woman wearing nothing but star pasties hops on his lap. What's he supposed to do? After all ... he's only human."

Nate chews his pizza, but the contemplative draw of his brow says he's chewing on the words I just said. This isn't helping.

"You think I'm right, don't you?"

Wiping his mouth, he shakes his head. "I didn't say that."

"But you're thinking it."

"Well, there you go, trying and failing to read my mind."

I level him with a glare.

"Fine." He takes another bite and chews it for a few seconds. "I was thinking that I don't know your boyfriend well enough to make any sort of judgment. However, based on what I know about you, I find it hard to believe any man would cheat on you. But …"

"But?"

He shrugs. "We are human. Claiming to be infallible is risky. A professor I had in college told her students that certainty leads to nowhere except one's demise. Sparingly use the words promise, guarantee, always, and never." Nate chuckles. "That philosophy makes the writing of wedding vows a little tricky. 'I vow to try to be faithful. I shall do my best to love you in sickness and health for as long as I can.'"

I grin, but I'm not sure why. "You suck at easing my mind."

"Sorry."

"Are you really?"

He covers his mouth with his napkin and nods. "I *promise*." The napkin doesn't hide his smirk.

"You're terrible." I punch him on the arm.

His body shakes with laughter.

"You owe me. Take my mind off how human my boyfriend is. Tell me a story … more Daisy."

"More Daisy, huh?" Nate leans back. A soft smile steals his mouth as his gaze meets mine. "I can do that."

Nathaniel Hunt Age 15

"WHAT DO YOU think?" I puffed out my chest, chin up.

Daisy circled the Camaro in the driveway, eyes shifting between me and the car my uncle left me when he died. I had three weeks until I turned sixteen.

"Well ... it's free." Her lower lip curled around her top lip, a goofy look that she gave me when she tried to be honest without telling the whole truth.

"It could use a little work." I shrugged.

"A little." She circled it a second time, arms crossed over her chest.

"I'll take you for a ride."

"You don't have your license yet."

"Just around the block. My dad won't be home for hours." I tugged open the passenger's side door.

She flinched, sticking her fingers in her ears. "Might need to spray something on the hinges."

"Stop being such a prissy cat. Get in."

"A prissy cat?" She laughed. "I'm not being prissy. But I think I should call home first and ask my mom when I had my last tetanus shot."

"It's just a little rust."

She eased into the bucket seat. "I think you don't know the meaning of 'little.'"

I shut the door and hopped in behind the wheel—a wheel with peeling black tape all over it, but nevertheless, my wheel.

"It smells like a forest fire in here." Her nose wrinkled.

I ignored her complaining. I had a car. That's all that mattered. My uncle was a chain-smoker and there were a half dozen pine-scented air fresheners hanging from the rearview mirror, but she didn't need to make a big deal of it.

We drove around the block and pulled back into the driveway. "She's not a bad ride." I stretched my arm out behind Daisy's headrest.

"You're crazy." She shook her head, but no amount of prissiness could hide her grin.

"Do you want to make out in the back seat before my dad gets home?"

"No."

"No? Really? Hmm ... so unlike you." My fingers drummed on the steering wheel.

"Yes, so unlike me. I'm *always* wanting to make out in the back of junkyard cars."

"Shh ... don't be offensive to Georgia when you're in her."

She giggled. "Georgia? Please tell me you did not name your car."

"My uncle did. He bought her in Georgia and drove her to Wisconsin with his first wife, Savannah."

"No." Daisy shook her head a half dozen times. "I'm not buying that story. Your uncle did not buy this car in Georgia and his first wife was not named Savannah. You're making this up as you go. It's a terrible story. *You* are a terrible storyteller."

"Swear to God."

"Your dad would not approve of you swearing to God. And when he gets home, I'm going to ask him about Savannah, Georgia."

"Go ahead."

"Whatever." She crossed her arms over her chest and stared ahead at our one-car detached garaged. "Last one in the back seat has to be on bottom."

It took me two seconds to process what she meant, by the time I did, she had already shimmied her way between the front seats. I took the bottom as we made out for the next fifteen minutes, exploring each other and nudging new boundaries.

After we righted our disheveled clothes and climbed out of a backseat that was not made for making out, we grabbed sodas and sat on the back porch in old blue lawn chairs.

"I left my jacket in the tree house last week, so I rode my bike over there yesterday afternoon to get it."

I frowned. "I thought we agreed never to go alone."

"I was careful. I didn't even get near the lake, and I made my way up and down the ladder slooowly."

"You should have at least told me you were going."

She kicked my leg. "Are you going to let me finish my story?"

"Yeah, yeah, go ahead."

"Anyway … on my way out of the gate a car pulled in the driveway—an old silver station wagon with a rattling motor and chipped gray paint with almost as much rust on it as Georgia."

I bared my teeth, ready to snarl at her for poking fun of my car.

"Scared the living daylights out of me at first. The guy got out and he had this creepy child-molester look."

"I don't know if child molesters have an actual look."

"I think they do. Chubby belly. Smelly. Clothes that have not been washed for weeks. You know … when jeans get that oily sheen to them? Bad dandruff. Crooked teeth with really red gums. And a mustache that's thin and cheesy." She shivered. "Creeps me out."

"Again … none of that means he's a child molester, but your parents would ground you for life if they knew you were there at all, but definitely if they knew you went there alone. Did you get out of there as fast as possible? I hope so."

"Not exactly."

"Morgan." If I called her Morgan then the situation was serious.

"I kept a good distance. It was still light outside. And I didn't get off my bike. But he asked me what I was doing there. Before I could answer, he smiled and said, 'Ah, let me guess … the tree house.' I nodded. It's all I could do. Stranger danger and all that. But then he started telling me about him and his dad building the tree house together. I'm not saying he's not still creepy, but—"

"No. Don't say 'but' anything. You need to stay away. We're done. Tell everyone else too. We've been trespassing."

"I told him." Her nose wrinkled. "He wasn't mad at all. He thought it was cool that someone was getting some good out of the tree house and the lake. His mom died a few years ago and his dad recently died of a heart attack. He's staying at the house for a while to figure out what to do with their stuff. Then he's going to sell the place, but he said we can still play in the woods or swim in the lake until it sells."

"No."

"Nate, don't be such a party pooper."

"Promise me you won't go back there."

"Nate—"

"Just promise me."

"Ugh! Fine. I'm going home. I have to clean my room or else I can't spend the night at Danielle's house this weekend."

"Slumber party, huh? A long night of talking about boys?"

"Maybe." She stood, tossing her ponytail over her shoulder.

"What do you say about me?" I held open the back door for her, and we set our empty cans on the counter.

"I don't talk about you. We only talk about real boy-friends." Dang, she loved to put me in my place.

"That's fair. When I hang out with my friends we only talk about girls with big tits."

She whipped around, clutching my shirt. "What's that supposed to mean?"

"I don't know. What do you think it means?"

"I think you're saying I have small tits."

"If the training bra fits ..."

"Take it back."

"No way." I laughed as she attempted to shake me, but I was twice her size. She wasn't going to budge me. "Oh, Daisy, Daisy, Daisy ..." I hugged her to me as she tried and failed to wriggle out of my hold. "I hope you love me this much in another five years."

"Let go of me, you big jerk! I'm not going to love you in another five seconds." She punched my gut until I released her. "You're on your own for food. I'm done feeling sorry for you."

My smile didn't waver, but that truth sucked the air from my lungs. She deserved a boyfriend who could buy her things. Real boyfriends didn't need handouts.

"You should be done feeling sorry for me. It's a waste of your time. Especially when your room is a mess."

"You know what I mean."

I turned, grabbing some trash from the counter and tossing

it in the garbage.

"Yeah, I know. Better get going."

"Are you mad?" She grabbed my arm.

I tugged it away. "I'm fine."

"You're not fine. Just look at me." She grabbed my arm with both hands.

I stilled, looking at the floor.

"Don't be mad. I didn't mean it."

"I'm not mad. But ..." I looked at her. "You're probably right. You should get a real boyfriend."

"Are you breaking up with me?"

I didn't know if I was breaking up with her. My young age prevented me from understanding the dangerous part of my brain called the ego. That ego flipped some switch. We went from making out in the back of Georgia to joking about tits to the sobering thought that Morgan deserved someone better than me.

"We can be friends."

Her head jerked back. "Friends. I see." She nodded. "So we'll hang out, but I can find another boyfriend and you'll find a new girlfriend?"

I shrugged. "Sure." I wasn't going to get another girlfriend until I had a job, until I could not seem so needy, until I could take a girl to a movie that wasn't at the dollar cinema.

"Wow ..." She backed away. "So I guess I'll see you around."

"I guess so." I was such an idiot, a stubborn, hardheaded idiot on the verge of losing the best thing ever.

She left. I strapped on my Walkman and went for a run. I lost the girl.

SWAYZE DOESN'T BLINK. I don't know if she realizes my story is over. How is it possible for her to not remember Daisy? My childhood revolved around the sassy little blonde. If she's channeling my thoughts from over twenty years ago, then she has to see that they were all about Daisy.

"I remember the car." Her eyes shift to meet mine.

"I wish you remembered us."

"Us?" Her voice trembles and all color leaves her face.

I let it hang in the air for a few moments. She saw the book on reincarnation in my nightstand drawer. I replayed that feed over and over, but the camera was at her back. I couldn't see her face. Every time I think of mentioning it to her, I lose my nerve. She has to know that I suspect she's Daisy. But I won't bring it up. I want her to make the connection. I *need* her to be curious and open to the possibility. But I won't force it.

"Daisy and me." I save her from the awkwardness.

She blows out a slow breath and smiles. "Me too. So you broke up."

I nod.

"And you're just going to leave me hanging? Did you get back together?"

"I need to pack for my trip. My flight is at six a.m. There are two guest rooms. Take whichever one you'd like. Towels are in the bathroom."

"Want me to put Morgan to bed?"

I stand. "Nope. I want to do it."

Her lips press together, failing to hide her grin.

"What?"

"Nothing." She shakes her head.

"Tell me." My arms cross over my chest. This girl rattles my curiosity.

"Just thinking about the Don't Hold the Baby rule you had when I started working for you. Now you hold her, cuddle her, and *want* to put her to bed even when you have stuff to do. You've come into your own and it's…" she shrugs "…nice."

I nod. From any other twenty-one-year-old girl, that would feel like a condescending compliment. Swayze's known me longer than she realizes, so it means the whole damn world to me that she thinks I'm doing okay at what is unequivocally the biggest challenge of my life.

"Thank you. It was a rough start. I read too many books on parenting, setting schedules, and self-soothing. I think I forgot to use my intuition. This bossy nanny helped me see the error of my ways."

"I'm surprised you didn't fire her."

"She has a lot of dirt on me."

Swayze's smile grows. "Do you think they'll take away your PhD if I tell them you cheated on that Spanish test?"

"Not likely." I chuckle. "Especially when they realize you weren't alive when that happened."

Her lips twist to the side as her gaze shifts to Morgan. "Hmm … that would be hard to explain, especially when I can't explain it to myself."

"I have a theory."

She fidgets with the hem of her shirt while a nervous laugh comes out as a soft cough. "I'm sure there are lots of theories, but none of them make perfect sense. I'm not sure we'll ever know. But … I'd better let you get Morgan to bed so you can pack for your trip."

"Do you want to hear my theory?" Dr. Albright's warnings

go unheeded in my head as my need to connect with the girl I knew grows stronger every day.

Swayze picks up her overnight bag, leaving her back to me. "I don't think I do."

"Why?"

"Just a feeling," she says, looking down at her feet.

"Are you scared?"

"Every day."

I hold in the words I'm dying to say as she fades into the shadows of the hallway, taking a right at the guest bedroom.

CHAPTER TWENTY-THREE

I'M A HOSTAGE in Nate's guest bedroom. He wants to talk about reincarnation. I'm not ready to shatter his hopes of reconnecting with his childhood friend. I know nothing of her except what he's told me. She doesn't exist in my head the way he does. If we make the journey back to another life, surely we remember ourselves more than anyone else from our previous life. What happens when he realizes I'm not her? Will the stories end? Will I become nothing more than an imposter in his already stressful life?

I slip on a pair of pajama pants and a camisole top, grab my phone, and plunk down on the bed to call Griffin.

"Hey, I was just getting ready to call you."

"Likely story." I grin.

"True story. We arrived about an hour ago. It's insane."

"Apparently. I can barely hear you." I cringe. There's no need for me to yell and wake Morgan. I'm not the one trying to speak over a party of people mixed with revving motorcycles.

"Sorry ..." His voice muffles a bit. "Better?"

"Yeah."

"I stepped into the bathroom. Well ... porta potty."

"Ew ..."

"Yes. It smells fucking awesome in here."

"Then I won't keep you. I just wanted to say goodnight. I'm staying at the professor's place tonight because he leaves so early in the morning."

"In your own room, I hope."

I laugh. "I should be offended that you feel the need for confirmation, but I want you thinking about me while you're gone—while women parade their naked bodies around you, while the booze flows a little too much."

"Is that a yes that you're sleeping in your own room?"

"Really, Griff? Do you really think I'm spooning with the professor tonight?"

"I'm not worried about *the professor*. He's old, Swayz. Probably needs a pill to get it up. But I'd be lying if I said the thought of you spending the night with *Nate* doesn't give me a few moments pause. I told you ... he's been thinking about your mouth around his dick ever since you sent him *my* text."

"He's thinking about someone, but it's not me."

"What's that supposed to mean?"

"I'll tell you when you get home."

"Dude! You got the shits?" A man's voice fills the background.

"Fuck off!" Griffin grumbles.

"Have fun." I giggle, but my grin falls sober. "But not too much fun."

"I'll do my best. I'd better go."

"Griff?"

"Yeah?"

"Are we good?" Insecurities suck. But they make you fight to keep the important things in life. They're a solemn reminder that emotions are not a choice; they're a toxic mix of chemicals running amuck in our bodies, playing roulette with our relationships.

"We're good. I love you."

"I love you too."

He disconnects the call, but I keep the phone to my ear. I want to hug it—hug him. When I'm convinced he's no longer on the phone, my attention shifts to the stolen picture. It's bowed and curling at the edges. I shouldn't carry it around in my pocket, but I have this sane and well-thought-out idea that twenty-something Nate in my pocket might tell me all of his stories. That's how it works.

Photo Nate talks.

My ass listens.

An undiscovered way of ass-to-brain communication relays the information to my mind.

I chuckle. Stranded on an island by myself? No problem. I'm one hundred percent self-entertained.

Had I found this photo as a teenager, I would have blown it up and pinned it to the ceiling of my room. I would have dreamed about this sexy surfer-looking guy and his contemplative look. I would have convinced my zit-faced, pigeon-toed self that he was thinking of me.

"What is wrong with you?" I toss the photo on the bed beside me and rub a hand over my face.

In need of a glass of water, I slide the photo under the pillow and slip out into the hallway. My feet root to the floor as the sight of Nate rocking Morgan to sleep replaces my thirst. One hand cradles her to his body while the other hand holds *Goodnight Moon*.

I'm in love.

It's hard to explain, even to myself. Jenna's death has brought me here. I'm certain fate played a role. I don't know what drives fate. And I certainly don't know what I am to learn from this. But I am in love with the story of Nathaniel Hunt.

It's so tragic, until moments like this that could not be more beautiful.

I can't stop thinking of *this*.

It's a song that loops in my head.

It's a movie I want to watch until I have every scene—every line—memorized.

It's my favorite book where all the words have been read and reread in search of something new, something more.

However, this isn't a fangirl moment over a book, a song, a movie … the love I have for whatever *this* is goes so much deeper. I'm connected to it in a way that's the same yet different than my love for Griffin. This love belongs to me too. I'm not merely an outsider looking in—admiring and wishing it were my life.

This is big.

I know it. I *feel* it. And I can't let go.

Nate sets the book aside. I move beyond the doorway so he can't see me.

"I love you, my sweet baby girl."

I smile, my back flush to the wall as I crane my neck just enough to peek around at him easing her into her crib. His fingertips feather her cheek.

"I need you to be the one to stay," he whispers.

Stay?

"I need you to live a long life, many years beyond mine."

"Nate …" I whisper so softly that only the gods can hear me. Blinking away this sudden rush of emotion, I pad to the kitchen for my water.

"She's asleep."

I nod, keeping my gaze focused out the window on the halos of solar lights lining the front walkway.

He opens the freezer then shuts the door. I turn toward his narrowed eyes, halting mid step.

"I think you took something that belonged to me."

The photo.

My back was to the camera. Maybe there's more than one camera in his bedroom.

"I … I just wanted to look at it."

Nate steps closer, sending my head back to keep eye contact with him. "Just look at it?" His head cocks to the side.

I nod, swallowing my tongue and some unexpected fear. Why did I take it? Such a stupid move.

"You didn't want to taste it?"

"Um …" Please don't let this be about the text. I don't want Griffin to be right.

No blowjobs for Nate—not even a taste.

No spooning.

No pills to get his cock ready for action.

Nope. Not happening.

"What if I give it back and we just forget I ever took it. It was a curiosity thing is all. It's eye-catching. My mom is a photographer. I … I don't know. But—"

"Eye-catching?" He laughs. "Are we talking about the same thing? Because I'm confused as to how you plan to give me back the last ice cream sandwich."

This is not about his cock. Thank god!

"It will be replaced with a new box by the time you arrive home Sunday night."

"So you did eat it?"

"I did."

"After you admired its beauty?"

I clear my throat and lift my chin. "The silver packaging

with blue lettering is a great design. I notice things like that." Someone please shoot me now and just put me out of my misery.

"Did you take a picture of it? Or did you save the wrapper for your mom to take a picture of it?"

"No. I'll tell her the brand. That's what she does. I told you this, right? She's a product photographer?"

Nate nods slowly. "You said she hasn't picked up her camera since your father died. Are ice cream sandwiches wrapped in silver with blue lettering going to inspire her to get back in the game?"

"Ya never know."

He twists his lips, failing to completely disguise his amusement. "Well, let me know. I'm going to be on pins and needles waiting to see if my impulse buy inspired something so miraculous. In the meantime…" he jerks his head toward the hallway "…why don't you help me pick out a tie for my trip."

"You mean tie it before you pack it."

"Correct."

We stroll down the hallway. He shoots me a grin over his shoulder. I divert my eyes to the floor.

Ice cream sandwich. Gah!

"Blue or red?" He holds up the ties.

"Red. The blue one has something on it."

He flips his wrist and frowns at the dark smudge. "Well damn. I wonder what that is. I haven't wore this tie in a long time."

"Probably food. Don't you tuck it into your shirt or flip it over your shoulder when you eat? That's what my dad did."

"No." He tosses the soiled tie on the floor and snakes the red one around his neck, chin tipped up while he looks down at me.

"You're serious? I need to tie it for you?"

"I think five grand should include a Windsor knot."

Taking a step closer, I grab the ends to his tie and tug them. Nate grins. It's so familiar. If I could freeze time, I would press pause on this exact moment, letting my eyes see beyond the familiar to the absolute, letting the fingers of my mind grasp something concrete. Every day it feels like I'm chasing a butterfly. Sometimes I think I could follow it over a cliff and not feel the loss of earth beneath my feet.

Professor Nathaniel Hunt shares space in my reality. Nate lives behind closed eyes, in the recesses of my memory— haunting my conscience, unraveling my existence.

"It probably should." I twist my lips, trying to remember what I saw on the how-to video. "But I didn't tie a Windsor knot, just a simple knot. Is the Windsor knot a requirement for you this weekend?"

He chuckles. "No."

My gaze remains fixed on the red silk between my fingers, but I sense his eyes on me. The only thing more disturbing than the familiarity I feel toward him is the way he looks at me like he knows all of my secrets—even the ones I don't know.

"I feel like an enabler. You know the saying about giving a man a fish versus teaching him to fish?"

"You know that saying about the more you know, the more that's expected of you?"

I laugh, making a quick glance up at his cocky grin. He's so handsome, especially when his lip quivers a bit as he attempts to control his amusement with me.

"I ate the ice cream sandwich," I say with a meaning be- hind my words that's greater than the actual words.

"Yes," he says, drawing out that one word into something greater as well.

My focus returns to the tie. "I took something else too."

"I know."

"You do?" I whisper, adjusting the knot, feeling the heat of his chest beneath my fingertips.

"Yes."

"How?"

"Because there's nothing special about those silver and blue wrappers."

I'm scared to look at him. I'm scared to not look at him.

"I stole a photo of you." I inch my gaze up to meet his.

He studies me with the exact look he has in the photo.

Spellbound gaze.

Parted lips.

Vulnerable.

After a few moments, he nods slowly. "Okay."

Okay? That's not the right answer. I confessed to stealing something. What photo? Why? Those are the right responses. Not "okay."

"Don't you want to know why?"

He shakes his head, a soft surrender in his expression.

"Don't you want to know which photo?"

He shakes his head.

"Why?" I whisper.

"Because Morgan—Daisy—used to say, 'If I'm snoopy then you're Charlie Brown.'"

"I don't—" As I release his tie, his hands cuff my wrists.

"You said that to me."

"Professor—"

"No. Not Professor. Nate."

"What are you doing?" I close my eyes and bite my lips together. Whatever this is … it's wrecking me from the inside out. I want to pull away, but I can't because Nate's touch comforts me in a way that it shouldn't.

"Do you feel it?"

"No." I force myself to pull away, turning my back to him. "I have a boyfriend."

"Swayze, that's not what this is and you know it."

My lungs draw in a shaky breath. I don't know what this is, but it scares the ever living hell out of me. And it hurts. The unexplainable should be miraculous and exhilarating—giving birth to promise and something greater than ever imagined. But *this*, whatever the hell *this* is, feels like it's ripping me apart. Maybe Griffin's right; I should walk away. But the memories will follow me.

"Yeah, well … I don't know what this is." I stab my fingers through my hair, taking a slow breath that fails to soothe my nerves. "I don't know why I took a picture of you. And I don't know why I can't stop staring at it." I turn. "And you don't care that I stole something from you. You don't care that your wife died months ago and now there's this stranger in your house, watching your child, rummaging through your stuff."

Creases line his forehead as his gaze slides to the floor between us. "For the record … I care a whole goddamn lot that my wife died."

"Nate, I didn't mean—"

His head snaps side to side, jaw clenched. "And I went through the proper process and background checks to hire you. I didn't pick you up off the street to watch my daughter." He brings his attention back to me. "Take whatever you need to take to figure this out."

A stifled laugh breaks from my chest. "Me? What happened to *us* figuring this out? That day in the garage when I told you about the Spanish test you said we would figure it out."

Nothing.

All he offers is a long look interrupted by the occasional blink.

"You think you have it figured out."

"Yes," he whispers.

I laugh. "Well, you're wrong. So keep figuring."

"I haven't told you what I think. How can you know I'm wrong?"

No. I'm not acknowledging this. The words will not come from my mouth. "Goodnight."

"Do you know how many times a day I think of the irony of your name being Swayze?"

Fuck him for going there. He's going to ruin this.

"Yeah? Too bad my parents didn't give as much thought to my name before they branded me with it."

"Her eyes were brown."

Keeping my back to him, I cover my face and shake my head.

"She was feisty and completely incorrigible. You have a meeker personality. That's what makes you so good with Morgan. But with me ... I see the spirited girl. You're ballsy with me. I guess some things never change."

"I'm not her," I whisper to myself. She doesn't exist in my head outside of the stories he tells me. I'm an extension of his mind. I see a part of his past. My ballsiness with him is me, not Daisy. He doesn't know me. I'm not meek.

"Can you look at me?"

"Goodnight."

"Ask me something about her. Anything."

I'm not her. I'm not her.

"Did you have sex with her?"

"No. Ask me another question."

He's baiting me. I need to walk away, but I can't. This story of their childhood together has become my addiction.

"Do you think she loved you as much as you loved her?"

"Yes. Another one."

"Did you love her more than you loved Jenna?"

"No. Another one."

"So you loved Jenna more?"

"No. Another one," he demands with a bite of anger to his tone.

If my questions anger him, why keep insisting I ask more?

"You loved a fifteen-year-old girl as much as you loved the woman you married? The woman who's the mother of your child? That's insane. You were fifteen."

"We don't love with our brains, we love with our hearts. We love on instinct. Love is undefinable and resides in all of us. There are no requirements to love someone. Daisy was my first love. Jenna was my last love. Morgan is my forever love."

I glance over my shoulder at him. "Did you make up with Daisy before she died?"

Emotion reddens his eyes as his Adam's apple bobs once. "Goodnight."

Do all the answers lie between his limit and mine? We may never know.

CHAPTER TWENTY-FOUR

"Swayze?"

I dream of Griffin getting in a motorcycle accident. I'm not sure it's a dream. It feels too real, the worst pain ever.

"Swayze?"

I stand next to his family as mourners file through the funeral home to give their condolences. The shiny metal casket is closed. People who die in motorcycle accidents don't have open casket funerals.

"Swayze?"

As I blot my eyes with the same handkerchief my mom held at my father's funeral, Nate appears, holding Morgan. She's wearing a dress. It's yellow like a Daisy, not black. I'm glad he didn't dress her in black. Babies shouldn't wear black. He holds her in one arm and pulls me in for a firm embrace with his other arm. My hand presses to his tie. It's gray. I wonder who tied it for him?

After he squeezes another round of tears out of me, he tells me how sorry he is, but that he'll be waiting whenever I'm ready. Ready for what? Then he leans in once more and whispers, "I love you, Daisy."

"Swayze?"

"What?" I startle and bolt to sitting, squinting against the light shining into the bedroom from the hallway.

It was a dream. I blink back the tears that sting my eyes.

Fucking hell, it felt real. I need to call Griffin.

"Um ..." Nate clears his throat then looks back over his shoulder toward the hallway, rubbing his neck. "I'm leaving and ..."

I start to adjust the spaghetti straps to my nightshirt and realize half my right boob is sticking out—half of my boob but *all* of my nipple. "Oh my god! You just saw my—"

"It's fine." He risks a quick glance before settling his gaze back onto my covered chest.

"It's fine? Are you referring to my boob or are you brushing it off as no big deal?"

Meek personality my ass.

Nate's eyes snap to mine. "Neither. Both." He shakes his head. "The light's off, I didn't see anything. I just wanted you to know I'm leaving so you know to listen for Morgan."

"Okay."

"Okay." He nods. "I'll see you tomorrow night. And ... I didn't see anything."

"You're a liar." I pull the sheet up to cover my chest just for safe measure.

"I'm not lying." He retreats to the door.

"I still don't believe you."

He chuckles. "Fine. When I get home tomorrow, I'll sketch what I saw ... which was your mouth open, snoring, one arm like a goal post by your head and the other draped over *your chest*. I don't know why you had your boob out."

I throw the pillow at the door, but miss him. "I didn't have it out. It just ..."

"Bye, Swayze." He grins and disappears around the corner.

Without giving a second thought to the time (4 a.m.), I call Griffin. I need to hear his voice.

"Yeah?" His groggy greeting wraps around me like a warm blanket. It's not sexy. It's not filled with excitement. I'm not sure he looked at the screen to see it's me.

But minutes ago my mind mourned him in the worst way. Stupid nightmares. He doesn't have to be awake, sexy, or excited. I just need him to *be*.

"Hey," I whisper past the lump in my throat, wiping away the tears running down my cheeks.

"Baby, is everything okay?"

"It is now."

"Swayz ... it's the middle of the night. Why are you awake?"

"The professor just left for the airport. I'm going to go back to sleep, but I needed to hear your voice. I ..." I sniffle.

"Baby, are you crying?"

"Bad dream. That's all." I wipe more tears. "Promise me you'll be careful."

"Did something happen to me in your bad dream?"

I nod, unable to speak past the pain. It felt so real.

"Swayz?"

"Y-you ... died." I hold back the sob that's dying to escape.

"I'm fine. Okay?"

Another nod that he can't see. "Go back to sleep. I just needed ..." I bite my quivering lower lip.

"I *need* you too," he says.

Yeah. That. Exactly that.

"I don't deserve my grocery store guy. But can that be our little secret?"

He chuckles. It's a sleepy rumble. "You were a mess that day in the grocery store. Everything came out of your mouth was a string of words tripping over themselves like dominoes. And you eye-fucked the hell out of me."

"What? Not true." My back straightens.

"Totally true. I felt thoroughly violated by the time I pulled out of the parking lot."

"Griffin Calloway, you're drunk or hungover. Where is this coming from? You've never said this to me before. Ever …"

More chuckles ensue. It makes my cheek miss his chest, my ear miss the thrumming of his heart. I love it when I'm sprawled out on his bare chest, our bodies tangled in sexed-up sheets while we talk about something that makes him laugh.

"It's true. I thought, 'Man, she's a fucking disaster—a mumbling mess of hormones who has stripped me ten times over with those eyes that I think are blue, but I don't know for sure because her gaze hasn't ventured any higher than my chest.'"

"Thanks, Griff. I'm starting to feel less brokenhearted over you dying in my dreams."

"But … are you ready for the good part?"

"Oh, wow! Is there really a good part to this?"

"The good part was dinner with my parents the night after we met. My mom asked about my day …"

I grin in spite of myself. That's where he gets it.

"I told her I met a girl. Couldn't stop thinking about her. It was just a feeling. *You* were this feeling inside of me that shook me to the core. It wasn't any one thing—your looks, your words, your voice, your demeanor—it was all of it … or none of it. I still don't know. I just felt like I'd arrived somehow. And I still feel it every fucking day."

Right here, on the other end of the phone, is my old soul of a grocery store guy. "Come home to me in one piece. Okay?"

"I'll try."

"If you don't, I'll die."

"That's tragic. Don't die, Swayz."

"Just … come home. I want to play house with you."

Griffin chuckles. "Play house, huh?"

"Yes. I'll cook. You clean. I'll do the laundry—"

"I'll do the laundry."

"That's what I meant. You'll do the laundry and clean. Well … let's be honest. You'll do most of the cooking as well."

"Sounds like what I've been doing. How do you fit into the equation?"

"I'll watch you work. Drool. Distract you with my body. Lick you up and down. Just … stuff like that."

He clears the frog from his throat. "This could work."

"I think so too."

"Go to sleep, Swayz. I have dirty dreams to have about you before the sun comes up."

"I love you. Don't die, or I'll kill you. Okay?"

"I'll see what I can do. Love you too."

He ends the call, and once again, I hold the phone to my ear just a bit longer, until I fall asleep. I want to dream of us, but I don't. Hours later I awake to a crying baby and a line of sweat along my brow. I dreamed of Nate, not Daisy's Nate or Morgan's daddy. I dreamed of the photo Nate.

Young.

Hot.

Sexy Nate in the photo that's still under the pillow.

I bolt to the nursery as if Morgan's life depends on it, but in reality, I'm running from the dream—the one where I was having sex with twenty-something Nate.

What. The. Fuck?

"Good morning, sweet baby." I hug her to me. "Are you

hungry? Or did you have a bad dream? Bad dreams are going around."

Dreadful dreams.

Inappropriate dreams.

"We should get you a dream catcher. Maybe we both need one." I change her diaper and mix up her bottle of formula.

Griffin is my world. A living fantasy. The winning lottery ticket. I need more scans of my brain. Something is wrong with me. I should never *ever* have sex dreams starring any other man than Griffin Calloway.

I didn't steal the photo to fantasize about Nate. I took it to feed my curiosity and maybe find a spark of recognition that could piece this craziness together.

My phone chimes as I settle in the recliner to give Morgan her bottle.

Professor: *Made it to the hotel. Give Morgan a good-morning kiss from me. Message me if you need anything. Try to keep it PG and professional. ;)*

"Oh for the love of …" I shake my head. He's all guy. I will forever be the nanny who sends blowjob texts by accident to her employer—and then has sex dreams about him.

Swayze: *My mom is coming to have dinner with me and Morgan. I have to be on my best behavior. So don't sweat it.*

Professor: *Don't forget to show her the silver wrapper with blue writing.*

Swayze: *If you weren't my employer, I would say something snarky.*

Professor: *I'm waiting in a mile-long line for coffee outside of the conference room. Humor me. What would you say if I weren't your employer?*

I grin. He's good at baiting me. I shouldn't take the bait. But …

> **Swayze:** *How's your tie? If anyone compliments you on it, don't forget to tell them your 21 yr. old nanny tied it for you.*
>
> **Professor:** *Low blow*
>
> **Swayze:** *Low blow would be the old man shoes you packed. Where did you get those? An orthotics store?*
>
> **Professor:** *Lies. All lies. My students think I'm the coolest professor on campus.*

I don't doubt it. Professor Hunt is the teacher all the girls want to screw. Good thing I'm not his student. I only fuck him in my dreams.

I cringe. My stupid brain won't let that go. He has a blow-job text. I have a sex dream. We're even, only he doesn't know it. And he never will.

> **Swayze:** *I remember what you looked like with zits. Not the coolest.*
>
> **Professor:** *Two. Three zits tops. Your memory is not the greatest.*
>
> **Swayze:** *Go be smart. I get to play with the world's cutest baby. She loves me. Be jealous.*
>
> **Professor:** *Incredibly envious of both of you. Have fun!*

"Both?"

Morgan kicks and tugs at the nipple, a grin sneaking up her face.

"Why is your daddy envious of you?" I tickle her feet. "Because you get to spend the day with me? That's crazy."

It is. Right? I wish I could control my mind, but I can't. It's skipping backwards to this morning's dream.

Stop thinking about that dream!

How did my mind go from Griffin dying to sex with twenty-something Nate? I force my thoughts into all things baby: dirty diapers, spit up, tummy time, stroller walks, naps. Over the next seven hours we do it all. With each passing hour, I become more attached to this little girl. I feel like her mom. It's not right. I'm not her mom. I never will be her mom. But I'm the mother figure raising her at the moment.

If Nate finds love again, that new person in their lives will not have rocked Morgan to sleep, comforted her during fevers, insisted that her dad hold her more, or made her giggle for the first time. Those are my moments.

I'm not in love with Nate, in spite of my dreams, but I'm in love with Morgan. She doesn't make me want to have a baby, she makes me want *her.*

"My mom's here!" I nuzzle Morgan's neck, eliciting giggles as I carry her to the door. "Oh … wow … what's this all about?" My jaw drops.

My mom smiles, so does Sherri, Chloe, Hayley, and Sophie.

"Surprise!" Sophie throws her arms up in the air.

"It's a huge surprise." I step back and gesture for them to come inside.

"A little birdie told us you could use lots of company…" Sherri wraps an arm around me for a side hug "…and lots of hugs."

"Gimme, gimme, gimme." My mom kisses me on the cheek then steals Morgan. "She's adorable."

Chloe, Hayley, and Sophie give me a group hug.

Griffin. He did this. I blink back my emotions. This makes me love him even more and miss him. God … I miss him so much already.

"I can't believe you're all here … on a Saturday night. Hayley, you're giving me a prime night." I loop my arm around hers and lead everyone to the great room. "I'm not worthy."

"Griff said he'd be forever indebted to us if we got with your mom and organized a girls' night. But…" she grins "…we wanted to anyway."

She pulls away from me as all of them huddle around my mom and Morgan.

"Are you guys here for me or Morgan? Be honest."

"Both." Hayley shrugs.

"Well, make sure you wash your hands before touching hers. The professor is a stickler on that."

"The professor?" Sherri glances over at me.

"Morgan's dad—my boss—is a professor of anatomy. His name is Nathaniel Hunt, but I like to call him Professor." And Nate because I know stuff about him, and I've had sex with him in my dreams.

Stop going there!

"How's he doing? He lost his wife didn't he?" Hayley asks as everyone lines up to wash their hands and play pass the baby.

"He's doing well, I think. It's different with a baby. He can't just move forward and focus on his work or think ahead to finding love again. He's not just a single guy; he's a single guy with a baby."

"And an awesome nanny." My mom winks at me while handing Morgan to Sherri.

"And that." I smirk.

"Whoa!" Hayley studies the pictures on the mantel. "Is this the professor?"

I laugh. "Yes."

"I hope my professors look like him."

Everyone except me gathers around the mantel.

"He's handsome," my mom says.

My mom. I can't believe the woman who has been unable to think or talk about anything or anyone else except my dad just called another man handsome.

"How old is he?" Sherri leans in closer to the picture.

"Thirty-six."

"If he shows interest in dating again, you should introduce him to Krista." Sherri gives a suggestive look to my mom.

I can't breathe as I wait for my mom to gasp or show some sign of being offended. She's not over my dad.

Mom bites the corner of her lip. Why is she biting her lip? What is going on here?

"Do you think I could pull off the cougar thing?"

What. The. Fuck?

They're drooling over Nate. My Nate. Internally I flinch. He's not actually my Nate, yet he sort of is. It's complicated. But it's wrong—so wrong—for them to suggest my mom and him should … what? Date?

I had sex with Nate this morning in my dreams. Yes, so wrong too, but there has to be a universal law against a mother and daughter having sexual thoughts about the same man.

Gross. No. Just … no.

"You don't look a day older than him. Of course you could pull it off."

My mom is beautiful, not just for a woman in her forties, for a woman of any age. I hope I look even half as good as her when I reach my forties. But … still no. No Nate for her.

"I don't think the professor will be ready to date anytime soon. He has a demanding job and a baby. Mom, I think you should look into online dating."

My shift of topic lures them from the mantel back to the sofa and chairs. Sophie, Hayley, and Chloe steal Morgan and play with her on the floor with her mat and mobile.

"Dr. B suggested that too."

Good ol' Dr. Bunz.

"I have several friends who are on dating sites." Sherri sits next to my mom.

I'm not sure if it's the best or the worst timing, but my phone rings and it's the professor.

"I'll be right back." I smile and retreat to the bedroom, bringing the phone to my ear. "Hey."

"It would seem that in spite of my orthotic shoes, the women you've invited into my house find me attractive."

How did I forget about the stupid spy cameras?

"Cocky isn't becoming of you, Professor. Besides, we're talking about my boyfriends' seventeen-year-old sister who is still in high school and two middle-age women—one is my mom and the other is Griffin's mom. I'm not sure you can puff your chest out too far just from that."

"You sound hostile."

I take a deep breath and chew my thumbnail. Do I really sound hostile? "Why would I be hostile?"

"Maybe it's just you being protective of me. You're right. I don't have time to date or the emotional strength to even think about letting another woman into my life. Between my mother, Morgan, and you, I'm at my limit."

"Me?" I cough a laugh.

He sighs. "I don't want to dance around this anymore. Denying it won't make it go away."

"Nate—"

"I'm not asking you to do anything more than acknowledge it's the only logical explanation."

"Stop, just—" I shake my head and close my eyes, gripping my phone like I hate it, and I need it to shut up.

"You have my best friend trapped inside of you!"

And there it is, out in the open, hanging like smoke, blurring everything, and suffocating me.

"I'm not her," I whisper.

"You are. I'm sorry you can't see it. Your memories—"

"I have to go. Stop drinking. It's messing with your mind."

"I'm not drink—"

I end the call and fight for air. Where did it go? Who sucked all the oxygen from the room?

Nate did. He's trying to take things that are not his to take. He can't have Daisy because she's dead. He can't have the air in this room because he's not here to use it. And he can't steal my sanity no matter how tiny the thread is that I have left of it.

Laughter crawls toward me. I wipe the emotion from my eyes and turn.

"She filled her pants. We'll change her diaper." Hayley, with her sisters in tow, looks from doorway to doorway for the nursery.

I nod toward Morgan's room. "You're stealing my job. I may have to share my wages with you."

"Really?" Sophie asks.

"Sure. I haven't taken my favorite girls shopping. I think we should plan an outing."

Sophie claps her hands. "Yes!"

Hayley rolls her eyes at her sister while Chloe tries to act cool, but I don't miss the excitement pulling at the corners of her lips.

"Everything's at the changing table. Let me know if you need help."

"I've changed a gazillion diapers. We've got this," Hayley says while laying Morgan on the changing table.

"Make sure one of you is watching her at all times. She could roll off."

"We've got it. Really."

I nod. I had it too when I was Hayley's age. But now I have the protectiveness of a mother with Morgan, so I feel compelled to say everything, even the words I shouldn't have to say.

"What's for dinner? Are we ordering in?" I ask Mom and Sherri, avoiding the camera in the corner. I refuse to look at it—at him.

"Pizza?" Sherri suggests.

"Works for me." I glance at my phone.

Professor: *Have a good evening. Thank you again for staying.*

Why does he make it so hard to be angry with him? I slide my phone in my pocket.

"Sherri said you're moving."

Making eye contact with my mom, I grimace, as does Sherri. If Griffin told her, of course she'd assume I told my mom.

Sherri holds up her hands. "In all fairness, I just found out this morning when Griffin called. He asked us to check in with you and to see if you needed help moving anything to his place before he gets back home."

"I was going to tell you tonight."

My mom waves me off. "It's fine. I'm sure you were." She folds her hands in her lap. "Moving in together. Things must be serious."

I give Sherri a tight grin. She's never hidden her love for me. I know there's nothing she would love more than for Griffin to ask me to marry him. It's my dream too.

But my mom is more reserved. That's fair. I'm her only child. She should feel protective of me. The fact that I realize this makes me pretty damn proud of myself.

"I think we're serious. Most of the time he's at my apartment or I'm at his house, so it makes sense to just live together and save on rent."

"So you're having premarital sex?"

What?

The evil women before me do a stupendous job of keeping serious expressions as I disappear into the chair under their scrutiny.

"Are you serious? You bought me condoms and lubricant for my nineteenth birthday." I remain unblinking for a few seconds until my mom cracks a smile.

"She did?" Hayley startles me.

I glance back. This conversation is not appropriate for young ears.

"Wow, Mom, and you won't even let me get a tattoo."

Sherri rolls her eyes at Hayley. "Letting you get a tattoo won't prevent you from getting pregnant."

"So …" I stand. "What kind of pizza does everyone want?"

CHAPTER TWENTY-FIVE

I T'S BEEN AN unforgettable weekend. What started out as me mourning my vacation with Griffin has turned into lovable baby time with Morgan and a night of laughter with my family. I don't have to marry Griffin to call his family mine. I love them. I love him for making last night happen when he could have been pissed that I didn't go.

He's always thinking of me.

However, all the fun and laughter is about to end as the back door opens. My boss is home.

Hand over the baby and get out.

"Hey …" Nate sets his suitcase on the floor and goes straight to the sink to wash his hands, depositing a bouquet of flowers on the counter.

I bounce Morgan in my arms. She has a few drunk-on-milk smiles for her daddy. It calms my nerves, but just a little.

Hand over the baby and get out.

"Trade." He holds out the flowers to me.

I take them as he takes Morgan. "These are for me?" I don't mean to sound so breathless, but once again he's taken all the oxygen from the room.

"For staying."

I shake my head. "I thought the five grand was for staying."

"The money is business. The flowers are personal. I know you didn't stay just for the money. You stayed because you care for Morgan."

I shrug, but I don't look at him. I can't. "I stayed for the money."

I stayed for Morgan. Who am I kidding? I stayed for Nate because he needed me.

Fuck.

I shouldn't have stayed. My mom is my family. Griffin is my family. His parents and sisters are my family. Nate and Morgan are not my family. I need to remember this.

"Well..." he clears his throat "...you're good at what you do."

I nod, keeping my gaze on the flowers. My feet won't move. They're rooted to the floor. Nate holds me captive without touching me. The force of his past is greater than my strength to walk away. It won't let go.

"She's out," he whispers.

I glance up. Morgan's asleep on his shoulder. I knew she was getting close.

"Don't go yet." His gaze locks with mine for a few moments before he carries Morgan to her room.

This is my chance to run. I should. Nothing good can come from the two of us alone. But my legs won't work.

His shadowy figure ghosts toward me. I will never let this be more than an unspoken thought, but I love looking at Nate—the one in my head, the one in the picture, and the one before me. And it breaks. My. Heart.

I love Griffin so completely. He's everything. What's left when you have everything?

Nothing.

That's the logical answer. That should be the only answer. But the rules of reason don't apply to me because I see things I shouldn't see, I know things I shouldn't know, and the answer to what's left when I have everything is ... Nate Hunt.

He walks with this swagger that's unintentional. That's just him. He's quietly confident. When he stops in front of me, once again invading my space, I suck in a silent breath. He doesn't speak. It's as if his proximity says it all—he thinks I'm her. He would stand this close to her. She would let him.

"I think you miss your wife," I whisper, staring at our bare feet an inch from touching.

"Terribly."

His response grips my heart.

"I think you miss Daisy."

"More than words."

The hair on the back of my neck shoots up.

"Nate ..." My chin inches higher until our eyes meet. "I'm afraid of what's going to happen when you realize I'm not her."

He cups the side of my face with his hand. I can't breathe. If he kisses me, I will shatter.

"I'm afraid of what will happen when you realize you *are* her." He closes the space between us.

Don't kiss me.

Kiss me.

Don't.

Do ...

He brings my cheek to his chest the way he did in the garage, but this time his lips press to my head. Griffin's girlfriend doesn't want to kiss Nate, but the girl who wants to know why Nate lives in her head—that girl wonders if a kiss would bring the past to life, bring clarity to confusion.

I don't hug him, but I want to.

I don't speak because there are no words for this.

I live in his embrace until he releases me. And when he does, I rest my palms on his chest to steady myself. It's there, in our touch—undeniable—like I've touched him a million times. That's why he thinks I'm her.

Nate gives me a sad smile when my eyes shift to meet his. "The memories you have ... they're not mine. They're hers— they're yours."

I shake my head slowly.

"Yes." He grabs my wrists as I start to step away and presses them back to his chest. "Everything you know about me is what Morgan knew. You know what she saw. You know what I shared with her. You know what my dad shared with her about the hockey camp. You say things that she said. You called the birthmark on my stomach a heart—she's the *only* one who ever said that. I don't know how ... but you have her memories of me. And I don't know why you don't remember her—or you—in that life, but ..."

"I have to go." I take a step back without moving my hands from his chest. I'm connected to this man in a way that defies all logic.

His chin dips as we both stare at my hands on his chest.

Undefinable.

Magnetic.

Life-altering.

Slowly. Painfully. I fist my hands and drop them to my sides. "What time tomorrow?" I whisper.

"Six."

I nod. "Goodnight, Professor."

WE DON'T SPEAK of Daisy for the rest of the week. I keep the photo in my pocket. Of course, I don't know why. My Don't Know List has grown exponentially in the past few months. For someone who started life intellectually advanced, I have fallen into a dark hole of the unknown.

I know Nate holds a part of me I never knew existed. But after a week, I also know that I don't function well without Griffin. He called me from someone else's phone three days ago to let me know his phone was stolen. I haven't talked with him since.

"I'm sure he'll be here soon." Sherri hands me a plate of food. It smells good, but my appetite died when I lost contact with Griffin.

"You really didn't need to do this." I give her a guilty smile.

His family and my mom helped me move my stuff into his house yesterday. Now they're serving me dinner at "our" house while we wait for his arrival, which is uncertain since no one has talked to him in three days.

"Your nerves are palpable, Swayze. He asked us to keep an eye on you and that's what we're doing. You're family."

I force a smile and rearrange the food on my plate with my fork, eating at most three peas and one bite of chicken. The past week messed with my head, making me question my existence, my identity, my purpose. Griffin grounds me. I find the best version of myself rooted in his love. Thinking of Nate loving Jenna and Daisy the same way I love Griffin is unbearable.

"I should have gone." I push back my chair and stand, shoving my fingers through my hair. "He should be here. Why isn't he here? Why didn't he get a new phone? Why ... Gah! I'm going crazy. Motorcycles are dangerous. He's a sitting duck on the road surrounded by idiots on their cell phones or drunk … or falling asleep at the wheel or—"

"Hear that? He's here." Scott grins at me as I have a full-fledged meltdown in front of him and Sherri.

"He's here?" I whisper, frozen in place as I listen.

The familiar rumble grows louder.

Scott holds the door open for me. Smart man. I will mow over anyone who stands in my way.

My heart explodes as Griff eases off his motorcycle and pulls off his helmet. Over six feet of leather covered muscles, a week's worth of beard, the whitest smile, and sable eyes are about to get tackled by five feet six inches of crazy love.

"Aren't you a sight for sore eyes." He grins, tugging at the fingers to his gloves, but I'm not waiting another second to be in his arms. "Oof!" He catches me, wobbling a bit to keep from stumbling back into his bike.

"I can breathe again," I whisper into his ear. My senses devour him. There's a million things I want to say, but my mouth needs his. My appetite has returned.

He gives me everything right in front of his parents. It's probably not the most polite thing to do, but I don't have time for manners.

I. Need. This. Man.

His tongue dives into my mouth. One hand cups my ass and the other fists my hair. A low growl vibrates his chest as he deepens the kiss. I missed him asking about my days. I missed watching him work in his garage. I missed him cooking for me. But more than anything, I missed my lover.

"You should have been with me …" he says between labored breaths, resting his forehead against mine, hand still fisted in my hair like he needs to reclaim what's his.

Just as breathless, I nod my head against his. "Yes. I should have."

Sherri clears her throat. "Should we come back in an hour or so?"

Griffin and I both grin at each other.

"We're not old like you guys," he says. "Hours. We need hours … maybe all night."

My skin heats to a blood-red shade of complete embarrassment.

Scott chuckles. "Chip off the old block."

Kill me now.

"Since when?" Sherri laughs.

Griffin lowers me to my feet.

"I have cobbler and ice cream." Sherri gives Griffin a hug when I step back.

I don't need the cobbler, but ice cream sounds perfect. Things feel pretty hot between me and Mr. Sex in Leather. I want to peel every inch of it off him and lick him like a—"

"Hungry, Swayz?" Griffin nods toward the house, holding a bag in each hand.

I nod, watching his parents go inside. "More than you can imagine."

He struts his sexiness in front of me. "Oh, I'm pretty fucking sure I can imagine."

I want to pounce on his back, tackle him to the ground, and have him in a hundred different ways right here on the lawn. But, I don't. Instead, we have cobbler and ice cream. Sherri and Scott gave me the impression they knew what Griffin and I needed, and it's not ice cream and cobbler. Yet here we sit, across from each other in the living room, talking about the trip while eating ice cream and cobbler.

I don't want ice cream and cobbler. I want to scream while riding Griffin's face and his cock and—

"Swayze's boss lives in the most exquisite house. Have you seen it yet?" Sherri asks Griffin.

When did we get on this topic? Probably between Griffin's teeth teasing my nipples and his tongue circling my clit. Best daydream I've had in a long time. But the mention of Nate ruins my moment.

"I have not." Griffin gives me a slight grin, tight lipped and uneasy.

"You will. I want you to meet the professor and Morgan. You'll like them." This is code for I don't want to talk about "Nate" so let's stick to "Professor" and his daughter so as soon as your parents leave we can fuck like rabbits on crack instead of playing twenty questions about my time at "Nate's."

What is my deal? I have never been this mad for sex. When did it become such a drug to me? Oh yeah … the day I met my grocery store guy.

Dear Mr. and Mrs. Calloway, I love you to pieces. I want to be your daughter-in-law someday soon, but would you please please please leave so I can do really kinky stuff with your son?

"Do you like his house better than *ours*?" Griffin's lips purse slightly as his eyes narrow.

If he knew where my mind is at the moment, he wouldn't give a shit about what I think of Nate's house.

I shrug. "Four walls and a roof. It's what you do to make it a home that matters." Like fucking me against these four walls.

Whoa!

I'm a mess. My mind doesn't crawl around in the gutter like this. What's happening? Was there something in the food? No. I barely ate. The ice tea did taste a little different. Maybe

someone slipped an aphrodisiac into it. No. That can't be …
Sherri doesn't look like she's ready to dry hump Scott's leg.

This is all Nate. He's messed with my head. The way he
looks at me. The things he says. It's twisted my thoughts.
Nightmares. Sex dreams. I'm not myself. I don't know who I
am. But I know I'm ready to orgasm just looking at Griffin. I
smell him like a bloodhound in heat.

"You look flushed. Are you feeling okay?" Sherri's head
cocks to the side, concern etched into her forehead.

"Um …"

"Were you allergic to something in the cobbler?" She gets
me a glass of water.

An allergic reaction? Maybe. I've never had one. I thought
allergic reactions caused swelling … well, my breasts feel heavy
and so does a certain area between my legs. "I … maybe I
should go lie down. I am feeling a little feverish."

I gulp down half of the water and stand.

Griffin grabs my wrist, but I can't look at him. I pull out of
his hold. "Thank you for dinner and dessert. And helping me
move my stuff. You've been amazing."

I feel Griffin's scrutinizing gaze, but I don't acknowledge it.
"Goodnight."

"Goodnight," Scott and Sherri say.

Oh sweet mother of mercy, even walking is painfully
stimulating. There's no way I look flushed, not when every
ounce of blood has merged between my legs. I take a left into
the bedroom, strip off my shirt—because holy hell it's hot in
here—remove my leggings, and crack the bedroom window,
desperate for the cool air to hit my skin.

One breath.

Another breath.

It's not working.

Voices mumble, but I can't make sense of them past the thundering of my pulse. I close my eyes and block out everything except what I need. My hand slides down the front of my panties.

"God ..." I pant, sliding my middle finger over that little bundle of nerves.

"Fuck me, baby ..."

All the muscles in my body clench as I jump, eyes flying open. I make a quick move to pull my hand out of my panties. Griffin arrests my attempt, covering my hand with his and sliding them both back under the white, lacy-edged cotton.

Turned on.

Embarrassed.

Ready to die.

Seconds from exploding.

I don't know which feeling demands my attention the most.

Flecks of gold and brown sear me as Griffin's gaze holds mine a few seconds before his head dips, lips brushing my ear. "Spread your legs more," he whispers, guiding my fingers beneath his. "Let's make you come."

All of those feelings bleed into each other when his mouth takes mine. We communicate in deep moans and the slide of our hands, the tip of my pelvis, the commanding hold he has on the back of my head.

His tongue flicks mine, teasing it over and over, making me feel it lower ... *so* much lower. My knees buckle. Breath hitches. Eyes roll back.

This unraveled, completely intoxicated feeling leaves me paralyzed. He steps back, putting the wall in charge of keeping me upright.

"You have never looked sexier." He grins, eyes roving the length of my body as he pulls off his bandana revealing short, dark hair.

I love him shaven and smooth, but I love him with thick dark shadows covering his head and face too. Griffin does it for me *any* way.

He loses the white tee next, gaze affixed to something below my belly. My hand is still in my panties, resting there like it's a pocket. I'm *that* out of it. I slide it up.

"Don't you dare." He shakes his head, bending down to remove his black boots.

Leather pants.

Black briefs.

They pile up beside him as my eyes get reacquainted with his tattoos, the lines of his muscles, and the steely erection begging for my mouth.

He frowns in disapproval at my hand leaving my panties as I step toward him.

"Don't give me that look, Griff." I push his chest once.

He takes a step backwards.

"No more games. You have somewhere you need to be." I shove him again.

He surrenders, easing back onto the bed. "Where's that?"

I crawl over him, ghosting my lips over his skin, my tongue tracing the length of his erection.

He groans, flexing his hips.

"Here." I kiss his pecs, up his neck, and hover over his lips. He's hard and warm in my hand. I stroke him a few times until his eyes leaden. "This is where you need to be." Sinking onto him, I close my eyes.

Before I can relish the illusion of control that he's given me, he grips my hips and rolls us over, pinning me to the mattress. For the rest of the night I don't think of the girl I'm not, the woman I am, or the memories that don't belong in my head. It's just me and my grocery store guy doing what I'm certain we do better than anyone.

CHAPTER TWENTY-SIX

"GOOD MORNING." GRIFFIN hands me a cup of coffee. I fear it's decaf. I'm a junk food junkie in love with a health nut.

"You're showered and dressed." I frown. "It's Sunday. We were supposed to wake up together—naked."

He leans over and pulls out the kitchen chair next to his, depositing a slow kiss on my lips as I ease to sitting. "I worked out. Felt a little flabby after my week away without exercise."

I chuckle. "Flabby? Yes. I thought the same thing about you."

"We can do naked the rest of the day if you want." He shoots me a playful grin before sipping his green tea. Health nut.

My eyes roll as I sip my decaf. "No. That's fine. Staying in bed is lazy. Getting back in bed feels overindulgent unless we're on our honeymoon."

"I see." He nods. "Where should we go on our honeymoon?"

This guy has proposed to me on more than one occasion without actually asking me to marry him. It's equal parts exciting and confusing. "I don't know. And I don't want to know. When the right guy asks me to marry him, I want to plan the wedding and I want him to plan the honeymoon. I want it to be a surprise."

"The right guy?" Griffin stands, shoulders back, chest puffed out, towering over me. "Are you suggesting I'm a stand-in until you find the *right* guy?"

I bite my lip to keep from grinning. "Yes. A real boyfriend."

I didn't say that. No, no, no … I didn't just say that. *She* would say that. I'm not her. Nate has told me too many stories. She's in my head because of him. That's all.

Griffin nudges my chair with his leg, turning me to the side and easing onto my lap, straddling me while supporting most of his weight in his solid, jean-clad legs. "Marry me."

I laugh. "Sure. When and where?"

"I'm serious." His eyes confirm it.

"This is it?" I chuckle. "This is your grand proposal? No ring?"

Whisky eyes search mine. I love this man with all that I am, even on the days I don't know who that is. And he loves me. I knew it before he ever said it. It's something I've felt in the way he holds my hand and smiles at the crazy things I say and do. It's in the way he looks at me when he doesn't know I feel his gaze on me.

"Do you need a ring?" He circles his calloused finger over my left ring finger.

I shake my head. "I need you."

"Am I the one? The *right* guy?" He feathers his knuckles along my cheek.

"Yes." I whisper, leaning into his touch.

He slides his hand into the front pocket of his jeans and pulls out *a ring.* "I got one just in case."

"Oh, Jesus …" I breathe out, my tear-filled eyes flitting between the ring and the most sincere expression I have ever seen on the face of another human. "You're really doing this …" I shake my head. "Right here, in our kitchen. Sitting on my lap. Next to the worst cup of decaf coffee ever."

He grins. "Right here. Right now. Because we've never been conventional. And you owe me for your groceries."

I laugh. "I bought you lunch."

"I think your groceries cost more than the lunch you bought me."

I nod. "And if I agree to marry you, we're even? My debt will be paid in full?"

"Yes."

I fist his shirt and pull him closer. "Then, yes. I will be Mrs. Grocery Store Guy Calloway." I brush my lips over his and trap his lower lip between my teeth.

He growls, standing and scooping me up in his arms. "I was wrong. It's a naked day after all." He tosses the ring on the table. On … the … table. And carries me off to the bedroom. I don't care because he really is all I need.

"IT'S A GOOD idea to do reds separately, but if they've been washed quite a few times, it's okay to stick them in with other darks like blues and blacks." Griffin loads the washer as I watch him from my spot perched on the dryer.

"I like that you do laundry in just your underwear. That fascinates me."

"Are you listening?" He squints at me.

I could not care less about his laundry sorting rules. Domestic Griffin is my porn. "Yeah, yeah, I got it. Reds on hot and washed with whites."

Griffin starts the washer and lifts me from the dryer, tossing me over his shoulder. "Just continue working on your cock-sucking skills and leave the housework to me." He smacks my ass.

"Ouch!" I laugh and smack his butt just as hard, blood running to my head. "I know how to do laundry, cook, and clean on a need-to basis. And there's nothing wrong with my cock-sucking skills. I'll be a fine wife. Just wait and see."

He drops me on the bed. "Get dressed. Let's go get the last few things from your apartment so you can turn in your keys."

"When are we going to tell my mom and your family?"

"After we elope." He pulls on a T-shirt and jeans.

"Excuse me?"

"We're living together. Weddings are expensive. You said all you needed was me. I *know* all I need is you."

How did this happen? I open my mouth, but nothing comes out.

He grabs his wallet off the dresser and bends down, kissing me on the cheek. "I love the simplicity of our love. It's almost dinnertime and you haven't taken the ring from the kitchen table and slipped it on your finger because that's not what matters to us."

No. No fucking way. I slide off the bed and throw on my clothes, yanking and pulling them like they did me wrong.

"Ready?" he asks as I stomp toward the back door, hands balled, jaw clenched.

"I'll get the rest of my stuff later. I'm going to my mom's … *alone*."

"Whoa … what's going on?" He grabs my arm as I shove my feet into my sneakers.

"Nothing's going on." I attempt to jerk out of his grip.

"Look at me." He grabs my other arm, forcing me to face him.

I glare at his chest.

Silence settles between us as he refuses to let me go and I refuse to look at him.

"You want a wedding?"

I don't respond.

"Swayz?"

Nope. I'm not going to move. Not one blink. How dare he be so presumptuous? Now the truth will make me sound greedy, selfish, and materialistic.

"Would you look at me?"

Biting my tongue and holding my breath, my gaze works its way up to meet his.

"Is that what you want? If so, then that's what we'll do. I don't care."

"No." This time he lets me wriggle out of his hold. "You don't get to say that. You don't get to completely dismiss my dreams—crush them—and then take it all back with a simple I don't care. You don't get to own a truck, a motorcycle, and a house then make me feel like wanting a wedding is impractical and excessive."

My voice continues to escalate as I cross my arms over my chest. "And the only reason that ring…" I glance over at the table and then back to him "…is still sitting on the table is because you should have the fucking decency to get down on your goddamn knees and put it on my finger like the *right* guy would do. And the right guy would care. He would want to see me in a stunning white gown walking down a long aisle toward him. He would want to dance with me to a song that meant something special to us. He would want to take off that stunning white gown like unwrapping the best gift he'd ever received."

Griffin doesn't move, not even the expression on his face. "Fine." He nods after a few seconds of silence and grabs the ring from the table.

"Hell no." I shake my head as he starts to get down on one knee.

He stops halfway to the ground.

"You cannot make this right. Not now. It's too late. Now I have to decide if this is it … do I marry the man I love in spite of the botched-up proposal or do I hold out for something better so I don't spend the rest of my life envying epic proposal stories of other couples?"

He stands slowly and bites his lips together.

"I'll call you or maybe see you later. I don't know." I open the back door and head toward my car parked on the street.

A strong arm hooks my waist before I make it to the end of the driveway. Griffin backs me up against the door of his truck.

"Let go of me."

"No." He clenches his jaw while grabbing my hand.

I try but fail to pull it away. He shoves the ring onto my finger.

"You said yes. That was the deal. You owe me for wine, chips, chocolate, and tampons." He holds my arms to my sides, keeping me from going anywhere as he kneels in front of me. "Will you please marry me?"

I glare at him through squinted eyes.

After a few seconds he swears under his breath and stands. "You said yes earlier. There's no taking it back now." He interlaces our fingers and presses my hands to the window of his truck next to my head. "There will be a wedding and a white dress. You will take my fucking breath away a million times before we make it to the reception. We'll dance to the sappiest love song ever composed. You'll pitch the bouquet to a group of jealous women. Then I will stand in the middle of a ridiculously expensive hotel suite like an idiot in awe of the fact that the kindest, most beautiful woman ever said 'yes' to me."

He loosens his grip on my hands, but I don't move them.

"Then I'll unwrap you like the gift you are and always have been to me. I'll thank the food gods every day for bringing us to checkout lane number three a little past five on a sunny Thursday afternoon in March."

I blink, releasing a single tear. He kisses it away.

"But this is it … this is the epic proposal that you'll tell our kids and grandkids. You pinned against my truck, in tears and pissed off at me. And me refusing to let you go. I will *never* let you go."

I swallow back as much emotion as I possibly can. The rest stays lodged in my throat. "I can't believe you remember the time of day and checkout lane number," I whisper.

"I remember all life-changing moments."

Like this one … this is a life-changing moment. I will remember it forever. But I hate that I'm sharing it with Nate. Griffin resides in my heart and the forefront of my mind. My desire to spend the rest of my life with him is indisputable.

What I fear is Nate. What if he lives in my soul? Even worse … what if *she* lives in my soul?

"I'm sorry," he murmurs, completely releasing my hands.

I wrap my arms around his neck and he hugs me to him.

"Let's go to my apartment."

"WHAT'S GOING ON?" I say as Griffin parks his truck up the street from my apartment building. A swarm of emergency vehicles blocks the road, along with crime scene tape.

We worm our way through the small crowd of onlookers.

"Sorry, you'll have to stay behind the tape," a police officer says.

"I live here. What's going on?"

"I'm not at liberty to share any information. I'll need to see some identification before I can let you in the building."

Griffin rests his hand on my lower back as I dig my wallet out of my purse.

The officer inspects my driver's license. "Barnes?" he calls.

A shorter man in uniform turns and walks toward us.

"Swayze Samuels. 2B." The first officer hands me back my driver's license.

"I'm Detective Barnes. I'll escort you to your apartment, and then I need to ask you a few questions."

"What's going on?"

He doesn't answer. He just turns and heads toward the entrance surrounded by police officers and a few other tenants I recognize. One of the ladies wipes her red, tear-stained eyes, giving me a grievous look as I pass her.

Griffin's hand goes from my back to interlacing his fingers with mine as we make our way up the stairs. When we reach the top by my door, I twist around toward the voices above me.

"No ..." The air explodes from my lungs, leaving me gasping for my next breath.

There's a few more officers outside of Erica's apartment, which is blocked off with crime scene tape.

I tear my hand out of Griffin's and run up the stairs.

No. No. NO!

"Ma'am—"

I charge my way past the officers, catching them off guard, past the tape, and into the apartment filled with more police and a few other people in suits, including a guy standing in her hallway taking photos, his lens directed into the bathroom.

"Miss, you can't be in here."

I move faster than the officer trying to get my attention. I need to know what's in Erica's bathroom.

"Swayz …" Griffin's voice is nothing but an echo as I see it—her.

I can't fucking breathe.

"No …" I pant, gasping for air. Desperate to make sense of what I'm seeing.

The photographer says something to me, pointing me away from the bathroom door. It's all echoes. Every voice.

My vision blurs.

A hand wraps around my arm and another around my waist, ushering me out of the apartment.

Echoes everywhere.

The room spins but it doesn't erase what I saw. Erica's naked body in a bathtub of water. No blood.

It's Griffin. He's guiding me to the stairs. I think he's saying my name. I'm not sure. The door to Dougly Mann's apartment is open. He's sitting on his sofa talking to an officer in the chair next to him, jotting down notes.

Scar-faced, clown-haired, creepy neighbor glances up as I pass his door. He winks.

The. World. Stops.

"Come on, Swayze." Griffin's voice sounds like it's underwater.

I don't move. I can't move.

Dougly winked at me. I've seen that wink before. His nose twitched when he did it. He's not that good at it. But the last time I saw him wink, the scar on his face was not pink and pearly-edged. It wasn't a scar at all. It was a bleeding wound. Blood running down his neck. Blood pooling at the corner of his mouth, and when he grinned there was blood covering his teeth. But he winked and his nose did that weird, unmistakable twitch.

"You killed her," I whisper.

He keeps his eyes on me.

"You killed her," I say louder, pulling away from Griffin.

"Swayze …"

The officer in his apartment turns and looks at me.

"You killed her!" I run toward him and the officer stands and blocks my way, holding out his hand.

"Can we get some help in here?" He looks over my shoulder.

"Swayze?" Griffin grabs my arms and pulls me back. "Erica? You think he killed Erica?"

I shake my head while fighting Griffin's grip so I can reach my phone.

"Miss Samuels, we need you to come with us." Detective Barnes jerks his head toward the stairs as I fight to hold my ground in the hall outside of the murderer's apartment.

"Swayze, let's go to your apartment."

I shake my head, swinging my elbows as Griffin tries to pull me toward the stairs.

"It's here," I mumble, my shaky hands move over the screen of my phone. "Here." I hold up my phone toward the door to Doug's apartment.

"You. Killed. Her!"

Doug squints his beady eyes and slowly stands, moving past the officer, keeping his gaze on the screen of my phone.

I try to move closer to him, but Griffin doesn't let me budge.

Doug stops, blinking slowly several times at the screen of my phone. He doesn't say anything. He doesn't have to. It's him. He knows I know it. I see the recognition in his face as he looks at the photo.

"Let's go." Griffin loses his patience, grabs my phone, and pulls me down the stairs.

I keep my head turned as Doug stares at me until the door to my apartment closes. Even now. I stare at the door, unblinking.

"Miss Samuels. We need to ask you some questions."

"Swayz?"

I slowly turn toward Griffin and Detective Barnes.

Griffin holds up my phone. "Who is this?"

Blink.

Blink.

Blink.

"It's Morgan Daisy Gallagher."

End of Book One

Also by Jewel E. Ann

Jack & Jill Series
End of Day
Middle of Knight
Dawn of Forever

Holding You Series
Holding You
Releasing Me

Standalone Novels
Idle Bloom
Only Trick
Undeniably You
One
Scarlet Stone
When Life Happened
Look the Part

jeweleann.com

Receive a FREE book and stay informed of new releases, sales,
and exclusive stories:
Monthly Mailing List
www.jeweleann.com/free-booksubscribe

About the Author

Jewel is a free-spirited romance junkie with a quirky sense of humor.

With 10 years of flossing lectures under her belt, she took early retirement from her dental hygiene career to stay home with her three awesome boys and manage the family business.

After her best friend of nearly 30 years suggested a few books from the Contemporary Romance genre, Jewel was hooked. Devouring two and three books a week but still craving more, she decided to practice sustainable reading, AKA writing.

When she's not donning her cape and saving the planet one tree at a time, she enjoys yoga with friends, good food with family, rock climbing with her kids, watching How I Met Your Mother reruns, and of course…heart-wrenching, tear-jerking, panty-scorching novels.

Printed in Great Britain
by Amazon